I0693160

The Taken

by

Donnette Smith

Spirit Walkers Series

This is a work of fiction. Names, characters, places, and incidents are either the product of the author's imagination or are used fictitiously, and any resemblance to actual persons living or dead, business establishments, events, or locales, is entirely coincidental.

The Taken

COPYRIGHT © 2023 by Donnette Smith

All rights reserved. No part of this book may be used or reproduced in any manner whatsoever without written permission of the author or The Wild Rose Press, Inc. except in the case of brief quotations embodied in critical articles or reviews.
Contact Information: info@thewildrosepress.com

Cover Art by *Debbie Taylor*

The Wild Rose Press, Inc.
PO Box 708
Adams Basin, NY 14410-0708
Visit us at www.thewildrosepress.com

Publishing History
First Edition, 2023
Trade Paperback ISBN 978-1-5092-5148-3
Digital ISBN 978-1-5092-5149-0

Spirit Walkers Series
Published in the United States of America

Her body reacted to the demand, even though her brain was caught up in a fog. She practically flew over the two steps and scurried across the patio, sharp rocks cutting into her bare feet. She didn't care. She hit the lawn, forcing her legs to sprint so quickly her muscles burned.

Shouting fanned out among the group of men, and one voice overshadowed the others, "Get her, you idiot!"

Someone was huffing and puffing. The grunts of exertion were so close behind her it prickled the hairs on the nape of her neck. Whoever was back there was gaining speed like a rocket. She drove her muscles to the brink, but she somehow sensed it wouldn't be enough.

She was snatched in mid-air and thrown to the ground. The feel of the earth against her cheek was a cold reminder these bastards weren't ever letting her go. The recollection of Luisa's words the day they'd taken her here hit her like a freight train. These guys are very good at what they do. No one will ever catch them. It was true. She did everything she could to escape. But in the end, she was still their captive. Meredith was right. They owed her.

Praise for Donnette Smith

"…Smith's creative writing style will have you engaged from the very first chapter. I couldn't help but fall in love with Jenna and Cole. It definitely had me on the edge of my seat. I cannot wait to read more of Jenna's and Cole's story!"

~ Booklover

~*~

"…From page one I was pulled in & wanting more. The characters and their interactions flow very smoothly. I was gasping in surprise, smiling, or "YESing" in my head. Donnette Smith has done an excellent job writing to illicit the emotions of the reader. An absolute must read."

~ Kathi Adam

~*~

"…Donnette Smith's character and world building is on point. I could picture everything in my mind and felt connected to the characters. It was very suspenseful with some twists I was not expecting. it was perfect. Brilliant author."

~Kelly Boudreaux

Dedication

I began the plot of this book as a way of raising awareness for the countless women and children who fall victim to the dehumanizing abuse of sex trafficking that takes place every day around the world. There are an estimated 26.7 million victims abducted by traffickers and forced to live a life few of us could ever imagine. In the US alone, only a small percentage of human traffickers are ever brought to justice. It has exploded into a crime that has become the second most profitable illegal activity in the United States.

But while I was in the middle of writing this book, tragedy struck my life. I lost my beloved daughter, Nichole, to a fentanyl overdose. One of the characters in this story is a recreation of her. This character is a symbol of my daughter's long-fought battle with addiction, and a reflection of my own struggle as I watched helplessly over the last few years while addiction changed my daughter into a person I barely recognized. Although this story was written with the intention of bringing awareness to one tragedy gripping this nation, it inadvertently shed light on another that is rapidly stealing the souls of our children.

For every individual who has become lost to the overpowering influence of drug addiction, there is a desperate loved one waiting somewhere, who would give up everything they own if the person they once knew would only come back to them.

Chapter One

Why couldn't she be normal like everyone else?

From the moment loud crying spilled out from the adjoining bathroom, Jenna Langley's sixth sense awakened like a dinner bell for a pack of starving hounds.

Then, from out of nowhere. the whimpering stopped.

She froze in place in front of the full-length mirror, gazing at herself in her wedding dress, one hand poised above her head. The pearl hairclip was clutched in her hand so tight it was surprising she didn't snap the damn thing in two. She waited for that dreaded paralyzing state to wash over her the way it always did when a psychic vision came calling.

The clock on the wall ticked out the seconds; one, two, three. Nothing happened. She released the air trapped in her lungs with a loud *whoosh.* Perhaps one of the guests' kids sneaked into the bathroom and was to blame for the sobbing, and it had nothing to do with a clairvoyant episode at all.

But if that was the case, she would have seen the child since the only way to enter the bathroom was through the room where she was changing. Barbara, her maid of honor, was the only one who had swept through here. Maybe the little heathen managed to sneak past Jenna without her knowledge, but that couldn't account for the atmospheric change she'd detected right about the time the crying rang out. It was a phenomenon that pinged her clairvoyant meter as if it was pounded with a hammer.

She swallowed the lump in her throat. Where the hell was Barbara anyhow? In their haste to get to the chapel on time, she'd gone to fetch the veil they'd left at the Blazing Saddle Ranch. She should have been back twenty minutes ago.

A sound came from the bathroom. Not a yell, exactly. Something…

Pull yourself together. This is your wedding day.

She took a deep breath and told herself that the butterflies dancing in her stomach were the cause of her hearing things that obviously weren't there. Nothing, absolutely nothing, would get in the way of her marrying Cole this time.

I'll have a little less panic attack with my side of wedding jitters, thank you very much.

Now, shouts came from the bathroom. "Oh, God! Why is this happening to me?"

Jenna spun around. Her lips trembled as she called, "Barbara? Is that you?"

Her best friend didn't answer. And she wasn't going to. Barbara was many things but for damned sure she wasn't some magic fairy with the ability to float through walls without being seen. She hadn't entered this room; therefore she couldn't be in the bathroom.

A voice yelled, "Hey, whoever's out there. Can you hear me?"

An eerie sensation crawled across Jenna's skin like the tiny legs on a centipede. This entity might not be a swamp creature, but it damn sure had a set of lungs.

"Who's there?" she demanded, taking measured steps toward the bathroom.

Dead silence.

As Jenna stumbled into the bathroom, the hairs on the nape of her neck stood on end. A presence lingered here. There was no doubt about it. A sudden chill bit into her flesh; puffs of cold smoke billowed from Jenna's mouth. She hugged her body to fend off the cold, but the arctic environment was nothing compared to the adrenaline that lit her up.

She scrutinized all three bathroom stalls. All the doors were shut, but her psychic ability drew her to the one in the center. Her hand shook like a leaf in a storm as she lifted it up and placed it against the door. As she gave the door a shove, the hinges creaked—ever so slightly. A flash of dread twisted her gut as the door slowly drifted open.

The sight of an ill-defined something, perched on the lid of the toilet, sent out an ear-splitting scream.

Jenna back pedalled, thudding against the cold, porcelain sink.

The shape took form before her eyes. The edges became sharper, clearer—until the girl with blood oozing from a hole in the center of her forehead shot to her feet like a rocket, her dark eyes as big as saucers. "You can see me, can't you?"

"Who...who are you?" Jenna stammered.

When the girl took a few steps toward her, Jenna instantly raised her hand to stop the creepy image from advancing. "You st...stay where you are. Don't take another step."

"Who are you talking to?" someone asked.

Jenna spun toward the door. Barbara, her best

friend in all the world, stood there, a white veil hanging from her fingers, and a puzzled expression etched into her face.

"I-I think she's dead."

"Who?" Barbara asked.

"Her." Jenna rounded back toward the stall where the gruesome apparition had stood just seconds ago. The only thing that greeted her was an empty space. "She was right there," she insisted, rushing into the cubicle to investigate. "I swear, she was sitting on the toilet when I opened the door."

"A dead girl." It wasn't a question, but more an atonal statement.

Anger flashed through Jenna. "Don't," she warned, sashaying past Barb and into the room. "I'm not crazy and you know it." She sat on the chair next to the mirror; Barbara sank down beside her.

"Hey, we're besties, right? I know you're not crazy. It's just these psychic visions of yours take a little getting used to."

"I'm not sure it was a vision."

"What do you mean?"

She shook her head and let out a deep breath. "Anytime I've had visions in the past, I see it like a movie that's playing right in front of me. My body becomes paralyzed. I can't move until the vision ends. But this time I saw a dead girl, and she talked to me. None of the other stuff happened like it usually does. In fact, since that day Cole brought me back to life, you know, when I died, I haven't had a single psychic vision. Until now. And this one didn't feel like a vision. Not like the ones I've had before."

"God." Barb gazed off into the distance. "I still

can't believe Cole's brother buried you in a makeshift casket and left you to die. All because he was jealous that Cole had a better upbringing than he did. And I can't believe I was so fooled by him that I dated him."

Jenna recalled that day ten months ago while tears slid from her eyes and threatened her carefully applied makeup. God had answered her prayers while she lay in that shallow grave, begging for a second chance at life, a second chance with Cole, and a second chance to watch their daughter, Emily, grow up.

She squeezed Barb's hand. "Dunstan fooled all of us, including Cole. Nobody knew his long-lost brother would come strolling into town one day with a vendetta the size of Texas and an appetite to see his evil plan through. But he's in prison and that's where he'll rot. As for me, Cole found me and hauled me out of that grave. He resuscitated me and brought me back."

"All right then. This is the way I see it." Barb stood to draw Jenna out of the chair, turning her so they faced the mirror together. "You and Cole have waited a lifetime for this day. You two have triumphed through your mother separating you as teenagers. You prevailed against a serial killer who did everything he could to kidnap and kill you. Then you beat the odds again when a different lunatic put you in a grave. Are you going to let some dead girl in a bathroom stall keep you from marrying the man of your dreams?"

Barb was right. If the world crumbled right now, she'd still shuffle her ass out there and say those vows to the man who meant everything to her. She was going to become Cole Rainwater's wife today come hell or high water. And there wasn't a person out there, dead or alive, who was going to stop her. Not this time.

Soft knocks drummed against the door before it opened. Jenna's father stepped in. He was a handsome sight in his black tuxedo and slicked back, gray hair. She smiled, pride filling her chest.

"They're ready for you, sweetheart," he said, in a voice that told her he was on the verge of breaking down. "You're breathtaking. Standing here staring at you reminds me of your mom the day I married her. Back when she was a young woman."

She sniffled and swiped at her tears.

Her father put his hand on his hip, extending his elbow in a gesture that said he was ready for her to loop her arm around his and take that walk toward the first day of the rest of her life.

"Hold on," Barbara said, affixing the veil to the crown of Jenna's hair. She swirled Jenna around to face her. The tears streaming down her best friend's face caused Jenna's lip to quiver.

"Oh, no you don't," Barb admonished, sniffling, and getting control of herself. "Don't you dare mess up the face I worked thirty minutes to perfect."

Shared laughter helped them regain control. Barb said, "Let's go do this. And by the appearance of you, Cole is going to fall in love with you all over again."

While Barbara swept past them into the hallway to get in her position as the maid of honor, Jenna faced her father and took a deep breath. She stood at the back of the line of attendants, jitters bouncing around her belly like a tennis match, until her daughter, Emily, threw a glance in her direction and beamed. The ten-year-old mouthed, *you're beautiful, Mama.*

Jenna mouthed back, *Thank you. So are you.*

The child glanced down at the basket of rose

peddles and busied herself by fluffing them with her fingertips. So many times she'd told her parents this was the day she'd waited for…like *for…ever.*

As the music started, Jenna focused on breathing to calm herself. The exhilarating notion that Cole Rainwater would become her husband today welled in her chest, causing butterflies to bat their feathery wings again. He was everything she'd ever wanted. And after all the setbacks leading to this day, she found it incredible the time finally came. She was going to take his name, and she, he, and Emily would become an official family. Just the way it should have been eleven years ago.

The line went forward, and she got closer. Jenna did her best to remember how she'd practiced her walk down the aisle during the many rehearsals. Shoulders back. Head up. Take a step, count to one. Take another step, count to two. Breathe slow and easy. Smile.

All the bridesmaids were escorted down the aisle, and Barbara, as the maid of honor, made her way. The only ones left were the ring bearer, and Emily, the flower girl.

The young girl stepped onto the red carpet—head turning toward the people seated on both sides of the aisle—and gently tossed the rose pedals to the ground.

Jenna's father stayed her arm, signaling for her to come to a stop.

The world was suspended in time. She waited in the narthex of the church, the pitter-patter of her heart beating in her ears.

Then the organist pounded out the beginning keys to "Here Comes the Bride," and her heart took a lurch. She swallowed hard, telling herself she ought to not be this nervous. Surely, Cole wasn't this nervous, was he? They might have been getting hitched, but it wasn't like anything would drastically change in their relationship.

She had to wonder where the blasted tension was coming from then? Why was she sweating so profusely? It was a wonder she hadn't drowned in a puddle of perspiration by now. Then it occurred to her just as her father urged her to get moving down the aisle. Someone or something would jump out of the shadows at the last minute and stop her and Cole from getting married…again.

She chastised herself for being so ridiculous. Cole was standing past those doors waiting for her. So what if she saw a dead girl in the bathroom? Out of all the many disturbing visions that had haunted her in the past, staring at a deceased woman sitting on a toilet seat should be a walk in the park.

Keep your shoulders stiff. Head up. Pace your steps in succession with Dad's. Pay attention to the guests in the pews. Smile. You're doing great.

She spotted the dead girl sitting at the end of the center pew, staring at her as if she was an exorcist. Jenna's breath caught in her throat. Her feet locked in place; static electricity threatened to set her on fire. She squeezed her eyes hard enough to make tiny lights flash behind her lids.

Go away. Please, just go away!

The words, "Are you all right?" rang in her ears. And it dawned on her that her father was talking to her. "Jenna. Is everything okay?"

Her eyes opened, and her head swung toward him. Dazed for a moment, she looked into his eyes. His reassuring smile grounded her. Her attention reluctantly drifted back to the middle pew.

The horrific sight that was present a moment ago was gone. She scanned the confused faces of the guests, searching for the dead girl. She was nowhere to be found. Who the hell was she and why was she interrupting their wedding?

Her dad leaned down to whisper into her ear. "It's okay, sweetheart. Just take your time. I'm here with you. We'll do this together."

She leaned against the support of his arm and forced herself to stand straighter.

Her attention cut a trail up the aisle, and the second she locked gazes with Cole, relief cascaded over her. The love and patience emanating from his smokey, gray eyes steadied her heart. She didn't think he'd ever appeared so proud and at peace. He stood as strong as an ox in his black tuxedo, a red bowtie at his neck, and a white rose pinned to the lapel. She took a mental snapshot in her mind of him as he looked right now. He was mesmerizing and she couldn't tear her gaze away from him—nor did she want to.

Keep staring at his face. Walk. Breathe. You're going to get through this.

The warmth of his hand as he laced his fingers over hers sent a wave of heat coursing through her. He leaned over, brushed a kiss against her cheek, awakening that primal craving she'd always had for him. "You are stunning, my love. And every inch of you is about to be officially mine forever."

Just like that she no longer feared seeing a dead girl. What concerned her now was that his intoxicating nearness would cause her to forget her vows. But thank God the preacher was there to save her with his words of *repeat after me.*

Before she realized it, the last *I do* was uttered, and the preacher announced that the groom should now kiss his bride.

She stood at the altar with the love of her life. There were no more visions of dead people, only Cole's handsome face as he lifted her veil, gently molded her body against his, and took her lips in the most intimate, spine-tingling kiss she'd ever been hit with. By the time he let her come up for air, she was certain her legs had turned to rubber.

His hand was on the small of her back, gently directing her to face the crowd with him. The preacher boomed, "Ladies and gentlemen. I now present to you, Mr. and Mrs. Cole Rainwater."

The guests came to their feet, applauding and cheering.

Their daughter traipsed over and gathered them against her. When both Jenna and Cole knelt to the child's level, Emily said, "Can you believe it? We're a real family. This is the happiest day of my life."

Cole lifted his daughter into the air, and kissed the tip of her nose, saying, "It's the happiest day of my life too, kiddo."

****

Cole took Jenna's hand as they burst through the doors of The Vine of McKinney and ran toward the awaiting limo. The sun had dipped low in the sky, setting the backdrop afire with an orange glow as they exited the building where they'd spent the last few hours with friends and family celebrating their wedding.

He couldn't have been more relieved the festivities

were finally over. He'd been waiting to get Jenna alone from the moment she came down the aisle in that white dress, appearing so lovely it stole his breath. Standing so close and not being able to touch her in the way he wanted nearly drove him to madness.

Once they approached the limo and spun to face the crowd on the wide, concrete steps of the venue that were gathered to see them off, he threw up his hand and waved. Emily blew them a kiss, and Jenna's parents gathered round her, waving, and smiling. Cole chuckled as his best man, Dylan "Texas Ranger" Cruz, saluted them.

The limo driver stepped around and swept the door open. The man was unusually tall with the face of a mischievous child and an infectious grin. "Mr. and Mrs. Rainwater, paradise awaits."

"After you, Mrs. Rainwater," Cole remarked, holding out his hand to the open space beyond the door.

Laughter bubbled from her chest. "I don't know if I'll ever get used to that title. It feels like a dream." She shuffled in, and he joined her, shutting the door.

The vehicle lurched forward, and his hand roamed to her bare leg. He massaged her flesh, and she glanced at him, a flush rising in her cheeks. "What? Does me touching you make you nervous?"

She swallowed, peering down, and whispering, "You touch me, and every normal thought runs out of my head. How do you do that?"

His heart skipped a beat at her confession, and an adrenaline rush wound its way through him. He cleared his throat. "You'll have to forgive me then, sweetheart. I've been dying to get my hands on you all day."

The limo eased to a stop, and although Cole

couldn't see a thing through the heavily tinted windows, he imagined they'd braked at a traffic light. The glass window separating them and the driver slowly ascended. The mechanism buzzed until meeting its end. The dark reflection of the partition offered a stimulating view of his bride's slender neck. She wore a white blouse with a high collar. Her tan skin was exposed down to a few inches above her breasts. There was a tiny, blue flower nestled between her perfectly shaped cleavage.

His heart hammered and sweat broke out all over. "Jenna."

She flashed her blue eyes, and he swore it was his undoing. He let his hand travel up her neck, cradling the back of her head, and he tugged her close. He explored her lips with his mouth. She opened for him, and he slid his tongue inside, instantly drunk on the taste of her. Her soft moan reverberated against his lips, and he was sure he'd lose his mind.

He couldn't control the movement of his other hand as it slid across her shirt, cupping her breast. He found a hard nipple—even under layers of clothes— and twirled his thumb around it. His lips abandoned her mouth, and he dragged them along the side of her neck, dropping soft kisses here and there.

As her chest expanded, he realized she'd been holding her breath, as if in anticipation of his next move. Cole forced the limit. His hand skated up her leg beneath her skirt and encountered the soft, moistness of her inner thigh. His fingertips grazed the silky material of her panties.

She closed her eyes, leaning against the seat, finally letting go of the air trapped in her lungs with a low groan. "You can't do this…here," she whispered breathlessly.

"Can't do what?" he said gruffly, drawing her thighs apart. "This?" His fingers worked their way beneath her panties, and he stroked the wetness between her legs.

She moaned softly. "Oh, God, Cole. You really shouldn't…you have to…" But the hunger in her eyes when she glared at him, the slightly parted lips, and the way she spread her legs told him the last thing she wanted him to do was stop.

He slipped a few fingers inside, moving them in a circular motion and carefully examining her reaction. Her response only heightened his carnal need to draw her panties down to her ankles, free the bulge tightening against his slacks, and thrust himself deep inside of her. He grabbed her hand and molded it around his hard cock. "Oh God, baby. This is what thinking of you has done to me all day."

The whine of the partition window echoed throughout the cab, and Cole instinctively straightened up, moving away from his bride. The remnants of touching her so intimately was still aching in his loins.

Jenna cleared her throat, and he noticed how flushed she was as she made quick work of tugging her skirt down.

The driver's voice sounded like a bullhorn through the haze floating around Cole's brain. "We're approaching the airport."

Great. If he couldn't get this boner under control, it was going to be one hell of a flight.

****

After settling in their seats for flight 209, Jenna

peered over at Cole who looked ready to jump out of his skin. *Oh shit, how could I forget. He hates to fly.*

She slid one hand over his, and rubbed his arm with the other. "Are you okay, honey?"

He squeezed her hand, and settled back against the seat and closed his eyes. "Did I ever tell you I flew in a helicopter to rescue you when my brother buried you behind my father's house?"

"You flew in a helicopter for me?"

He still didn't open his eyes. "Here I am, flying again for you, Mrs. Rainwater. If it was up to me, we'd be on a bus right now."

She stifled a laugh. "At least we'll be there in a few hours instead of twelve."

"You're right. It could be worse. You could have chosen to fly to Paris for our honeymoon. I guess I should be thankful you wanted to go to Pensacola, Florida instead."

It warmed her heart he would have flown anywhere with her that she wanted to go. Now she was thankful she didn't pick somewhere out of the country. The poor guy might not have survived it. The plane lifted from the runway, and his Adam's apple bobbed in a deep swallow.

Even though she realized he must be fighting his fear of flying, for the most part, he appeared calm and collected. "It's okay. The plane will level out. I'm right here with you, babe."

Breathing slowly and deeply, he kept his eyes closed. "Yep. Just give me a minute."

"Would it make you feel better if I told you I was shirtless?"

One eyelid popped open. That sly grin of his came

out of hiding. "You're such a tease."

"There, you see. The plane has leveled out. No more bumps. You can relax."

A blonde flight attendant stopped at their seats. "Is there something I can get for you?"

Cole's eyes finally sprang open. "What's the strongest alcoholic beverage you have back there?"

Jenna couldn't help the laugh that escaped her. "You'll have to excuse him. He's not too fond of flying."

"Oh," the woman said with an understanding nod. "We're through the rough part. It'll be smooth sailing from here. But I know just the thing that will calm your nerves. I'll be right back."

As she sashayed away, Cole complained, "Why don't you go ahead and tell the pilot? He has an intercom and can share it with everyone."

"Oh, gosh, honey. I'm sorry. I didn't realize you were so sensitive about it. I'm sure the people who work here deal with this kind of thing all the time."

"That may be, but I don't make a habit of broadcasting my weaknesses."

She found it charming this big, strong man didn't want anyone to know he was petrified of flying. She wouldn't embarrass him by forcing the issue.

Jenna focused her attention ahead. Her gaze fell on the full head of straight, black hair belonging to the girl sitting in the seat directly in front of her. Fear hit her like a mighty punch to the gut. The woman twisted her face slightly to the side, and her dark complexion, coupled with the blue feather earring resembled that of the dead girl she'd seen at the church. Could the ghost have followed her here? Trepidation shook her to her core. She stretched out her shaky hand and touched the back of the person's hair.

The woman spun around and stared at her. Brown eyes bore into her. But no bullet hole in the forehead. It wasn't the same girl. Although a wave of relief reeled through her, so did the awkward sensation of making an idiot of herself.

The woman, sounding none too pleased, said, "Can I help you with something?"

"Sorry, my mistake."

The stranger sighed with irritation and spun back around.

Cole said, "Someone you thought you knew?"

The last thing she wanted to do was bother Cole with another one of her visions, or whatever the disturbing episode had been, especially on the day of their wedding. But she figured they'd had enough of not being honest with one another the last go-round. What they didn't need to do was hide things from each other ever again. "I saw something at the church while I was waiting for Barbara to bring the veil."

Cole frowned, concern pinching the corners of his eyes. "A vision?"

"Not really. I heard a woman crying in the bathroom. When I went to investigate, I saw a girl sitting in one of the stalls. The woman in the seat in front of me resembled the one I saw at the church." She shook her head. "It was really stupid of me to think that could have been her."

Cole straightened and focused his full attention on her. "Who was this girl, Jenna?"

"I don't know. But I could tell she wasn't alive."

"You found *a dead girl* in the bathroom?"

"It wasn't like that. It was the spirit of someone."

"How could you tell it was a spirit?"

"I could tell because she had a bullet hole in her head. And when Barbara walked in, she disappeared into thin air. I noticed her again sitting in one of the pews as I was heading down the aisle."

An understanding expression crossed his face. "So, that's why you appeared so confused for a minute there. I got a little concerned you were going to bolt and leave me standing at the altar."

"I was hoping you didn't notice my misstep. I was more horrified by the thought that some damn clairvoyant episode of mine was going to prevent us from getting married."

"You know I love you with all my heart, right? There's nothing that could have stood in the way of us being together. Whether we have a marriage license or not. A piece of paper and a ceremony wouldn't make a damn bit of difference when it comes to how much I love you, Jenna. Always remember that, okay?"

She nodded, more grateful than anything she had the love of this man to fall back on.

The flight attendant carried the drinks over, handing a snifter half-full of brown liquid to Cole, and a wineglass to Jenna. She said, "Wine for the lady, and a brandy for you." She leaned in and whispered, "Brandy always does the trick to calm my nerves."

After she sauntered away, presumably to serve the next passenger, Cole took a sip. "Why didn't you say anything about your encounter with this dead girl in the limo?"

"Hmph. That would have been a little hard to do with you distracting me."

He cocked an eyebrow, appearing intrigued. "I've got plenty more, sweetheart."

"I'm not a member of the mile high club, Cole Rainwater, and neither are you."

"I hear they're giving free memberships in the bathroom right now. Wanna follow me there?"

She rolled her eyes. "You would, wouldn't you?"

"In a heartbeat."

Chapter Two

From the second Jenna stepped into their room at the five-star, beachside resort where they would stay for the next two weeks, she was blown away. She recalled Cole had left the reservations for this trip up to Cecilia, the grounds manager at The Blazing Saddle Ranch, the estate he'd recently inherited from his great-grandfather, Hershel.

The woman was accustomed to handling such accommodations, as she'd done for Cole's great-grandfather many times when he was alive. If there was one thing Jenna could be sure of, it was that Cecilia had impeccable taste and spared no expense to have made their honeymoon as extravagant as was humanly possible.

Jenna marched into the exquisite bathroom with its vaulted ceilings and white marble countertops that stretched on forever and unzipped her travel bag of toiletries, putting her stuff away. Cecilia had been baffled at her choice of destination for their honeymoon. *"You know the sights in Paris are fabulous, Ms. Langley. I can book you and Mr. Rainwater on a first-class flight to France if you'd like."*

The woman attempted to convince her Pensacola, Florida wasn't nearly as glamorous and romantic a place for a young, wealthy couple to spend their honeymoon when compared to a location such as Paris or Rome or the British Isles. It didn't matter how many times Cecilia dropped little hints, reminding Jenna that the fortune she and Cole now had at their disposal put them into a different category than what they'd known before.

Jenna made peace with the fact she was an ordinary girl before this newfound prosperity, and she'd remain an ordinary girl long after, even if she could admit it was nice sometimes to have fancier things. Besides, Pensacola held special memories for her. She and Emily had spent many spring breaks right here, close to the vicinity of where they were right now. Of course, where they vacationed before wasn't nearly as glamorous as this place. Nor did it offer its own private beach, but it was nice for the two of them. The memories mother and daughter built would last a lifetime.

Concerning their daughter, she wondered if she and Cole made the right decision to spare the child the awful details of what happened six or so months ago. Did Emily really need to know Jenna had been kidnapped and put in a grave by the crazy uncle she never even met? At this age, her daughter was already a worrywart, just like her mom. Jenna realized that kind of news would give Emily anxiety attacks every time her mother got two steps away from her.

She took a minute to stop and stare at herself in the mirror. With her hands braced against the counter, she leaned in and said out loud, "Not telling Emily was the right decision. You are going to put all of this out of your head and enjoy this time with your husband."

But even as the words left her lips, the dead girl

she spotted at the chapel popped into her mind. Maybe she'd get lucky, and the gruesome sighting of that woman would be nothing more than some strange occurrence that happened, and she'd forget all about it by morning.

Just then, Cole's voice floated through the opened door of the bathroom. "You okay in there?"

She stepped into the bedroom to find him standing over the bedside table, a brochure in his hand. God, he was hot in those jeans and that black polo shirt that stretched across his torso, showcasing the ripples of his lean, muscular frame. He peered over, catching her staring at him, and said, "What is it?"

You're so scrumptious I could spend the rest of my life tangled up in bed sheets with you. Her stomach growled right on cue.

A lopsided grin developed across his face. "Hungry?"

"You heard that, huh?"

He held out the brochure. "You're in luck. There's a gourmet restaurant downstairs."

"I don't care if they serve fast food. I'll take it." She peered down at herself, realizing her skirt became a little wrinkled from the flight. "Do you think it will be all right if I go like this?"

"Honey, you could strip down naked. You won't hear a complaint out of me."

"Somehow I don't think the guests would appreciate that as much as you."

He tossed the brochure on the table before taking slow, lazy steps toward her. "Maybe we should order room service instead."

If she didn't put some distance between them now,

they'd never get a decent meal. "I'll go change," she said, backstepping her way toward the bathroom.

Right before she closed the door, Cole groaned, and she grinned deviously. He could go another hour without jumping her bones. Besides, a little payback for getting her all hot and bothered in the limo and leaving her to suffer the whole flight was in order.

And he was the one who called her a tease.

****

After peering around at the other restaurant guests, Jenna was glad she made the decision to change. There wasn't a person seated at any given table dressed in casual attire. The atmosphere resembled more of a country club than a place to dine.

She wondered if she'd ever get used to their newfound well-to-do status. She'd sworn from the beginning the millions Cole inherited from Hershel would not affect the way she lived to the point it might change her personality. They both had been raised in a small, country town, growing up around kids who wore cut-offs and cowboy boots. On a typical Friday night, the main attraction was a gathering of local teenagers hanging out in the middle of a cow pasture, drinking home-made moonshine, attending a homecoming football game, or checking out the rodeo. They didn't borrow their daddy's shiny sports car on the weekend, play golf, or crash parties at extravagant homes that could have doubled as palaces.

Sometimes she felt like a square peg being crammed into a round hole. The staff that ran the massive ranch Cole inherited didn't make it any easier for her to remain true to herself with the way they waited on her and Cole hand and foot.

It was a constant work in progress where Cecilia Dowers was concerned. She was determined to train that woman one way or the other there was no need for her to manage every facet of Jenna's life. Christ, she could pick out her own wardrobe for the day, make a phone call, and run an errand. Although she acknowledged some of the assistance Cecilia offered was warranted and appreciated, much of it was overkill. She was surprised the woman hadn't instructed her on the eve of their wedding night on the proper way to make love to her new husband.

Hmm. The idea of sexual exploits with Cole made her blush. She glanced over at him. And knew instantly, her reaction to aberrant thoughts wasn't lost on him.

"What is churning around in that brain of yours?" he prodded, a mischievous sparkle in his eyes.

"I'm thinking I'm going to faint dead away if I don't get something to eat soon. What is taking them so long? We turned in our order thirty minutes ago."

"You know how it is in a place like this. Everything has to be cooked to perfection."

She blinked, and it struck her that he was getting quite accustomed to this kind of life. "This really doesn't bother you, does it?"

He took a sip of his whiskey. "What? Eating in a place like this?"

She shook her head. "No—it's the whole thing. We weren't raised in the extravagant life we now have."

"Does it bother you?"

She drew her expensive shawl tighter around her shoulders, wanting to curse the uncomfortable thing. "It just seems like the last ten months things have changed so dramatically it makes me wonder if we're losing ourselves in all this glamor."

"The only thing that's changed is that we have more money now than we've ever had in our lives. Do you think I'm not the same person you met and fell in love with eleven years ago?"

She shook her head, realizing his personality was still the same. But his expectations had changed. Unlike her, he was content to hand numerous responsibilities over to the crew at The Blazing Saddle Ranch. It was probably the reason she was getting such a fuss from Cecilia. If it didn't bother Cole to allow the paid help to cater to his every need, why should it bother her? After all, the staff acted like the people working there were more knowledgeable in such matters.

"Cole, our daughter is attending a private school that costs more than the average new car. She's letting the staff buy her clothes. Have you seen the price tags on the stuff she wears?"

"Have you noticed attitude changes in Emily?"

His question caused her to pause. Now that she considered it, she couldn't say she did.

Cole frowned at her show of hesitation. "I'm confident we are raising Emily with strong, moral values. She's a good kid. Hell, she's wiser than both of us put together. This life we have hasn't changed her because she has deep-seated roots. I don't doubt for a minute that our daughter knows exactly who she is. No one or nothing will ever influence that."

In Jenna's heart she recognized the truth in his words. But still she worried. God knew her mother, Amanda, always acted as if she had to have the best of everything. On her husband's mediocre income, it often stressed the family's budget to the brink. Jenna recalled with a heavy heart that it nearly tore her and Cole apart forever when Amanda insisted Cole was not good enough for her and snatched her away from Texas to prevent them from being together. The last thing she wanted for Emily was for the girl to embrace her grandmother's attitude. She did her best to raise her daughter to have a giving heart, and to appreciate the things she'd been given.

Their food finally arrived, and the waiter, dressed in a natty suit and tie, delicately placed their plates in front of them, and topped off their drinks. "Thank you," Jenna said, and before he could ask if all was well, she added "This will do just fine."

He nodded curtly, spun on his heels, and strolled away. The food in front of her appeared mouth-watering. She took a bite and had to admit it was worth the wait.

"How's your steak," Cole asked, cutting into his.

"It's really good, babe."

He grinned knowingly. "I told you, cooked to perfection."

Okay, so he was right about that. Was he also right about their way of life not changing their daughter for the worse?

"You know, sweetheart," he said in between bites. "It's perfectly okay to enjoy our blessings and not feel guilty about it. It was you who convinced me I should accept my great-grandfather's inheritance, remember?"

Yeah. There was that, wasn't there? "It just doesn't feel like us, you know. Things have suddenly become so…complicated."

"What can I do to make it better for you?"

She could tell he was sincere. He'd always gone

out of his way to make sure she was as comfortable and content as possible. It was one of the reasons she adored him so much. He didn't have a selfish bone in his body. She didn't speak for a minute. Perhaps there wasn't one specific detail she could point to that was the cause of her discomfort. Maybe if Cecilia would back off a little, she could breathe again.

"It's Cecilia, isn't it?"

She frowned, picking up her glass of wine and taking a sip. "How do you do that?"

He rolled the bottom of his glass against the table, appearing completely at ease. "What?"

"Read my mind, is what."

Now he shrugged, slicing another chunk out of his steak. "Is that what I did?"

"It's what you always do."

"You complaining?"

She snorted. "It just baffles the mind."

He slid his hand across the table and touched her, and a hot sensation ricocheted through her like a ping pong ball. "When a man loves a woman as deeply as I love you, he just knows."

It took a minute to recover from the contact, especially when he continued to wind his fingers around hers, and gently rub the top of her hand with his thumb. "I can talk to her if you want."

"Are you always going to solve all my problems?"

He leveled her with that famous Cole Rainwater expression. The one that melted her insides every time. "If you let me, babe. I'd love nothing more."

"As tempting as that is. I'll handle this one on my own. I don't expect you to fix everything for me. Some things I need to figure out for myself." She slid another chunk of steak into her mouth. While she chewed and swallowed, she noticed he didn't take his gaze off her. His laser-focus skated from her face to her breasts. It hovered there, as if he was imagining stripping off her clothes, layer by layer.

She remembered the sensation of his hand as it traveled up her shirt in the limo and cupped her breast, fondling her hardened nipple. She sighed inwardly, incredible heat winding through her as she recalled the sexual gratification that rocked her when his fingers found that intimate place between her legs and he stroked her maddeningly. She had been on the verge of an orgasm right when the driver rolled the window down. She hadn't recovered since.

She swallowed, and said breathlessly, "Aren't you hungry? You're not eating."

He focused his attention on her, and the lust in his eyes was like a gun firing a shot directly into her soul. His voice was hoarse when he said, "I'm starving. But what's on my plate isn't going to satisfy me."

He left no doubt as to what he meant. Then he put up his hand to flag down the waiter. The man strolled over, and he handed him payment for the meal, voicing his desire to leave as quickly as possible.

The waiter marched away, and he once again fixed his attention on her. "We have unfinished business, me and you. No more stalling."

****

The door to their room shut with a thud. Jenna's shawl floated toward the floor, and Cole's hands glided up the supple flesh of her arms. The heat of her skin against his palms did this thumping thing to his heart that he realized would never cease as long as she was near. He leaned into her ear. "Do you have any idea how difficult it was for me to eat and carry on a normal conversation with you across the table from me in that naughty little dress of yours?"

She took a deep breath in answer.

"I've been wanting to devour you all day, sweetheart," he confessed, his lips pressing against that sexy spot along the side of her neck, right below her ear. "Do you remember what I was doing to you in the limo?"

Now, her hands found the hem of his shirt, and she lifted it up. He helped her release it from over his head, and let it fall to the floor. Her feathery touches started at the upper portion of his chest, and worked their way down, molding over each ripple of his abs. His breath caught with a gasp, and he closed his eyes. Every time she put her hands on him, it lit a fire that burned out of control.

"Speaking of that," she said in a breathy voice, "You didn't know it, but I almost…"

"Almost what?" He manipulated the strap of her dress until it slid off her shoulder, and then tugged on the bodice, releasing a creamy breast from the material.

He leaned over, and his tongue traced around her hardened nipple. She threw her head back and moaned, letting him have full reign to do what he pleased. "Almost what?" he pressed, dragging his lips back up to the base of her neck.

Once there, the pressure of his mouth against her skin took on an urgent caress. He couldn't help it. The mere scent of her this close was like a wrecking ball to his resistance. And he'd been holding on to control by a thread since he'd opened his eyes this morning and the first thought of her popped into his mind. He worked his way to her mouth, and rested his lips loosely against hers, demanding again, "Tell me. You almost what, Jenna." He needed to know what his touch did to her.

"I almost had an orgasm," she admitted, her voice a tortured whisper.

If he thought he was wrapped in ecstasy with her now, her confession was his complete undoing. With his pulse pounding, he loosened the other strap of her dress. With one, effortless tug, the garment slid down around her ankles. The sight of those womanly curves sent blood rushing to his midsection. And the swelling against his jeans throbbed to the point of intolerance. The straps of her lacy underwear curved around her high hipbones, setting off the tones of dark flesh in perfect contrast. He slid his hand down to her midriff, noticing the way her stomach muscles retracted to his touch. He buried his fingers inside her panties, and she inhaled sharply.

He discovered how wet she was and it turned him on even more. He drove his fingers in and out of her, and closely examined her expression. Her reaction to the fondling made him as hard as a man could ever get.

"Oh, God. That feels…amazing," she called out, urging him on by spreading her legs.

He continued the sweet torture, sliding his fingers in and out while his thumb fondled her clitoris.

Her sighs of pleasure that were once soft and whispery, now heightened into intensified cries. He muffled her gestures of gratification with the covering of his mouth, until her moans were trapped in his throat. He took her lips in a bruising kiss as his need to have her escalated with each show of desire she displayed.

He allowed her to come up for air, and she begged, "Make love to me, Cole. I need you inside of me now."

He needed no more encouragement. She stepped out of her panties, and he unzipped his jeans, finally releasing the bulge she was responsible for all day. He lifted her off the ground and settled her around his hips, walking her forward. The second her backside thudded against the wall, he drove his cock so deeply inside of her that an instant fear struck him he might hurt her.

But she called out, demanding more. He continued to withdraw out of her sheath of warmth and plunge back in. Every thrust became harder than the last, until the pictures on the wall rattled. "Oh, God, baby," he groaned, "you feel so good."

She tightened her legs around his hips, taking every rock-hard inch he pounded into her. Her head thrashed from side to side, and she called out in ecstasy. He rode her harder than he'd ever ridden her before. The first wave of an orgasm hit, and he called out in a hoarse voice, "Cum with me, Jenna."

His body tensed, and he rode the wave of the most powerful orgasm he swore he'd ever had in his life. The intensity in her eyes told him she was in the grips of climaxing. He held her tight as she cried out one last time. Her body writhed, and her vagina tightened and pulsated around his shaft.

She sagged against the wall, and he held her there, remaining buried inside her, and basking in the aftermath of such a powerful release. Sweat glistened on her flesh, and he leaned into her, taking her mouth in a slow-burning kiss. "Thank you," she finally said, "You don't know how bad I needed that."

He chuckled. "I have a pretty good idea. I've been

walking around with a hard-on all day. And it's all your fault. You shouldn't tease me the way you do."

She raised one eyebrow. "And how exactly do I tease you?"

"Every time you walk, talk, breath. I could go on."

She sighed, her gaze floating toward the ceiling. "There's no hope for you."

He helped her to the ground, and she headed toward the sliding glass doors.

He couldn't peel his gaze away from that sensual tush sashaying away from him. See, he told himself. There she goes teasing me again.

She glanced over her shoulder, saying. "I'm going to try out the jet tub. Care to join me?"

A grin the size of Texas crept across his face. "I thought you'd never ask."

****

The cold air crept into Jenna's nostrils. She tossed and turned, hugging the covers tighter around her neck. Although she couldn't be sure when the temperature in the room changed, she realized it must have been the cause of her being roused out of a deep, comfortable sleep.

Cole stirred in the bed beside her, then nestled closer. She imagined the chill had hit him, too. After waiting a brief minute, the soft drone of his snoring continued. Did he turn down the thermostat before they'd finally slipped into bed last night? A glance at the digital clock next to the bed told her it was one in the morning. They'd gotten into bed a little after midnight. If her husband changed the temperature before they headed to bed for the night, it would have been freezing in here very shortly after. Could he have done it recently, while she slept?

The answer to her question came in the form of a moving figure creeping across the floor near the foot of the bed. She bolted upright, heart racing, and a high-pitched ringing pounding in her ears. She caught the slight advancement of someone or something heading straight for the sliding-glass doors. And then it, or they, vanished. But the doors never opened.

The chill in the air disappeared. The revelation of who the intruder was settled in her gut. She glanced at Cole, laying there in the bathing light of the moon streaming in through the same glass doors the dead girl she recognized from the church yesterday had just exited. The idea of shaking him awake was tempting. But they didn't get to bed until late, and he was exhausted. He'd drifted off to sleep within minutes. She already suffered from enough guilt that she'd dragged him into the middle of her sighting of the dead girl yesterday on the flight. It was their honeymoon. And before she left Texas, she'd promised herself nothing would get in the way of their time together.

Too much of their lives had been disturbed by her damn visions. She just wanted this one special occasion to belong exclusively to them, minus the insanity of her clairvoyance that was a constant interruption. Getting him involved this time was not an option. She'd handle this herself.

Jenna carefully tossed the covers aside, being mindful not to wake her husband, and placed her feet on the floor. She snatched a white robe from the chair a few feet away from the bed and slipped it on. It was time to deal with this now. It was obvious at this point the girl was a lost soul. Jenna had no idea why she'd chosen her to haunt, or how seeing this phantom was even possible—it's not like she had a manual for this crap since she'd never seen dead people before—but she was damn sure going to march out there and find out what this random ghost wanted with her.

Jenna stepped through the frame of the sliding-glass door, and the dead girl stood by the farthest end of the iron railing encasing the jet tub. The woman's back was facing her, and her head was down. "Who are you?"

The girl swirled around, staring briefly at her as if she was expecting this encounter, and then spun on her heels, continuing to face the lights of the city beyond the railing. "My name is Luisa Florentino."

Jenna noted she had a strong Spanish accent. By her appearance the last time, when her eyes went the size of salad plates, she could tell the girl was of Latina heritage. "Why are you following me?"

"Because you're the only one who can see me." Now she faced Jenna, her hands spread out in front of her. "How you can see me when no one else can."

"I don't know."

Luisa appeared hopeful for a moment. "Do you know my brother?"

Why in the world would she think I know her brother? "Who's your brother?"

"Diego Florentino. He lives here in Pensacola."

Jenna shook her head. "I'm sorry. I don't know him. Did you live here, too?" She munched on her lip before continuing. Did the woman know she was dead? There was only one way to find out. "I meant…before you died."

Her shoulders slouched; her voice darkened to a

growl. "Before those *bastardos* shot me in the head? Yes. Me and my family have lived here all our lives."

Wait. If she lived here, what was she doing all the way in Texas, showing up at her wedding ceremony? Was there some connection she was missing? "Do you know me somehow?"

"I have no idea who you are, *mujer blanca.*"

"Then why are you here?"

She shook her head, frustration and confusion flourishing in her intense eyes. "I was drawn to you for some reason. I dunno why. Maybe you can tell me."

Jenna was dumbfounded. "Why would someone kill you, Luisa?"

"Because of those girls," she said, becoming agitated. "They kill them, you know, like unwanted livestock. Use them up, then throw them away when they're done." Her body shook, eyes twitched, and lips quivered.

Jenna took a step back, seeing the storm brewing in the dead girl's body language. "Who?" she asked, becoming fearful for reasons she couldn't identify. "Who do they kill?

Luisa stalked toward her, trembling with anger and wagging a finger. "I told you! Those girls! They kill those girls!"

Terrified, Jenna stepped back. Her foot caught on the aluminum track of the door, and she fell backwards.

Someone caught her from behind. Cole's voice boomed in her ears. "Hey now, what's going on? Are you okay?"

She twisted in his arms, clinging to her husband's strong embrace. An uncontrollable shiver seized her, and she couldn't rid herself of it.

"God, honey, you're trembling like crazy. Tell me what happened?"

She glanced up at his face and could tell he was deadly serious.

"Who's out there, Jenna?"

She was too stunned to answer.

He settled her to the side and stepped out onto the patio.

She stood by the door struggling to get the shaking under control, and he rushed over to the rail, peering down. Obviously, his search of the rest of the area proved fruitless, and he stepped back inside, asking again who she'd seen out there.

She hung her head and whispered, "It was that girl. The one I told you I'd been seeing from the morning of our wedding."

"Aw, honey." He drew her near, wrapped himself around her like a cloak. He ran his hands up and down her arms until the trembling stopped, and she was able to function again. "I'm so sorry, babe. This is all you needed to deal with on our honeymoon. I guess it was wishful thinking it would go away, right?"

As he swayed back and forth, she said, "I'm the one who's sorry. This isn't fair to you. I promised myself I would do everything I could to keep this from happening while we were on our honeymoon. Just this once I wanted everything to be perfect."

"Hey." He lifted her chin and gazed so deeply into her eyes that she could feel it down to her soul. "When you're here with me, nothing could be more perfect. Being with you is all I've ever wanted. I'm your husband, Jenna. Your problems are mine, and we will solve them together."

She reluctantly nodded, so thankful they found each other again after all these years.

"Come on," he said, sliding the door shut, and escorting her into the room. "Why don't you sit down on the couch, and I'll make us a cup of coffee. Then you can tell me what happened." He framed her face, leaned in, and gave her a tender kiss.

With her heart a little lighter, she headed toward the sofa.

Chapter Three

When the phone jangled, Jenna opened her eyes for the second time that morning. She grabbed the noisy device from the bedside table, and issued a raspy, "Hello," after placing it against her ear.

"Good morning, Jenna. It's Professor Delaney from the Paranormal Research Center. How are you holding up?"

With furrowed brows, she sat up in bed, her attention scanning the spot next to her where Cole should have been. He wasn't there.

"Can you hear me?"

Why was the professor calling, and what time was it?

"Jenna?"

"I'm here," she finally answered, sliding her legs over the side of the bed, and glancing at the clock. Jesus, it was eleven thirty.

"Did I wake you?"

"It's okay. I needed to get up anyhow." Why did Cole let her sleep so late? And where was he? She stumbled out of bed and grabbed the robe she'd flung over the chair at 2:00 a.m.

The professor said, "I would have called earlier, but I was with a student, and I just got the message."

Message? What was the woman talking about?

She slipped into the robe and tied the sash.

Heading toward the sitting area, her gaze scanned the room for the whereabouts of her husband. "I'm sorry, Professor. But I'm not sure what you mean."

"The message Cole left at about eight o'clock this morning."

Cole was sleeping in bed with her at eight this morning. Wasn't he? She stopped roaming from room to room and reflected on what happened after they sat up talking for almost an hour. They both agreed they'd deal with the ghost of a dead girl in the morning and crawled back into bed together.

It appeared Cole got up early. Why did he call the professor, and how did he get her number? *Duh, he searched the contacts in your phone, that's how.*

"He seemed worried about you," Delaney said.

"What did he say?"

"Just that you were experiencing some odd things and I should call."

Why didn't he tell her he planned to call the professor? Now she stumbled into the kitchen, headed straight for the coffee machine, and found a fresh pod already in the dispenser with an empty coffee cup sitting beneath it just waiting for her. There was a note lying beside it on the counter.

She picked it up and told the professor to hang on a minute as her eyes scanned the words. *Hey, babe. I ran to the store to pick up some breakfast. By the way, I called Professor Delaney. She should be calling you.*

Gee, thanks. He could have discussed this with her beforehand. That would have been nice.

She closed the lid to the dispenser and hit the button for the largest cup option available. A small part of her was glad the professor called though. If it was left up to her, she probably wouldn't have bothered the woman. Truth be told, she did need a little help from someone who specialized in this sort of thing to figure out exactly what was happening.

With a sigh she said, "It started just before the wedding. I saw a ghost, or some apparition, in the adjoining bathroom to the room where I was changing. I've had another two sightings since. The same girl. In fact, at about one this morning, I saw her again. She's talking to me, Professor, and she says I'm the only one who can see her."

"Has this ever happened before?"

"Should it have?"

"That's hard for me to say. I know from all the experiences we've had dealing with your psychic abilities in the past, you haven't mentioned that you've had any such encounters."

The spouting of the caffeinated liquid streaming into the cup was a welcome sound. She needed something strong enough to pluck her mind out of this haze. She grabbed the packets of sugar, tore into three of them, and poured them into the mug, along with a little cream, then she wandered to the table and sat down with the brew, taking a sip.

"Let's see," she said. "I've witnessed murders by way of out-of-body-experiences. I've had visions of people being stalked, including myself. A few times I've been so incapacitated by my visions that I couldn't move, which led to my kidnapping when I couldn't lift a finger to fend off the person abducting me because I was having a vision of them doing it right as it was taking place. But I haven't seen a single dead person walking around talking to me. Until now. And I have to admit, it's really creeping me out."

Her hands trembled, and she realized if the coffee wasn't so hot, she'd have downed it like a glass of wine and poured four or five more. "Why is this happening to me?"

"I think it may have something to do with the fact you died."

"Wait. How did you know about that?"

"Barbara," they both said in unison.

"Does she schedule appointments to discuss the juicy details of my personal life with you, or does she just randomly call when the mood strikes?"

"It's Barbara. She doesn't schedule appointments to do anything. She just does it."

Of course, she does. She should have learned long ago if you didn't want people to know about your business, you should, at all costs, hide it from the biggest motor-mouth in the Dallas-Fort Worth area. That would have been a little difficult to pull off though since Barb had been very much involved in the last threat to Jenna's life.

If it wasn't for her best friend visiting her in that grave Dunston put her in, during the time Barbara was in a coma, which led to her relating those whereabouts to Cole when she finally woke up, that casket would have been Jenna's final resting place. She doubted they'd have ever found her body if it wasn't for Barb's spiritual intervention, even though neither one of them had a clue how Barbara was able to wander from her body while she was lying in a hospital bed. She did owe the woman her life. That fact made her best friend's intruding nature a little easier to swallow.

Get over it. The girl has been this way all her life.

Jenna shook her head, getting back into the conversation with the professor. "I couldn't have been dead for more than a few minutes before Cole performed CPR on me and brought me back. How can that have anything to do with what's happening now?"

"I had a case once a few years back," Delany said. "It was a young patient we were monitoring. She had clairvoyant gifts similar to yours. She died in a boating accident but was resuscitated. After that happened, the dynamics of her abilities altered. She experienced much the same phenomena you are now. Spirits were drawn to her, and she was able to communicate with them."

Jenna was so stunned she almost spit out her coffee. "So, what are you saying? I brought something back from the grave with me?"

"A heightening of your psychic senses. It would be my educated guess when you left this earth, something in the hereafter latched onto you. You brought it back to the living with you."

"So, now I'm a walking target for dead people?" Just great. If she imagined things were complicated before, it was about to get a whole lot more interesting.

"It's a—"

She cut the professor off mid-response. "I know, I know. It's a gift."

It's not like she hadn't heard this spiel from Delany before, when by way of a series of out of body experiences, she'd had a front row seat to women getting viciously murdered. Too bad this time wasn't like a trip to the department store. You end up with something you don't want, you could always return it.

Sorry, lady, we don't have a return policy for dead people harassing you. You'll have to go upstairs and take it up with the big guy.

Good luck with that. "What can I do about it?

"There's only one thing you can do," the professor said, more on a sigh than any other sound. "But you're not going to like it."

"Go ahead. Hit me with it." Why not? She was already barreling downhill like a snowball headed for hell. She could have sworn that was a line from a country song.

"You need to find out what this girl wants. Only then will she leave you in peace."

"You're kidding." Christ, it was as if she was trapped in a horror film with an overused storyline. *Guess Hollywood isn't as full of crap as I always guessed they were.* "What if this girl's only goal is to follow me around and drive me insane?"

"Don't be ridiculous. There's a reason she hasn't moved on. Find out what that reason is."

"She's not going to be the only one." As that realization sank in, Jenna wanted to scream and tug her hair out. This was never going to end. If she managed to get past this one, there'd only be another one standing in line.

"We don't know that. Don't get ahead of yourself. Take a deep breath and try to relax. After all, you are on your honeymoon, right? It'll all work out. You'll see."

Jenna's bullshit detector rang loud and clear.

The creaking of the front door told her Cole had returned. "Thanks for the call, Professor Delaney. I have to go."

"All right, dear. If you have any more episodes, call me. Don't make your poor husband do it instead. You are never bothering me if that's what you think."

She nodded and issued a pleasant goodbye right as Cole stepped into the kitchen.

He entered the room and she stared at him. Both his arms were cradling bags of groceries. He set them on the counter and dug into one of the sacks, drawing out a dozen eggs and a tub of butter. She said, "When you mentioned you were going to get breakfast, I didn't realize you planned to cook it, too."

He frowned and plunged his hand into the shopping bag again. "I could tell last night you weren't too keen on the restaurant thing. So, I figured I'd whip you up a meal myself."

She rose from the table, wondering how she'd gotten so fortunate to find a man who cared about her as deeply as he did.

He set down the items as she approached, and he faced her. She took him into an embrace and lifted on her tippy-toes, giving him a kiss. "You didn't have to do that. I would have been glad to go to that restaurant and eat breakfast with you."

"You know I love to cook. So, it just gave me an excuse to do it."

She remained in that position and gazed into his eyes. "Next time you decide to call Professor Delaney, at least warn me first, please."

His stare drifted away from her. "I knew you'd never do it—your bad habit of not wanting to disturb someone 'n' all—so, I figured if I didn't do it, it wouldn't get done. And you needed to discuss what's been happening to you."

"At least tell me next time."

"You would have stopped me and you know it."

She groaned in frustration, letting go of him. "You

don't always know what's best for me, you know."

He leveled her with an expression that undoubtedly told her he most certainly did. "Was the professor able to help you figure out why this is happening, and offer any advice on what you can do about it?"

She drew her attention away, staring at the floor. A clear sign he'd made his point.

He kissed her forehead. "I rest my case, Mrs. Rainwater."

God, every time he called her that, butterflies danced in her stomach. He was her husband for better or worse, in sickness and in health, till death do they part. She wondered if there'd ever come a day when she'd become accustomed to being his wife. It was all she ever dreamt about from the time she was seventeen years old, back when they were sneaking off in his old pickup truck and fogging up the windows.

"So, what did she say," he wanted to know as she busied herself with putting away a few groceries. He gathered the ingredients for an egg omelet and grabbed a skillet.

"She thinks something changed with my clairvoyance when I died."

He spun around and stared at her. "How do you mean?"

She opened the fridge and leaned in to place a jug of orange juice on the shelf. Resurfacing, she answered, "The professor seems to think I may have brought a new psychic ability back with me from the grave. Now I can see spirits that have not moved on, whereas before I couldn't. She sighted a case she studied some years ago, where a young girl died, was resuscitated, and could suddenly communicate with the dead."

Surprisingly, Cole shrugged, as if that was the answer to all their questions. "Is that all?"

Jenna shut the fridge, staring at him as if he must be kidding. "Like that isn't enough."

"What I mean is, what else did she say? Did she offer any guidance?"

"According to her, I need to find out why this girl hasn't moved on. Only then will she leave me in peace."

"That's cliché, isn't it?"

"That's what she told me."

Cole cracked a few eggs in a bowl and produced a whisk from the drawer. "What are you going to do?"

She sat down at the table, wringing her hands. "I guess the next time this girl shows herself, I'm going to press her on it. Find out what she's after and what I can do to help. Now that I'm taking charity cases for dead people, they'll be coming out of the woodwork."

"I wish you wouldn't worry about that, Jenna. We can't predict that will happen. This could be a one-off."

The smell of fried eggs wafted in the air, reminding her how hungry she was. "God, honey, I hope you're right. But I just don't know. I didn't sign up for this. I don't want to live like that."

He laid an omelet in front of her, along with a glass of juice. His hands were on her shoulders, gently massaging the tension that saddled around her like a lead jacket. "Whatever happens, babe," he said, his fingers digging into her taut muscles, working their heavenly magic. "We'll deal with it together. You don't have to face it alone. I'm here for you."

She couldn't describe how comforted she was by his words. If she was forced to handle dead people harassing her, she was relieved to know he'd be there to help her through it. She peered up at him, saying, "Thank you. I really needed to hear that."

He nodded and winked at her. "It's going to be okay. We'll work this out. I promise." He stepped away and announced, "I made a call to the Pensacola PD this morning and talked to a sergeant there. When I mentioned the name Luisa Florentino, he told me she was a twenty-three-year-old Latina who's whereabouts became unknown a week ago."

She twisted in her chair and gazed at him as he strolled over with his plate of eggs and a glass of juice, taking a seat at the table. "What is that supposed to mean?"

"I asked if they'd opened a missing person's case for her. He told me she was a local addict who has a history of running off."

Jenna wanted to laugh out loud with incredulity. "Obviously, she hasn't run off, Cole. She's dead."

"I know. That's what I told him."

She almost dropped her fork. "You told him your wife is getting daily visits from a missing dead girl. I can only imagine how that conversation went."

He cut into his omelet, and took a bite, saying, "He hung up on me a few times."

"I bet he did," Jenna snorted and slid another forkful of eggs into her mouth.

"But I convinced him to meet with you."

Now she stopped chewing and stared at him. "How in the hell did you pull that off?"

"I told him you were a clairvoyant who works for a Texas police department, and that you helped solve the case of the notorious serial killer, Joseph Rainwater."

She frowned. "So, you lied?"

"I told him what he needed to hear to get our foot in the door. At least this way we may be able to get a little more information about Luisa. And besides, you did help solve that case."

"But I didn't work for the police department."

"You reported the sightings to me…who works for the police department."

"Clever." He never ceased to amaze her. "Did you tell him you were a detective in Texas?"

"When he stopped hanging up on me, yes."

After not taking her seriously the last time she'd had a vision about being buried alive, and the whole ordeal happened the way she envisioned it, he swore he'd never make the same mistake again. Her husband was true to his word. He not only believed her, but he was taking action this time. It was a good feeling knowing she would never have to worry about him doubting her again.

"Eat up, babe," he said, checking his watch. "We're meeting him at the station in an hour. That should give us enough time to have Pete, our limo driver, swing us by a car rental place to pick up a car while we're here. I wanted to spend some alone time with you without a limo driver intruding on our privacy."

The memory of what he'd done to her in the limo on their way to the airport spiraled back, sending heat creeping up her checks. "What do you plan on doing, having sex with me, and driving at the same time?"

He grinned a roguish grin. "That works for me. Just don't wear panties today. It'll make it easier."

"I wouldn't put it past you."

He winked at her. "You'd be wise not to."

She shook her head, indicating how much of a hopeless case he was, and helped herself to another bite of his scrumptious omelet, chasing it down with a sip of juice. Although she couldn't predict how things would go with the sergeant today, she was confident they'd taken a step in the right direction in solving this mystery.

****

Cole swung the rental car into the parking lot of the precinct and noticed right away an older man in uniform standing by the shrubs, slipping what appeared to be a pack of cigarettes out of the pocket of his shirt. The guy bumped the top of the pack, and a cigarette slid out. Once he removed it, he twisted off the butt, and threw the unwanted object into the standing ashtray, then he lit the cigarette without a filter.

Jenna and Cole approached, and the man tilted his head toward the sky, blowing out a stream of smoke. Cole couldn't be sure how he sensed this was the sergeant he'd talked to on the phone earlier, but his intuition convinced him it was.

They made their way up the walkway, and the man's brown eyes zeroed in on them. "Mr. and Mrs. Rainwater," the guy said, extending his hand.

Cole nodded and shook his hand, then said, "Sergeant Bancroft?"

The man's gaze slid over them as if he was sizing them up in one glance. "Call me Alan."

"It's nice to meet you, Alan," Jenna chimed in. "Thank you for meeting with us so quickly."

"No problem, ma'am," the sergeant said, knocking the cherry off his cigarette, and returning it to the pack he removed it from.

Cole studied his peculiar actions, and it wasn't lost on the guy when he added, "These damn things are so expensive nowadays, I do my best not to waste them."

Jenna said, "I used to smoke. Believe me, I know."

Cole said, "I see you don't care for the filters." His gaze drifted toward the ashtray that was full of discarded butts. "Why not buy cigarettes with no filers?"

"It's the taste," Bancroft said. "The flavor of the unfiltered things is awful. I prefer these, but don't care for the filters. Why don't you guys follow me into my office."

The sergeant led them to the back of the precinct to a stained-glass door with stenciled, black letters that spelled *Sergeant Alan Bancroft*. He opened the door, stepped in, and welcomed them inside. "Go ahead and have a seat."

After they shuffled in, he sank into his chair at the same time they took to the ones on the opposite side of his desk.

Cole's attention wandered around the man's office, from the picture on the wall of Bancroft in uniform, to the one sitting on his desk of an older lady with silver hair and a warm, trusting smile.

"That's, Cheryl, my wife," the man said, after he took notice of the direction of Cole's stare. "We've been married for forty years if you can believe that."

"Congratulations," Jenna put in. "We just got married yesterday. I hope forty years from now we can say the same thing."

Now, the sarge grinned pleasantly. "That's what your husband told me. You've come to Pensacola to spend your honeymoon?"

"I love this place. Me and my daughter used to vacation here quite often."

"We get a lot of visitors here, especially this time of year. The tropical setting brings tourists in by the droves. And it's certainly good revenue for our city."

"How do you like living in Pensacola?" she asked.

He leaned against his desk and frowned. "It's not so glamorous when you've been here as long as I have. Besides, in my profession, I get to see the not so desirable side of this town. Unfortunately, with the tourist traffic we get, crime goes up. And it's my department that deals with the low lives who come in with the tides."

"I can imagine," Cole responded.

"I bet you can, working for the homicide unit, Detective Rainwater." He focused his attention on Jenna and said, "From what your husband tells me, you're clairvoyant, and you were quite an asset to the police department in helping to solve a serial killer case in Texas."

Jenna nodded, twisting the leather tassels hanging from her purse in her lap. "It was a case in which they thought the killer committed suicide many years earlier. But as it turned out, it was the wrong man, and the killer was still running free."

"And from what I understand, it was your psychic abilities that aided in that discovery," Bancroft offered.

"I was having out-of-body experiences in which I witnessed him murder a few victims."

The sergeant frowned, appearing unpersuaded. "To be honest, Mrs. Rainwater, I've never really put much faith in the solving of cases using psychics. It's not as though the idea of that is foreign to me. I have heard of police departments using them on occasion. But I don't know of any cases that have ever been solved as a result of that."

"You have now," Cole remarked, eyeing the man as if he'd already been there and done that. "There was a time not too long ago, I had a problem believing it, too. But when I witnessed what my wife is capable of, I don't doubt it any longer. If it weren't for her, my father, Joseph Rainwater would still be out there killing today."

Bancroft clasped his hands around his arms in deep consideration. He studied Jenna thoroughly. "You saw Luisa Florentino, and you say she's dead."

"She came to me about one this morning," Jenna said. "When I asked, she told me her name. She made mention about someone killing young girls. Said *they* use them up like cattle and get rid of them when they no longer have use for them."

Bancroft leveled her with the look of a skeptic. "Hypothetically speaking, if I were to believe this, which I stated from the beginning, I'm not sure I do, what do you think she meant by that?"

"I have no idea. I think the important thing is that you open a missing person's report for her. She's dead. I saw the bullet hole in the center of her forehead."

Now, he stared at his desk. "Look, Mrs. Rainwater, you don't know this girl, but I do. She's acquired a nice little rap-sheet here in Pensacola. She's been arrested for everything from theft and prostitution to the sale of narcotics."

Cole glanced at his wife and immediately recognized familiar storm clouds brewing in her eyes.

"So, because she's been involved in criminal activity, it doesn't matter who killed her and why?"

If the sergeant figured he could placate Jenna with the excuse Luisa had been a criminal, therefore they weren't going to waste police time and resources to find out what happened to her, he had another think coming.

The sergeant adjusted his approach, leaned back in his chair, and straightened his shoulders. "This isn't the first time Ms. Florentino has come up missing. She has a habit of running off with different men. She'll go on a drug binge for a few days, a week, hell, even a month, then she'll resurface again. I can't tell you how many times she's done this previously. Recently, in fact."

Jenna didn't appear as if she was even close to backing down. "I can assure you she is dead, Sergeant. Perhaps, you should ask yourself why a stranger from out of state, like myself, with psychic abilities would come in here and tell you she saw and can identify a woman who just happens to have run off, as you put it, with a bullet hole in her head. Wouldn't you, at least, question how in the world that could happen? Or is it simply a coincidence because you refuse to accept there are people out there who can see things you can't?"

Cole wanted to stand up and cheer. Instead, he cleared his throat and said, "Don't you think it's at least worth investigating?"

The man lowered his head again, bobbing it with indecision. He jerked back up with all the appearances he'd come to a decision. "Okay. Maybe you're right. Perhaps, there is something to this. I'll have a few of my boys pound the streets, find out who saw her last, and see if they have any information on her whereabouts."

Jenna let out a sigh of her own. "That's all I'm asking."

A warning shrouded Bancroft's eye. "But don't be surprised if Ms. Florentino shows up, alive and well, before we get too far with this."

Jenna said, "Thank you, Sergeant. We really appreciate the effort."

"It's Alan," the man returned. "And here." He plucked something out of the billfold he'd taken out of the pocket of his trousers and handed it to them. "This is a business card for a well-known captain in these parts who owns one of the biggest cabin cruisers around. He does tours. Tell him Alan Bancroft sent you, and he'll give you a nice discount. I've been on one of his tours. Trust me, it's a memorable experience."

Cole took the card from the man, issued his appreciation, and studied the fancy writing. *Julian Finch. Captain of the high seas. Call for a tour.*

"You two are supposed to be on your honeymoon," the sergeant continued. "Enjoy the sights here in Pensacola; let me and my men worry about finding Ms. Florentino. I'll give you a ring if we find anything, okay?"

Jenna rose to her feet, expressing her gratitude once more, and they both strolled out together.

After they settled into the rental car, Cole's head swung around toward the passenger's seat, and he studied his wife. She sat there, hands folded in her lap, a distant expression on her face, and she gazed out of the windshield.

"What do you think?" he said, interrupting what he guessed were her solemn thoughts.

She took a deep breath before speaking. "I think he

just wanted to get us out of his office. He's not taking this seriously."

Cole slipped his hand in hers and squeezed. "I think we should at least give him a chance before we jump to that conclusion."

"I suppose you're right. It's only fair." Then she faced him. "Did you see the guy standing by Sergeant Bancroft's door when we walked out?"

He searched his memory. There were a few people examining them with curiosity as they strolled through the bullpen. Then the face of the person Jenna mentioned clicked in his mind. "The Spanish guy with the cowboy hat. Is that who you're talking about?"

She nodded. "The way he stared at me really creeped me out. Did you notice it?"

Cole started the engine and threw the gearshift in reverse. He backed out of the parking lot, and responded, "Now that you mention it, he was definitely staring at us. The guy was dressed in plain clothes. I got the feeling he was a civilian and didn't work there. Did you see the detective with brown, wavy hair sitting on the corner of his desk as soon as we exited the sergeant's office?"

She shook her head.

He braked at the intersection, threw on his blinker, and yielded to oncoming traffic. "I could tell he'd been sitting there listening in on our conversation with Bancroft. It was written all over his face from the minute I laid eyes on him."

"Is that odd behavior for detectives?"

He swung the car onto the highway and leaned on the accelerator. "That's not what was strange; it was the way he acted about it. He jumped up, pretending he wasn't listening. But it was as if he couldn't take his eyes off us. It just gave me a suspicious vibe."

"You're a detective. Isn't it in your nature to be suspicious?"

He laughed inwardly. She was right. There were times he was suspicious even when nothing warranted it. "Tell you what," he said, changing lanes and maneuvering around slower traffic. "Why don't we give this Captain Finch a call, see if he can fit us in today? We'll head back to the resort and slip into our swimming gear and spend the rest of the day on a beautiful boat, basking in the sun."

She smiled. "You don't know how heavenly that sounds. It's the perfect day for it."

He handed her the business card, and she punched the number in on his phone. With Bluetooth connected to the car, it rang through the speakers. A man announcing himself as Julian Finch finally picked up. Cole told him who he was, and who recommended him, and asked if he could fit them in for a tour today.

"You're in luck, Mr. Rainwater," the captain said. "I just got a cancellation for a tour. It was scheduled to start in an hour. It was my only tour of the day. Would you like me to pencil you in?"

Jenna nodded emphatically from the passenger's seat. His heart took a bump when he saw how happy this made her. He went back to Finch. "Let me know which marina; we'll be there."

Chapter Four

Jenna could not believe the size of the vessel waiting at the end of the dock. The name *Saint Marie* was stamped along the starboard side. She spotted two double-seated jet skis attached to the boat by what appeared to be a towing mechanism. A man and woman stood on the stern. They waved as Jenna and Cole ambled down the dock.

As the sunlight nearly blinded her, when Jenna came to rest near the boarding ladder, she stretched one hand over her eyes to get a good look at the two people. The woman, sporting a sheer, colorful wrap around her midsection and a neon, pink bikini top stared down, a warm smile lighted her face. "Hi. It's Jenna, right?"

If it weren't for her shimmering blonde hair and radiant glow of her dark skin, Jenna would have taken her for an ordinary girl. It was apparent though, that she took good care of herself even if her frame was a bit thick. She nodded.

The woman said, "It's nice to meet you. I'm Clara Finch, Julian's wife."

"Oh." Jenna wasn't aware the captain's wife would be joining them. All the better though. A little female companionship would be great. It was certainly better than spending the day on a boat with testosterone surrounding her from all sides.

Julian himself was stout, thick bodied and tanned,

with sandy-blond hair. He stretched out a hand and helped Jenna onto the stern, doing the same for Cole. "I hope you don't mind," he said, putting his attention on Cole. "Clara didn't have any plans today, so she agreed to accompany us. I thought it would be nice for your wife to have some girl flavor."

"Sounds great," Jenna replied. "Thank you."

"Here," Clara said, taking note of Jenna's hefty beach bag. "Let me show you where you can store that thing."

Leaving the men up top, Clara led the way into the cabin. It was stunning. The spacious sitting area was surrounded by light brown, glossy walls, leather furniture and plush carpet. Jenna's breath caught. "It's really beautiful in here."

Clara acted as if it wasn't a big deal. "Julian inherited this cruiser ten years ago from a business partner who passed away. He's been taking it out on tours ever since." She stepped around to the bar, opened a stained-glass cabinet above her head, and took down a few rocks glasses. After dropping a few cubes into them, she asked, "What's your poison?"

"Whatever you have on hand."

"Honey, we have more liquor on this boat than the local tavern." She shuffled over and threw open the doors of a huge, glass cabinet running from the top of the ceiling to the floor.

Jenna's attention cruised over bottles upon bottles of different whiskies. Clara wasn't exaggerating. She spotted a jug of a familiar brand and grinned. Old habits never died, she figured, remembering all those nights as a teenager she, Cole, and their friends would hang out drinking. "Southern Comfort would be great."

"You got it. What do you think your husband would like?"

"I'm sure he'll have the same."

"Great," Clara said, tossing a smile in her direction. "I guess we'll all have the same then." She pointed toward a hallway behind Jenna. "If you'd like to change into your bathing suit, there's a bathroom down the hall. There's a nice cove with a beach area where Julian would like to take us. He already has the place set up for us. Once we get close, he'll anchor the boat, and we'll take the jet skis the rest of the way."

Fun in the sun. It was the perfect recipe to take her mind off the weird events she'd been experiencing. For the first time since the wedding, Jenna felt at peace and looked forward to enjoying some serene time with her husband and this couple. It was nice to finally let go, allow the day to take her where it may, and not concern herself with visits from dead people. She'd nearly forgotten what life was like for normal folks. But today, on this gorgeous vessel, and blessed relaxation waiting on a beach somewhere, she was going to soak up every bit of it.

By the time she slipped into her bathing suit and strolled back into the formal living area, Clara was nowhere to be found but laughter spilled out from up top. She followed the sound, up the steps and past the hatch. The fresh air hit her with smells of the sea; a warm gentle wind blew against her face, ruffling her hair. Seagulls cried out in the distance. Immediately, her soul lightened.

"Hey, there," Clara said, peeking around the corner as Jenna climbed the last step. "The guys are up top navigating. But I have something to show you." She handed Jenna a drink. "Come with me."

Clara led her up to the upper deck where a breathtaking view overlooked the ocean as far as she could see. There was a step-down, and two lounge chairs nestled close to one another, a small, glass table separating them. Jenna noticed a metal bucket in the center, the bottle of Southern Comfort protruding from it. "These," Clara said, waving her hand out in front of her, "are the best seats on this boat."

Jenna had no problem taking her for her word. When she stepped over to the lounge chair on the left and sat, the warmth of the sun that penetrated the seat dissolved into her bottom and backside. The silver railing of the boat shined in the sunlight, and the bow stood proud, like a tall statue in a museum.

Jenna was mesmerized. "This is amazing. If I owned this boat, I fear I'd never leave it."

Clara chuckled. "I don't come out with Julian as often as I'd like. My career keeps me too busy."

"What is it you do?"

"I'm a case worker for the local office of Child Protective Services."

"Wow. I imagine that must be hard. All those misplaced children. It would break my heart."

Clara frowned, gazing off into the distance. "I'm afraid I was one of those misplaced children. My parents abused me from a young age. CPS stepped in when I was seven after one of my teachers reported all the bruises she'd seen too often. My father was both an alcoholic and a child molester."

"Oh, my God, Clara. I'm so sorry you went through that."

The woman shook her head and with it the bleak

expression in her eyes disappeared so quickly, Jenna questioned if it was ever even there. "When I turned seventeen," Clara went on, "I got word he was found in Shreveport, Louisiana, face-down in a bayou. Someone beat him so severely he didn't have much of a face left. They were able to identify him by a tattoo on his arm."

Jenna was so stunned she didn't know what to say.

Clara finally looked away and gave a half-laugh, half-sigh. "Geez, I'm sorry. Sometimes I'm too frank for my own good. Julian keeps telling me I should watch that. I have a tendency to shock people with the things that come out of my mouth."

"There's nothing wrong with honesty, Clara. "I find it refreshing."

"Truly?"

"If you don't mind me asking, how did your father end up in the bayou?"

She snorted. "It was a fight over another woman in a bar. The jealous boyfriend beat him to death and dumped him in the swamp behind the establishment. My mother died of an overdose soon after. I don't think I have a single memory of her when she wasn't out of it. To be brutally honest, the foster homes they put me in weren't much better. I was always nothing more than a paycheck for one dysfunctional family after another. I don't know how, but I finally reached eighteen, and I decided to do something decent with my life. I met a lady who worked for CPS. She convinced me that I could help children who were in the same predicament as me. I've been doing it ever since. What do you do for a living?"

"Nothing that noble, I'm afraid. I run my own consultant firm."

Clara appeared impressed. "An entrepreneur. How cool is that. So, what's it like now that you're married?"

A grin Jenna could not control spread across her face. "I've wanted to marry that man since I was seventeen."

Clara's eyes grew large with adventure. "Ooh, a teenage love story. Tell me all about it."

The woman topped off their drinks, and Jenna settled in, basking in the sun, and reeling from the effects of the wind rushing over her body. And she told this stranger the story of she and Cole while they laughed and sipped expensive liquor.

****

Once on shore, Jenna settled into a lounge chair next to Cole. She grinned with contentment, and the distant silhouettes of the captain and his wife waded out into the water. Her attention drifted to her husband who had his eyes closed, and his hand gripped a beer on the armrest of the chair. "You enjoying yourself?" she asked, causing him to open one eye and stare at her.

"I think this is just what the doctor ordered," he told her and then took a pull of his beer. "How are you and Clara getting along?"

"I can't complain. She's very easy to talk to and has been a gracious hostess."

He nestled into his chair, as if satisfied with her answer. "You hungry, babe?"

She eyed the grill next to the cement bench sitting a few feet away under some shade trees and recalled Clara telling her Julian previously packed the cooler with food in anticipation of their arrival here. "Perhaps a little, but I can wait. What about you?"

His attention slid up and down every square inch of

her. "Honey, I've been hungry since the moment I saw you in that hot bikini." He glanced at the bottle of suntan oil sitting on the table between them. "Want me to rub you down?"

She laughed. "Maybe we should go for a swim to cool you off."

He took another swig of beer, set the bottle on the table, rose from his chair, and stepped over, extending his hand. "C'mon, he said, "I want to show you something."

Cole led her away from the sand, and into a small patch of forest.

There, around the corner, Jenna noticed a few trees and a clearing. Off in the distance stood a towering waterfall, picturesque, as if it was ripped from the pages of a magazine. "God, it's amazing," she said, gazing back at him. "How did you find this?"

"I stumbled across it when I had to relieve my bladder. You like it, huh?"

"It's breathtaking."

He winked at her, flitting his eyebrows playfully. "Let's go check it out."

She hesitated. "Is there even a way over to it?"

He grabbed her hand. "We're about to find out."

After stumbling across a beaten path, Cole glanced back at her and said, "I think I found a way over there."

A two-minute hike uphill carried them to the end of the trail. They stood at the crest of a bluff, a pool of water rippling below, and a gentle cascade pouring over the jagged rocks of the waterfall in the background. The compression of dirt at the lip of the drop-off told Jenna people used this spot to free-fall into the water below. Shivers ran up her spine and she took a step back.

Cole stared at her. "What's wrong? Are you afraid of heights?"

She grimaced. "That must be an eighteen-foot drop or better. I don't want to slip and break my neck."

The sunlight played across his face, and he stood on the edge and observed her. "I would never let that happen. But if you're worried, we can go back."

She took a deep breath and weighed her options. It really was a stunning view. Like a tropical paradise. And it was nice to be out here alone with her husband. Although she'd never considered it before, most likely because she'd never been in a position to, obviously her reaction to standing at the edge of the cliff, staring that far down forced her to come to grips with the fact Cole was right. She was afraid of heights.

Cole searched her eyes and then arched in closer, brushing a stray wisp of her hair out of the way, and framing her face with his long fingers. "I don't like that you're uncomfortable. Let's just leave, babe."

He tugged on her hand, but she resisted. "Just wait a minute," she said, letting out a long sigh. "Maybe…"

"Let's just go back and get something to eat. I'm starving. Aren't you?"

"I'm tired of being afraid of things."

He stopped in his tracks and peered back at her. "Jenna, you have nothing to prove to me or anyone else. You don't have to jump into the water from up here."

"I know that. But just because I don't have to doesn't mean I shouldn't."

Besides, I can see how much you want to.

As if reading her mind, he said, "You don't have to do this for me."

She was silent for a moment, then, "Maybe I have

to do it for myself. I'm tired of letting fear rule everything in my life. I find myself backing away from situations because I'm not brave…because I can't predict the outcome. I always take the safe way out."

His eyes grew large with incredulousness. "You," he said, pointing at her, "You are the bravest person I know. I could have never survived half the things you have and lived to talk about it."

"And I was scared shitless every time."

"Jesus Christ, Jenna, you were stalked by a killer and then buried in a hole in the ground for over twenty hours. I would have been scared shitless, too."

"That's not bravery, that's handling something against your will because you have no choice."

"What do you think bravery is? Do you think any of us would willingly put ourselves in the path of danger? Bravery is the actions you take when you find yourself in those predicaments."

She stared at the ground. He had a point. But she couldn't ignore the fact she constantly erred on the side of safety. There was never any room for spontaneity, throwing caution to the wind and doing something for the hell of it, and not considering for a minute the consequences of those actions. She screwed up her face and said, "I'm jumping in, Cole."

For a minute she figured he was going to talk her out of it, but then his expression lightened. "Okay." He held out his hand. "Let's do it together."

She put her hand in his and they stepped to the edge, their movements causing a few loose stones to tumble down the embankment, splashing into the water below. As her heart raced and perspiration popped out on her forehead, she gazed toward the sky to keep from feeling woozy.

"Are you sure?" he said.

She took a deep breath and closed her eyes. "Stop asking if I'm sure. I'm here, aren't I?"

He gripped her hand tightly. "On three then."

The second he arrived at the end of his count she fought the urge to recoil but braced herself and allowed him to tug her forward. The effects of flying sent butterflies weaving throughout her stomach. She hit the water with a smack, and gravity took her down. Cole never let go of her hand.

Before she knew it, she emerged, gulping air into her lungs. She opened her eyes to find her husband no more than a few inches from her, grinning. "Look at that," he said, "You survived."

"Such a funny man," she retorted, leaving him behind, and swimming toward the waterfall.

Behind the steady stream of water, she was amazed to discover a hollowed-out area nestled underneath the rocks. It was a small cavern large enough to fit a medium-sized craft. She swam over, exploring the opposite side of the cave, where it opened once again into the ocean.

She made her way beyond the opening and spotted a lone black and white boat with a small cabin tied to what appeared to be a private dock. The craft rocked gently with the movements two men on the main deck were making, as one removed the protective seat covers, and the other swung open the hatch and ducked inside the cabin. She would have guessed it was nothing more than two guys headed out on a fishing excursion, if it weren't for the two young women perched on the edge of the dock having difficulty keeping their balance. The small blonde almost fell head-first into the water before one of the men noticed what was happening, and leapt onto the dock, grabbing hold of her at the last minute.

As the men hustled the girls into the boat, an eerie sensation crept over Jenna. Although the women didn't put up a struggle, something wasn't right. Their bodies were as malleable as rag dolls. The men shuffled them across the boat deck, and down into the cabin.

"What are you looking at?"

Jenna jumped, a gasp escaping her, and she twirled around to stare at her husband. "Good grief, you scared the crap out of me."

"I almost thought I lost you when I didn't see you inside the cave."

She returned her attention to the scene she'd been watching. No one resurfaced from the cabin yet. "There's two guys in that boat," she told him. "They just took two girls down there with them. But there's something wrong with those women."

"What?" He stared in the direction of her gaze.

"It looked like they've been drugged or something. One almost tumbled off the dock, and neither one could hardly walk."

Cole shrugged. "Maybe they're drunk. It's the weekend after all, and from what Julian told me people party out here all the time."

"Then why are the two men sober while the girls couldn't keep their balance?"

"Perhaps, the girls are light weights like you."

She glared back at him, then shoved him.

"What? There's nothing wrong with being a lightweight, honey."

"Hush," she admonished. "This is serious, Cole."

"Do you want me to swim over there and crash their party?"

She frowned. "I guess it's none of our business. It just gave me the creeps. The way they were practically dragging those girls into the boat."

"Were the women trying to get away?"

She shook her head.

"Then it seems to me they might have had a little too much to drink. The guys might be taking them home."

The vessel bobbed with the movements of people inside. It bothered her that the two girls appeared awfully young to be hanging out with those guys.

Just then the sound of an approaching motor caused Jenna's head to spin around. "There you two are," Julian said as he and Clara drove up on the jet skis. "We thought you guys might be out here."

Clara peered around and said, "It is beautiful, isn't it? Me and Julian stumbled across this place years ago."

"It's really something," Jenna agreed.

"We've grilled burgers if you guys are hungry," Julian said. "Why don't you hop on, and we'll grab a bite to eat?"

"That sounds great," Cole said and swam toward one of the jet skis.

****

The sun was setting on the horizon, and Cole pointed the rental car in the direction of the resort. He peered over at his wife who sat quietly, attention glued to the windshield. He said, "We don't have to go if you don't want to."

When she swung around and stared at him, as if

she didn't catch what he said, he clarified, "To the beach party Julian and Clara invited us to tonight."

The expression in her eyes told him she'd snapped back to the present. "I really like Julian and Clara, and it sounds like fun. Why wouldn't I want to go?"

"You seem distracted."

She finally took a deep breath, shook her head, and pasted on a smile as if instantly recovering from her profound deliberations. "I'm looking forward to going tonight. Aren't you?"

He frowned, putting two and two together, and hung a right on Bluff Boulevard. "You're still thinking about those two girls on the boat."

The cheery façade he imagined she'd staged for his benefit melted from her face and she looked down as if she'd been busted stealing a cookie from the jar. "It just bugs the hell out of me. I swear those girls were teenagers, and the guys were in their mid-thirties."

"You didn't mention that."

"To be fair, there was quite a distance between me and the dock where they were. The view wasn't the best. Maybe I was wrong about their age."

"You heard what Julian said about the area, right? There's drug activity and prostitution going on. He mentioned the police have been doing their best to crack down on it."

She shrugged, as if it could have been possible that was what she witnessed.

He swung into the parking lot of the resort, drove the car toward the valets standing out front, and tossed a reassuring grin in Jenna's direction. "Why don't we forget about all this craziness for one night, go up to our room, get a shower, and enjoy the evening with Julian and Clara? What do you say, honey?"

She nodded, and the valet opened Cole's door, greeting him with a "Good evening, sir."

Cole handed over the keys while another valet swept the door open for Jenna.

"That sounds wonderful," she finally said, and they strolled into the resort hand in hand.

Chapter Five

The gathering on the beach was a small crowd of perhaps one hundred people by Cole's estimation. He recalled Julian telling him it was a private party one of his regular customers invited him and Clara to. From what the captain explained, the guy was a millionaire who sold real estate across the world. When he was in town, he'd throw small parties on his private beach for friends and acquaintances.

Cole slid his hand across the small of Jenna's back, and they navigated their way through thick sand toward the cluster of lit lanterns hanging from strings attached to various poles. The reggae music floated toward the shore, and the excited shouts of the guests whooped and clapped at what he guessed was a live band.

He plodded along beside her and peered at his wife. Her hair was caught up in a chignon, with a few loose tendrils dangling below her chin. Her sundress was glittery white, and strapless, hugging her sensuous curves as if the manufacturer designed it with her in mind. Come to think of it, with the way Cecilia insisted she dress like a socialite, it wouldn't have surprised him if the woman hired a seamstress to measure Jenna's every curve. But then it was highly unlikely his wife would have let her get away with it.

He glanced down at himself remembering how delighted she was he'd chosen a pair of comfortable, cotton, drawstring slacks that happened to match the color of her dress, though completely accidental. He'd replied, "I'm not trying to be your twin if that's what you think." She shrugged, saying, "I figured you'd wear a pair of shorts. So, I'm not complaining about your formal wear. I consider it a plus they happen to match my dress."

He would have worn shorts if it weren't for the ankle holster concealing the Glock. Since he was not on active duty when he boarded the plane from Texas and would not have been permitted to travel with his gun, he made prior arrangements with a guy his best man, Dylan Cruz knew, to borrow a handgun while in another state. He'd swung by to pick up the gun on his way here. And although he hadn't worn a gun since the plane touched down in Florida, he realized they would be around a lot of people tonight, and he didn't like taking the risk of being unprotected in the event something unexpected went down.

Cole clutched Jenna's hand while they wound through a horde of people, weaving their way to the bar. It was an impressive set-up for an outside gathering. It was obvious someone took a decent amount of time to construct the makeshift bar, complete with a tiki hut, and a bartender who dressed like a surfer.

When someone clapped Cole on the shoulder, he turned to find Julian standing there, cradling a drink. "I'm glad you guys made it." The captain pointed to a cluster of tables off to the right. "Me and Clara are seated right there."

The captain's wife threw up her hand and waved excitedly. Jenna signaled back, and said, "Can you order me a margarita, honey?" Then she was gone, making her way to the waiting Clara.

"Women," Julian blurted out with a knowing grin, then tipped his glass to his lips, taking a swallow while Cole ordered a margarita and a draft beer.

"I'll tell you though," Julian said, "Clara has really taken to Jenna. Your wife is all she wanted to talk about the whole way here."

"I can tell Jenna has bonded with her. With all the crap my wife has been through recently, it's nice to see her relaxing and enjoying some female companionship for a change."

The minute the words left his mouth, Cole regretted them. It wasn't like him to be so loose lipped when it came to sharing information with strangers, especially when he was this far from home.

Julian expressed sympathy. "Clara told me the details surrounding Jenna's auto accident last year. So, she's clairvoyant, huh?"

Cole wanted to roll his eyes. It appeared *his* big mouth wasn't the problem here. He was sure he'd told Jenna not to share intimate details of their lives with anyone they met while here. The detective in him was aware in a strange place the less information you offered people about you, the better. You never could surmise what people's true intentions were, and you didn't want to unintentionally provide them with ammunition they might use later.

Julian nodded, signaling to the bartender he needed another drink. "From what Clara told me, the poor girl has been through hell."

Cole switched gears quickly. "So, how long have you been giving tours? And where did you get such a cool boat?"

Julian frowned, downing the rest of his drink, and setting the empty glass on the bar. "Me and a good buddy of mine went into business many years ago repairing boats. He had the financial backing and I had the brains. When he passed away, I inherited the Saint Marie. I realized the demand for offering tours in this area would prove to be much more lucrative than making boat repairs for folks. So, I got my captain's license, and here I am."

The bartender slid their drinks toward them as Julian said, "Clara tells me you're a detective down in Texas."

What else didn't Jenna tell Clara?

"What's it like catching bad guys?"

Cole shook his head and snatched up the drinks. He spun around, heading toward the ladies. "You stay stressed and lose a lot of sleep."

Julian chuckled, strolling alongside him. "You should be a spokesperson for young cadets wanting to join the police academy."

"The excitement fades away quick. Trust me. Dealing with the criminal nature of people day after day makes it challenging to keep one's faith in the goodness of humanity. It wasn't until I became a detective and I worked with a lot of victims, that I began to see the other side. The pain and suffering of those people. How they relied on me to bring justice to their families. I think it was at that time I felt my career had real purpose. It suddenly became more important to me to offer them a sense of closure than it did to take criminals off the streets."

"Most people don't think that way."

"When you work a homicide, you do."

After approaching the table, Julian stepped over to his wife, planted a kiss on her cheek, then sank into the chair beside her. "What are you two ladies gabbing about?"

Clara's attention floated toward him. "Jenna has been telling me about their daughter, Emily."

Julian cleared his throat and glanced away with an air of discomfort. The reaction wasn't lost on Cole as he sat down, placing Jenna's margarita down in front of her.

Clara eyed them, her expression crestfallen. Then she peered away, saying softly, "Although me and Julian have always wanted children, I can't have any."

Jenna said, "You work for CPS, right? Can't you adopt one of those children?"

As Clara and Julian stared at one another, Cole closely observed their reactions. The captain directed a stern warning toward his wife with the way his eyes narrowed. It was undoubtedly a threat to shut her up. How odd.

Clara glanced up again, and a forced smile pinched the contours of her face. "How's your margarita?" she asked Jenna, in an obvious attempt to change the subject.

"You know, I haven't even tried it yet." She put the cocktail to her lips and took a sip. "Mm. It's tasty. All right."

"You work for CPS?" Cole said, forcing the issue. Seeing the hushed way her husband responded to the subject when Jenna mentioned it, he wanted to gauge his reaction.

Clara stared at the table, losing her smile, and shifted uncomfortably in her chair. Before she could respond, the band struck up again, playing a slow melody. Julian took Clara by the hand, drawing her out of the chair, and urging her toward the makeshift dance floor.

Cole shrank down into the chair next to Jenna, his attention never wavering from the retreating couple. Julian tugged his wife against his chest, leaning into her ear, his head jerking with what could only be construed as heated words. Clara backed away, her eyes widening in anger, letting fly a few gestures of exasperation herself.

"What are you doing?" Jenna asked, drawing his attention away from the tense exchange.

"Did you see that?" he asked. "The way those two were acting when Clara's career was mentioned?"

His wife shook her head, taking another healthy gulp of her drink.

And it dawned on Cole her margarita was going down far too quickly. With the sensation of uneasiness now sinking into his bones regarding the strange behavior of the captain and his wife, the last thing he wanted was for Jenna to get intoxicated and not have full control of her faculties.

"It's probably nothing. I think they're a little sensitive about not being able to have children."

"I think Julian didn't want us to know Clara works for Child Protective Services."

She smirked, straightening the hem of her dress. "You're being overly suspicious again."

"What if I'm not?"

She stared at him as if he couldn't be serious. "We're here on our honeymoon. Once we leave and go back to Texas, we'll never hear from them again. So, why would they care if we know what Clara does for a living?"

"That's exactly my point. Why would they care? But Julian obviously does." He pointed toward her drink. "You've only had that margarita for five minutes, and it's almost gone. Maybe you should slow down."

"So, now you're going to monitor my drinking?"

He didn't appreciate her flippant attitude. He was just trying to keep her safe. They were in a strange place, and now the couple they'd attended this party with was acting out of sorts. He had every right to question their peculiar behavior and raise the issue that in this circumstance she might not want to get inebriated. And that was without adding the fact she'd blabbed to a stranger, telling Clara all about their personal lives. How reckless could someone be?

He glared at her, a warning flashing in his eyes. "All I'm saying is, we're in unfamiliar surroundings. It's not a good idea to let your guard down. Alcohol slows your response. You downed that pretty fast."

"What's that in your hand?" she asked, pointing to his beer. "It's okay for you to drink, but not me?"

Irritation crept through him. She was blowing this way out of proportion. "I've had one beer, Jenna. And it's still half-full. Since my body weight is different than yours, my alcohol tolerance is not the same. I don't plan on having another. Someone's got to be responsible and keep us safe."

Her eyes grew large. "Safe? From what?"

"I'm not getting a good vibe from these two. I can't explain it. I just need you to trust me."

"You're the one who told me to relax and enjoy myself. That was the reason we came here, isn't it?"

Her indifference frustrated the hell out of him. He was a detective and was trained in how to read these situations. Why was she giving him such a hard time? "I think we should leave."

"You're out of your mind."

"You guys are leaving?" Clara said, coming up from behind. She stood there, lips curved with disappointment.

Cole stared at Jenna, and she lowered her head in obvious embarrassment the couple had overhead the tail end of their conversation.

"Is everything all right?" Julian asked, drawing out a chair for Clara, and taking his usual seat beside her.

"It's fine," Cole answered. "It's just that we have a big day planned for tomorrow and we should probably turn in early."

"It isn't anything we've done, is it?" Julian prodded again, examining their expressions.

Jenna peered up and smiled reassuringly. But Cole could see the storm clouds gathering in her eyes. He'd sort things out with her later. For now, he sensed with everything inside him leaving was the right thing to do.

To his relief Jenna said, "Don't be silly. We have enjoyed your company more than ever. And we wanted to thank you for such an enjoyable day. But Cole's right. We really do have a busy day tomorrow. It's probably best we get some sleep."

Discontentment emanated from Clara's eyes. "Can you at least stay for one more drink? I promise we won't keep you more than thirty minutes."

Jenna relinquished with a nod. "I don't see why not." She glared at Cole; that, don't you dare make a spectacle, admonishment in her eyes. "What do you think, honey?"

Since she put him on the spot like that, what else could he say? "I'll go get the drink order."

The offer to make a trip to the bar to order another round was deliberate. He didn't want to hand Julian or Clara an opportunity to slip something into their drinks if either one of them was up to no good. Although he realized his guarded way of thinking was not an ordinary process for the average person, his duties as a homicide detective strengthened his perceptions, opening him up to clues most people would not pick up on. It was those sensitivities that saved his ass on more than one occasion.

He sauntered to the bar and couldn't shake the uneasy premonition that settled into his gut. Something about those two didn't set right with him. They hadn't acted out of character earlier in the day. They both portrayed themselves as an ordinary, happy couple. He recalled Julian telling him they'd been married for twenty years. The guy was sure free flowing with information about him and Clara before. Why now, the secrecy concerning what his wife did for a living? The man's reaction to Jenna's mentioning the subject was out of the range of normal.

An image of the captain speaking to his wife on the dance floor with ire raised the hackles on the back of Cole's neck. They were hiding something.

After waving down the bartender, Cole rattled off the drink order, leaving out a beer for himself. The festivities were over as far as he was concerned. He'd let Jenna finish her drink and they would high-tail it out of here. It peeved him to no degree that she'd questioned his instincts. She of all people, with her history of clairvoyance, should have known not to doubt someone else's intuition, especially that of a police detective. Why was she being so stubborn and unreasonable tonight?

Probably because she'd been through so much and was excited for this opportunity to relax and enjoy herself. After all, she was right. It had been he who suggested they go on this boat tour as a way of forgetting about the alarming experiences Jenna was having since the day of their wedding. But that still did not excuse the fact that when he told her his suspicions were raised, she refused to take it seriously.

He recalled her words from earlier, *it's okay for you to drink, but not me?* It was becoming clear she was still fighting for her independence, the way she'd confessed she was doing a few weeks in advance of their wedding the last time, before his brother's sinister deeds put their plans to marry on hold for the next ten months.

She had been on her own raising their daughter for so many years before they reunited, and he realized getting hitched and allowing someone else to share in the decision making was a big change for her. It certainly couldn't have been made any better with Cecilia's insistence she allow her to handle certain aspects of Jenna's life.

Although he understood the grounds manager was only attempting to fulfill the role she satisfied for years at The Blazing Saddle Ranch, even long before he and Jenna came along, her stubbornness to see it through so thoroughly was only making his wife more resentful. Both women had a take-charge attitude, and the result was constant clashing. He really needed to have a talk with Cecilia. Persuade her to back off a bit.

And he ought to give Jenna a break. He realized the vast change in their lives, going from a small-town couple, to becoming the owners of a wealthy estate with millions in the bank was not an easy transition. Especially for her, whose deep roots made her feel as if living this kind of extravagant life somehow made her untrue to the person she was. He'd dealt with the same emotions to begin with. But he learned to accept their newfound fortune, and all the adjustments that came with it. It wasn't so terrible letting those in charge do their jobs, while he investigated expanding their fortune.

He recalled the discussion he'd had with Dylan Cruz a month ago, and a grin crept across his face. The guy had his eye on a fifty-acre-tract of land in the country that was on the market for a good price. He'd presented Cole with a business proposition. With Cruz's background in construction, and Cole's financial backing, they could split the property into separate lots, build homes and sell them individually. With the way real estate was exploding in Texas because of the high demand for new homes, it was a sound investment.

"Here you go, man," the bartender said, breaking his train of thought. The guy slid his drink order across the bar.

Cole nodded his appreciation, and while balancing the tray, spun on his heels and headed back toward the table.

The closer he got, the more apparent it became Julian was the only one sitting there. His head spun in every direction, scanning the faces of the guests. Jenna was nowhere to be found. His heart skipped a beat, and he advanced toward the table, setting the drinks down. He stared at Julian who leaned back in his chair, a lazy grin on his face. "Where's Jenna?"

"She and Clara headed down to the shore to take a walk. They wanted us to join them with the drinks."

"How long ago?" Cole calculated in his head how many minutes ticked by while he waited at the bar. He couldn't have been standing there more than ten minutes. It would have been long enough for something to have happened to her.

An uneasy sensation slammed into his gut and Cole took off, winding his way around tables and chairs, dodging the cluster of people leisurely going about their business, and bumping into a few.

The captain's voice called out from behind, and Cole hit the shore, his feet sinking into the loose sand with every step he took. His gaze darted frantically around, but there wasn't a soul around, and it didn't matter how much distance he closed. The tide rushing in was the only sound.

Cole rounded a corner where a few beach houses stood on stilts. As he scanned the area, Julian called his name again. This time he realized the captain couldn't have been more than a few feet behind him. A chill ran down the length of his spine, and he remained as still as a statue. A formidable premonition gripped him. He couldn't for the life of him explain how he knew a gun was trained on the back of his head, but it was as sure as the waves crashing against the shore.

Before another second ticked by, Cole hunched over, acting as if he was attempting to catch his breath. He freed the gun from the ankle holster, spun and trained the Glock dead center of Julian's head.

Finch's mouth dropped open. Surprise lit his eyes, and the gun in the man's hand shook slightly.

"Where's Jenna?" Cole demanded, holding a steady finger on the trigger.

It was apparent the man was doing everything to regain control of the situation. "I can't tell you that."

"You have about five seconds to tell me, or I'll bury a slug in your forehead."

"What if I shoot you first?" he taunted.

"If you were going to shoot me, you would have already done it," Cole said.

"It wasn't supposed to go down this way."

No shit. "Where's my wife?"

"She's safe. Maybe we can talk about this. Work out a solution. Look, I'll put down my gun." Finch slowly held out both hands and lowered the weapon.

A boat fired up in the distance, causing Cole's head to swing in that direction. Within a split second, the click of a bullet being loaded into the chamber told him Julian was making his move.

Cole swung around and fired.

His target stood there, unmoving, the pistol slipping from his grip. Blood oozed from a hole in his forehead. The body crumpled to the ground.

Cole didn't waste a second. He sprinted across the sand, rounded another corner and spotted a man untying a black and white boat from the dock. It was the same small vessel he and Jenna spotted by the waterfall earlier in the day. The guy saw Cole and jumped onto the boat, hollering at the person behind the wheel.

Cole fired a few rounds in an attempt to stop them from taking off. It didn't work, and Cole ran up the dock just as the boat sped off.

He couldn't afford to waste time. Whoever was on that boat had Jenna. With the adrenalin pounding in his ears, he quickly scanned the area for another boat, and realized there weren't any. He hiked back to the gathering, and made a beeline straight for the bar, still gripping the gun.

Breathless, he shouted at the bartender, "Who has a boat?"

Loud gasps fanned out amongst the crowd, and people backed away as Cole quickly approached the bar with a gun in his hand. He imagined the guests were scared shitless. But he didn't have time to care.

The surfer-bartender threw up his hands and took a few clumsy steps back, his lips trembling. "I'm not going to shoot you. Someone on a boat just kidnapped my wife. I need to know if anyone has a boat here."

"I do," a voice said from behind.

Cole spun around to come face to face with a Latino in a straw cowboy hat. His shoulder rested against a wooden pole, and his long legs were crossed in front of him. His arms hugged his body leisurely, as if he was holed up there for a while, watching the goings-on.

As the man's identity clicked in Cole's mind, fire lit up every nerve ending in his body. He was the Spanish cowboy at the precinct earlier today Jenna mentioned was staring at her and giving her the creeps. Cole instantly raised his Glock to the man's head. More stunned cries rang out from the crowd, and the stranger blinked but remained unmoved. The few people who hadn't already fled the immediate area, scrambled for cover.

"You were the guy at the police station earlier. The

one who was staring at my wife. Who the fuck are you?"

Although cautious, the guy didn't flinch the way someone with a gun to their head would have done. His graveled voice was a little too relaxed for Cole's comfort. "I thought you said someone kidnapped your wife. I have a boat. Do you want my help or not?"

Cole weighed his options. He sure as hell didn't trust this guy, even if the expression in his eyes reflected no ill intent. The truth was, he didn't know who he could trust. But he desperately needed the use of his boat if Jenna stood any chance of being rescued, and it appeared no one else was willing to offer up their craft to a gun-waving lunatic. He had the Glock. If the man attempted anything funny, he'd leave him as dead as the guy he'd laid out on the shore earlier.

"Where's your boat?"

"Follow me, and I'll take you to it."

Thankfully, the stranger acted with urgency as both men sprinted down the shore and rounded a few beach houses. Up ahead in a cove, the light of the moon homed in on a small, aluminum fishing boat tied to a pole sticking a few feet out of the ground. They made a beeline for it, and Cole jumped in a few seconds behind the boat owner.

The guy fired up the engine while Cole untied the rope. "Which way are we going?" the man asked, folding the bendable cowboy hat, and shoving it into his back pocket.

Cole pointed in the direction the kidnappers fled.

They took off, and the craft sped across the water so fast, Cole braced himself to keep from being thrown over the side.

The stranger tossed him a life vest.

He wrestled into it, and the man hollered over the roar of the engine, "The boat your wife is on. Do you know what kind it is?"

"It's a black and white cruiser. Small. Maybe twenty-four feet."

They raced forward, and both men scanned the water for signs of any other boats.

A thousand scenarios ran through Cole's mind. Who took his wife and why did they take her? He recalled Julian's response to his question about where his wife was. *She's safe.* What in the hell did that mean?

Who were Julian and Clara Finch? They were not at all who they portrayed themselves to be. This whole thing, taking them on a tour, and then inviting them to a beach party later in the evening, was a set up from the beginning. He couldn't deny that much. But why? What did they plan to do with Jenna?

Disbelief slammed into him with the obliterating force of a tsunami. Things had been fine one minute, and the next his entire world was ripped from its axis and tossed into a state of utter devastation. His heart ached with such intensity it was hard to breathe. Everything in his being screamed for the safe return of his wife. And with the sense of awareness settling deep in his gut for the fear she must be experiencing right now, came a rising level of despair that he would not be able to find her, and she would be lost to him forever. Jesus Christ, this was all his fault. He had a feeling something wasn't right, yet he stuck around long enough to put her at risk. He'd known better than that. And now, here he was.

His wife's words when he snuck up on her as she was watching the mysterious boat by the waterfall earlier in the day, came crashing through his head. *There's something wrong with those women,* she had said, referring to the girls the two guys took down into the boat cabin. She described them as being drugged. Jesus, was that what they were planning to do to Jenna? Did those men kidnap those girls? Then realization struck him. If the boat had been spotted by the waterfall before, maybe that's where it was headed now. It wasn't far from here.

"Head to the waterfall," he told the Spanish cowboy.

The man peered over his shoulder, and Cole explained, "Me and my wife saw that boat earlier today. It was docked on the other side of the waterfall."

The stranger nodded and steered the boat in that direction. The craft slowed and rounded the corner behind the waterfall. They drifted through the water, but nothing could be seen on the bank, or anywhere else. If they'd ended up here with Jenna, where could they have gone?

As if reading his mind, the guy mentioned, "There's a boat ramp up ahead."

Cole nodded, and they took off.

The lot beyond the ramp was completely deserted. Although it was dark, streetlamps lit up the parking spaces. Nothing more than an old beer cooler missing its top sitting off to the side, a few discarded soda cans, and some empty ice bags could be seen. "Where does that road lead?" Cole asked, pointing to the street leading out of the parking lot.

"To the highway. But we don't know if they used

this ramp. There are others. And I'm afraid they would have been long gone by now."

The boat softly idled, and Cole focused his attention on the stranger. It was time for him to answer some questions. "Who are you and what were you doing at the police station?"

With his back facing Cole, he answered, "My name is Diego Florentino. And my sister, Luisa, came up missing a week ago. I was at the station trying to get the sergeant to open a missing person's investigation. I've been there every day since she disappeared. They refuse to help."

Swiveling in his seat, he stared at Cole, appearing lost, desperate for answers that no one was willing to provide. "My sister is a heroin addict. She's been that way since our parents died in a car accident last year." He shook his head, lowering it to his chest. "After they died, she got mixed up with the wrong people. I wasn't there for her like I should have been."

"The people at the precinct think she ran off," Cole said.

Diego sat up. "Yes, Luisa did that a couple times. This time is different."

There was a determination in his dark eyes, as if the need to tell the truth was the single most important thing in his world. "She called me from a convenience store the night she went missing. *They* were after her. That's what she said. She was afraid they were going to track her to the store. She mentioned something about a tracking device in her arm. If she escaped, they'd find her. I told her to stay where she was. The store was only ten minutes from my house. But by the time I got there…she was gone."

Disturbing scenarios swirled around Cole's brain. What Diego described sounded a lot like what sex traffickers would do to their victims. The mentioning of the tracking device was a dead giveaway. That's exactly how they ensured none of the girls could escape. But why would they target Jenna?

Julian Finch knew he was a police detective, and he wouldn't just let her kidnapping go unanswered. The guy had to know Cole would gather every resource in the world to find his wife. Then again, Julian planned to kill him tonight.

There were tons of easy targets, like Luisa, who required much less effort and wouldn't pose any kind of a risk to their operation. Why go to all this trouble to kidnap a detective's wife? Killing a detective and abducting his wife was just asking for boatloads of trouble—not to mention the publicity it would bring down on them. And traffickers did not like publicity.

With him and Jenna being out-of-towners, maybe that's what made them an easy target. If no one ever found him or Jenna out here in Florida, the authorities may not have applied as many resources because it wasn't a LLEO—local law enforcement officer involved.

Then, there was a connection between Jenna and Diego's sister, Luisa. Although he couldn't be sure if Jenna may have told Clara about her chats with a ghost named Luisa, Jenna certainly had run her mouth about other personal things. Finch had disclosed enough of Jenna's discussions with Clara, if she'd blabbed about the dead girl, he would have said something.

Cole swallowed hard, doing all he could to hold on to his sanity. Suspecting Jenna was kidnapped by traffickers and not knowing what they were doing to her at this moment, was enough to drive him to complete madness.

"Do you have any ideas about who kidnapped your sister?"

He recognized a glimmer of hope in Diego's eyes, a look that told him that finally someone was taking interest. "When I got to the store that night, I spoke to the cashier. He said two men came into the store and grabbed Luisa. The taller of the two said he was her boyfriend, and that she was strung out on heroin. He was going to get her home and help her sober up."

"The cashier let them walk out with her?"

Diego lowered his head again and nodded. "There was a homeless man outside the store. Goes by the name of Greg. Greg the Grifter, he said. I asked him if he saw a lady struggling in the parking lot with two men. He said he watched the whole thing go down. She'd kicked the taller one in the shins and got away, but the other one grabbed her. It took the both of them to shove her into the back of an older model, black car."

Luisa's brother took a deep breath and clenched his jaw, as if he was coming to grips with the disturbing reality of what happened to his sister. "Greg told me it wasn't the first time he'd seen those guys roll up to the store with women in the backseat. Most of the time the girls were either out cold or so lethargic they didn't do much in the way of moving."

"Where is this Greg the Grifter?" If Cole could find him, he could question him for details a civilian might not think to ask.

Diego put up a hand as if to signal there was more coming. "The next day I saw on the news, Greg had been found dead, thrown into the dumpster behind the store.

So much for that.

Burning disappointment settled into his gut; Cole motioned for Florentino to continue.

"I returned to the store, day after day, watching to see if those guys came back. And sure enough, one of them drove up two days ago in the same car Greg described. I spotted a young girl with her hands tied in the backseat, and I pounded on the window to get her attention. But she didn't move. I don't know if she was dead, or out cold like the homeless guy said they sometimes were. Then the tall guy I'd seen go into the store came running out. He shouted at me to get away from his car. I got in my vehicle and followed him. And before I knew it, the bastard was shooting at me from the driver's seat. He slammed on the brakes, got out of his car, and came toward me with a pistol. I had no choice but to get the hell out of there."

Stunned, Cole sat there, listening while Diego finished his incredible tale. He knew beyond the shadow of a doubt they were dealing with a well-organized sex trafficking organization. And these monsters had his wife. Fighting a wave of panic mixed with rage and despair, he asked, "Do the police know all of this?"

Diego stood and threw out his hands. "I told them everything. They refuse to believe sex traffickers took my sister. They said there isn't enough evidence to point toward that. Told me to go home, that Luisa was just on one of her drug binges again, and she'd resurface. But I know what's going on here. The last time I spoke to my sister she sounded different than she ever did before. I knew she was telling the truth. I don't know how I knew that. I just did."

"I believe you, Diego."

To that, he slowly sat back down, shaking his head. "She's dead, isn't she?"

Cole didn't respond.

"I overhead your wife at the police station. She said she saw my sister and that she had a bullet hole in her head."

"Is that why you followed us here?"

His head bobbed in answer. "I'm not trying to be a stalker. I just wanted to know what happened to Luisa is all. And I thought your wife could provide that information. I had no idea how I was going to approach the two of you without coming off like a nutjob. But I figured it would come to me when the opportunity presented itself."

"Did you see what happened on the shore?" Cole asked, referring to the showdown with Julian Finch.

The guy shook his head. "I lost sight of you. I never saw you leave the bar, but after some time, I noticed you were gone. I wasn't sure where you went until I saw you coming back."

"I killed the guy—the boat captain—we were with. He pulled a gun on me just as I realized my wife was kidnapped. Do you know them? The couple we were sitting with?"

"I've seen the guy around. He gives tours on that fancy boat of his. But I don't know much about him. The lady. I've never seen her before."

"I'm sorry," Cole finally said, "Luisa might be dead. And I believe you're right. A sex trafficking ring is involved here. I think that's who took your sister, and now they have my wife."

From out of nowhere, Diego screwed up his face and, fighting back tears, announced, "Fuck the police. Let's go get her ourselves."

Cole planned to. But the police were going to get involved whether they liked it or not.

Chapter Six

Jenna hoped the shots fired outside the boat came from her husband in pursuit of her captors. Although they'd slapped a strip of duct tape over her mouth the moment they'd converged on her from out of nowhere, she fought them like a wildcat, kicking, pummeling, scratching, and kneeing.

It wasn't until after they'd settled her into the cabin, and Clara Finch flew at her and slapped her across the face hard enough to make her ears ring, that she'd halted her defense. The hatred emanating from her took Jenna's breath. She had no idea where such animosity could have come from. After slapping her, the captain's wife warned if Jenna didn't get control of herself, she'd slit her throat and be done with it.

Even as she curled up on the soiled seat that reeked of sweat and urine, hands and legs bound with duct tape, she had no idea what these men wanted with her or this woman's role in all of it. But the memory of those two brutes with the young girls who appeared drugged and confused, nagged at her. Whatever that was, it wasn't good.

Cole was right—and she'd blown him off. There was something seriously wrong with Clara and Julian Finch.

What could they possibly want with her? She could only surmise the reason for her being here was no different than those two girls she'd witnessed being swept into the cabin by the same men who took her now. Jesus, there'd be only one reason they kidnapped females. They intended to sell them to the highest bidder.

It was too late to downplay this in her mind. The whole thing had been a setup from the award-winning performances of the captain and his wife meant to lure her here, the boat docked and ready to take her away, and the men coming out of nowhere to snatch her up. Out of all the women they could have targeted, they chose a detective's wife. How foolish was that?

Cole would come for her. He had to.

As if reading her mind, Clara Finch, sitting in the seat across from her, a disdainful scowl dripping from her face, said, "I don't know what kind of shit your husband thought he was pulling back there, but where we're taking you, he'll never find us. He should have been dead by now. If he isn't, he will be soon enough."

So it was Cole who fired shots at the boat. Thank God he was alive. Jenna's fiery response came out as a series of muffles. She cursed the tape that trapped her voice. She wanted to tell this stupid bitch it didn't matter where they took her, Cole would never give up the search—and if she thought they'd get rid of him that easily, she had another think coming. After that, she'd love nothing more than to spit in the woman's face.

"Oh, stop blubbering," Clara said. "Nothing you say will make a difference anyhow. We have ways of getting what we want."

A voice came from the corner of the cramped cabin. "Why did you let them take you?"

Jenna's head spun toward the sound. She feasted

her eyes on the dead girl, crouched in a cubbyhole nestled in between the seat and the far wall, and staring at her with burning disappointment. "You realize you're as good as dead now, right? They'll never let you get out of this alive. They'll kill you just like they did me. Just like they did all those other girls."

Jenna started, back peddling against the cushion. A scream shot up her throat, only to be muffled by the tape.

Clara bolted off her seat, snatching off the tape with one fast rip. "Do you see the ghost right now? Is she talking to you?"

Confusion swirled around Jenna's brain. How did Clara know about Luisa's visits?

The captain's wife grabbed her by the chin and jerked her head up. "I asked you a question. You'd be wise to answer me."

"I-I don't know what you're talking about."

At this point, Jenna realized there was more to this abduction than she'd originally suspected. But if Clara could see Luisa, she wouldn't be asking if the girl was talking to her. So no, Clara couldn't interact directly with the ghost—but she was certainly interested to know if Jenna could. Best to keep the fact she could see Luisa under wraps until she could figure out the connection.

"You don't think I can tell when you're lying?" Clara said, leaning in so close Jenna could detect a slight glimmer of fear in her eyes. "You better start talking."

"What are you afraid of?" Jenna asked, holding back the urge to spit in her face as she'd wanted to do earlier.

"Hmph." The woman let go of her face with a fling. "You think you're so smart. You don't know anything about me."

"I know something's got you good 'n' spooked. You might as well tell me what it is. I'm probably not going to survive this anyhow, right?"

Through Clara's sneering grin, she noted anxiety breaking out around the seams. The captain's wife retook her seat, letting out a carefree chuckle. "What do I have to be afraid of? You, on the other hand, have every right to be scared shitless."

"Cole will never let this go. He will hunt you down. You can bet your sweet ass he will find you. And when he does…"

"Your husband will be dead by morning."

"He should have already been dead. But he isn't, is he? And he knows you took me away on this boat."

For a moment, the grin slid from Clara's face, and the emotion replacing it was pure nerves. "How about I just kill you right now?"

Jenna could not define the bravery that welled up, nor where it came from, but it was there, giving her courage to stand up to these monsters. "I don't think so. You brought me here for a reason. You'll never get what you want if I'm dead."

"You must really think you're something," Clara said. The boat motor whined to a low purr; the vessel rocked to a stop. "You're not the first little bitch who thought she was smarter than us. And just like the others, you will learn the hard way that we always get what we want."

****

Cole sat on a stump next to Julian Finch's lifeless

body and gripped the phone against his ear. Alan Bancroft's gravelly voice answered. It was around midnight; Cole suspected he'd awakened the sergeant out of a dead sleep. "You should know I killed that captain you recommended."

"Who the hell is this?" Cole could imagine the man sitting up in bed about now, his hand going for the lamp, an expression of bewilderment tugging at his face.

"Detective Cole Rainwater. Me and my wife were in to see you earlier today."

"I'm sorry. There for a minute it sounded like you said you killed the captain."

Cole's attention drifted over to the dead guy laying no more than a few feet from him and examined the blood coagulating around the hole in his forehead. "He looks pretty dead to me, sarge. Maybe you can tell me how well you know this guy."

"I don't...I mean I do...wait a minute. You killed him?"

"He pulled a gun on me and tried to shoot me. That was after his wife kidnapped Jenna."

"What are you talking about?" Bancroft yelped. "Finch's wife died from bone cancer seven years ago."

Cole expected the man to act stunned by the things he told him, even ask a few questions, but he didn't anticipate what came out of his mouth. If Clara wasn't Julian's wife, then who the hell was she?

"How do you know his wife died?"

"Because it was in the obituaries. Her name was Abigail. Listen, I've shared a few beers with Julian when I've seen him in the local tavern a few times, and I've chatted with him when I've run into him out and about. Me and Cheryl took him up on a tour once last summer. The locals speak highly of him and his services. That's why I recommended him to you. But I don't really know the guy. Did you say someone kidnapped your woman?"

Cole ignored the question. "Describe his wife."

"She was a redhead, skinny with lots of freckles. What happened to your wife?"

Clara was a blonde, and a little on the hefty side. They couldn't be the same girl. "Was Julian dating someone? This woman said she worked for CPS."

"No…I mean I don't know. I can't remember seeing him around with anyone since Abigail died. Where is your wife?"

"I think you need to get dressed and get down here, sarge. Call the ME. They'll need a body bag. We'll talk when you get here."

After rattling off his location to Bancroft, Cole slid his finger across the phone, ending the call, and stared at Diego who leaned against a nearby palm tree, his straw cowboy hat perched on his head. He was chewing on a twig, reminding Cole of a vaquero from one of those old wild west movies.

Diego stepped toward the corpse. "You sure did a number on him." He leaned down, going for the gun in the sand next to the dead guy.

"Don't touch that," Cole said, coming off the stump. "It's evidence. We don't want to smudge the captain's fingerprints. They might try to frame me for murder."

"Why would they do that?"

"Bancroft's the one who recommended Jenna and I take a boat tour with Finch. It could have been a trap, or it could have been coincidence. I can't be sure at this point. There are more people involved in this than what we see on the surface. This is a sex trafficking ring. Where there's this magnitude of money involved, there will be people with their hands out, willing to use their positions of power to help these assholes along and fill their own pockets."

Cole saw the lights go on inside Diego's head. "Damn. That makes sense, you know. Them not taking me seriously and refusing to open a missing person's investigation for my sister."

"Don't get ahead of yourself. We have zero evidence to back up our suspicions at this point."

"What do you say we get some?"

"I'm working on it," Cole murmured while he searched the contact list in his phone. He scrolled across Dylan Cruz's number and hit the call button.

"Hey, man," Cruz said after he finally answered the phone. "Do you know what time it is?"

"You realize there's only one reason you'd hear from me after midnight, right?"

A pause and then, "What happened?"

"Jenna's been kidnapped."

"Again? How the hell did that happen?"

His buddy's question caused the instant resurfacing of the fear and torment Cole felt the moment he realized Jenna was missing. It was like ripping a Band Aid off a fresh cut. There had been an overwhelming amount of activity going on since the kidnapping, and he'd focused so much of his energy on finding her. But the sound of Cruz's voice back home was just the thing to bring his emotions exploding to the surface. He bowed his head, choking back tears.

The thought of Jenna out there, scared and suffering, was enough to tear his heart out.

He somehow found his voice through the gripping pain. "These are some seriously bad people who grabbed her. When can you catch the next flight out?"

"Shit." Rustling echoed over the phone. Cole pictured the Texas Ranger searching for his glasses on the bedside table. "Any clue who took her?"

"She said her name is Clara Finch, but I'm sure that's not her real name. I shot her pretend husband. He's lying on the beach with a bullet in his head. I'm staring right at him."

"You're with him right now?"

"I'm waiting for the police to get here. I can't be sure if any of them are involved in this."

"What the hell is going on out there?"

"I think sex traffickers took my wife."

"You're kidding me."

I'm responsible for letting it happen. If I'd listened to my instincts, I would have gotten her out of this situation before any of this happened.

"I'll have my ass on the next plane out. I'll call you as soon as I land at the airport." A sigh and then, "Cole. Stay vigilant. Keep your eyes and ears open. Pay attention to the little things going on in that police department. If any of them are in on this, there'll be signs."

As Cole issued his thanks to Cruz, he reflected on the strange way the one detective had acted after he and Jenna stepped out of Bancroft's office earlier that morning. His investigator's hunch told him something was off. He'd strolled through the bullpen, feeling the stares bore into the back of his head. At this point, he honestly couldn't say if Bancroft was part of this. The guy acted straight forward and didn't seem as if he was hiding anything. But he couldn't say the same for the rest of them.

The people who took his wife had wanted him dead. With Cole out of the way they would have been free to do whatever they wanted with Jenna. Jesus. She's got to be frightened out of her mind about now. These monsters were the worst kind of criminals in existence. They were ruthless and abused their victims in unimaginable ways. He'd let her down again. Why did this keep happening to them?

Because they'd failed to get Cole out of the way, they might take her out of Florida to keep him off their trail. That was the problem with these trafficking organizations. They continuously relocated girls from state to state, making it damn near impossible to track them down. Although he'd never directly worked a sex trafficking sting before, being in law enforcement he had a decent idea how they operated. He would need to target one of their sources, and then bleed the bastard for information on Jenna's whereabouts, and he'd need to do it before her trail went cold. The clock was ticking.

****

Jenna lay curled on a soiled mattress. The only light in the room came from a nightlight plugged into an outlet on the opposite side of the room. The black pillowcase they'd finally snatched off her head after shuffling her into this room sat crumpled on the rickety bedside table. She recalled the two men slipping it over her head before they climbed out of the boat with her. No doubt the measure was meant to keep her from taking in any of the surroundings. They didn't want her to know where they'd taken her. There would be no use attempting to leave this room. The click of the lock told her they'd secured the door behind them after they left her in here alone.

"I escaped from here, you know."

Before Jenna bothered to peer toward the end of the bed, she already figured Luisa was sitting there. She wiggled around far enough to face the girl.

"They put me in this room, too," she said. "Kept me chained up on this bed to begin with. This is where they took the last bit of dignity I had left. They'd take turns raping me, pumping me so full of heroin that I couldn't even tell night from day. Then, after they completely broke my spirit, they led me into the bathroom and told me to take a shower because I had a customer waiting for me." She lowered her head, remaining silent long enough that Jenna opened her mouth to say something.

Then Luisa said, "I wasn't some innocent victim like you might think though. I brought this on myself. I've done some things in my life I'm not proud of."

"What could you have ever done to deserve that kind of treatment?"

She shook her head, then resettled herself. "I was hooked on heroin long before Simon came along. You have no idea how many times I've prostituted myself for more dope."

"None of that justifies what these animals did to you," Jenna said. "No one has the right to take you against your will, force you to have sex with men, then profit off that."

"The kind of life I lived opened the door to that

horror," Luisa admitted.

"It doesn't matter."

Luisa veered her attention away from her. Staring off into the darkness of the room. She snorted. "You have no idea the kind of person I am."

"I know you escaped from here because you didn't want to live like this. I know they used you and they had no right to do that. They're the monsters, not you."

"When Simon came along, he got me off the streets. Helped me to get clean. He moved me into this beautiful apartment. Life was good for the first time since my parents died. And then one day he invited a friend over. They sat me down and told me I was going to be a prostitute again, only they were going to collect the money and I wouldn't get any of it."

Sorrow sank deep into the crevices of Jenna's heart. She couldn't imagine what that must have been like for this poor woman.

"I tried to fight them," Luisa continued. In the brief bit of light a glistening of fresh tears streamed down her face. "But they threatened to kill my brother, and I knew they'd do it, too. After they brought me here, I wasn't as obedient as they wanted. So, they held me down and put a needle in my arm. And just like that, I was addicted to heroin all over again. It no longer mattered how hard I fought to put that miserable life behind me. Once they introduced me to it again, I begged them for more. They used the drugs as a means to control me. To get me to turn tricks."

"What they did to you wasn't your fault. They knew you were a recovering addict. And like you said, they used that weakness to get you to do what they wanted. You had no choice, Luisa."

The girl searched Jenna's face, as if seeking answers. "Then why do I feel so guilty?"

"Because as an addict you must have carried guilt around so often, that even when you became clean, you never let it go."

Jenna was surprised at her response. It wasn't as if she'd ever dealt with drug addiction, or knew anyone first-hand who did, but she could sense this young woman's anguish as clearly as she could identify her own. She had a sixth sense what was at the root of Luisa's emotional battle.

The dead girl didn't say anything for a moment. Then she shrugged as if accepting Jenna's hypothesis. "Do you know someone who was an addict or something?"

Instead of answering the question, Jenna asked one of her own. "Is Simon one of the men who took me?"

"The tall one with the dark hair." She gave a cautionary frown. "He can be very persuasive. He doesn't like to be disobeyed. Best not to cross him. Just do what he says and he won't hurt you."

Oh, she planned on disobeying him every chance she got. These bastards were going to rue the day they took her hostage. She damn sure wasn't going to make anything easy for them. She'd give them a run for their money, all right. At least until Cole came for her. And he would come for her, wouldn't he?

"You're not afraid of them. Are you?"

"I've been chased by a serial killer, buried six feet in the ground and held for ransom. And I died too. These assholes are the ones who should be afraid when my husband comes for them."

Luisa shook her head, appearing seriously

doubtful. "You don't get it. These guys are very good at what they do. They know how to fly under the radar. No one will ever catch them. Not even your husband, whoever he is."

For the tiniest fraction of a moment, the girl's words planted a seed of doubt in Jenna's mind as to her husband's ability to track her down to this place. But she stubbornly tossed it aside. She trusted Cole with every inch of her being. He was a good detective. And he would search the ends of the earth to find her. After all, he'd managed to save her when his brother put her in the ground to rot. Even when she figured it was hopeless, and she had lain in that tiny casket surrounded by darkness and misery, he came to her rescue. He resuscitated her back to life again. This time would be no different. He would come for her. She just needed to be brave and bide her time until he got here.

As an idea occurred to her, she focused her attention on Luisa. "You said you escaped from here. How did you do it?"

The girl shook her head as if she realized what Jenna was implying, that perhaps she could escape the same way she did. "That was a case of luck. They let one of the other girls bring a meal in here for me. She neglected to lock the door on her way out. To this day I wonder if she did it purposely." She appeared deep in deliberation, then snapped out of it with a sigh. "I opened the door and tip-toed down the hall. I noticed the only one here at the time was Simon. I waited until he was distracted, and I ran out the back door, through the woods, and was lucky enough to find my way to the road. There wasn't a single, stray driver in sight that day. So, I walked all the way to the nearest store, and called my brother."

She tapped her shoulder where Jenna saw a small scar about an inch in length. "But because of this tracking device they put in my arm, they were able to hunt me down. I think the reason I was able to get as far as I had gotten was because Simon must not have noticed my disappearance right away. They got to me before I could leave the store."

She stared at Jenna with a torturous expression. "My brother was on his way to get me. He didn't make it in time, and I often wonder how badly that must have affected him. Is he still searching for me? Will he ever know the truth of what happened? I have been trying to find him ever since they murdered me. But I've been running around in circles. I think I'm going somewhere, but I end up right back in the same place I started. Until I saw you in that church. I was drawn there for reasons I can't explain. Why are you the only one I can communicate with?"

"I'm psychic, Luisa. I think when I died something happened to me. I'm suddenly able to see people who have passed on, when before I couldn't."

The girl's eyes grew large, and Jenna could tell something of great importance just occurred to her. "Oh. My. God!"

"What?"

"That's why they took you. Meredith knew you could see me." Luisa scooted closer. "You remember how she acted in the boat when she made the remark about you seeing a ghost?"

So, her real name was Meredith. Clara Finch was just another cover name. Was she married to Julian—if that was even his name? They sure acted the part, even down to their cozy display of intimacy.

"Well…do you?"

Jenna snapped back to the present. She knew from the moment Clara…or Meredith inquired about whether she was talking to a ghost, the reason she was snatched had everything to do with Luisa Florentino. "I caught that, yes."

"I know what they want, and they can burn in hell before I'll ever give it to them."

Before Jenna could react to Luisa's unexpected statement, the key clicked in the lock and the door creaked open. Bright light poured in through the breach, exposing huge tears in the dirty linoleum floor. The nightlight in the room was so dim when they had forced her in here, she couldn't get a good idea of her surroundings. Becoming aware of the little bit she was able to view now, gave her the heebie-jeebies. No wonder the mattress she'd been held captive on smelled so atrocious.

The silhouette that lurked in the doorway, stepped into the room, clicked on a flashlight, and shut the door. Meredith leveled her with an all-knowing smirk. "We heard you talking to your little friend. We have some demands, and if you're a good girl and do as you're told, we'll let you eat and take a shower."

Was that so? She'd play their game, find out what they wanted, and in the process kill some time. "I'll have dinner out there," she said, pointing toward the door. After my shower." It would be a plus to get a good idea of the layout of the house in the event she had an opportunity to make a hasty escape, like Luisa.

"Hmph. That's not going to happen. You'll get dinner in here, before a shower, and only if you agree to do what we tell you."

"I'm afraid that won't work for me. I have demands of my own"

"Listen here, you little bitch," Meredith said between clenched teeth, and snatched Jenna by the arms, shaking her. "You'll take what we give you, in the order and under the conditions that we give it to you and be happy with it."

Jenna wrestled away from her, and said in a firm voice, "That shit doesn't work on me. I won't be intimidated by you. Are you worried your little henchmen can't handle me outside of a locked room?"

The woman's eye twitched at the corner; she appeared as if she'd like to seize Jenna around the neck and choke the life out of her. "Do you have any idea what I can do to you?"

"About as much as I realize I don't have to cooperate with you."

"You little—"

"Bitch, I know," Jenna finished for her. "So, do we have a deal or not?"

Meredith stood there for a good three minutes with hypothetical smoke rolling off the top of her head. The rage finally dissipated from her eyes, and she cleared her throat. "Leo will be in to get you for your shower in ten minutes." She shuffled out and slammed the door without another word.

Jenna listened with her heart in her throat for the sound of the lock engaging. It was silent and disbelief riffled through her. Did they forget to lock the door like they'd done with Luisa? Would it be this easy? But before she could rise from the bed and test the knob, the dreaded click echoed through the room. She sank back onto the mattress, disappointment stabbing at her heart.

It's going to be okay. Cole is searching for you right now. He'll get you out of here.

****

The ME and his team loaded Julian Finch's corpse onto a stretcher and zipped up the body bag. Cole stared at the goings on from a distance, while Alan Bancroft, bent to dig one hand into the sand and plucked out Jenna's sandal. The disturbance in the dirt made it obvious the scuffle took place right here.

"The Glock you had," he said. "Where did you say it came from?"

Irritation ran through Cole like a fast moving locomotive. He snatched his wife's sandal from the man's grip. "We've been over this. I obtained the firearm through legal channels. Why don't you tell me why you haven't listened to a damn thing Diego Florentino has been telling you?"

The man munched on his lip, the expression in his eyes hardening. "Given his sister's track record, we had no reason to believe anything nefarious was going on."

"What about when he reported the encounter he had with the suspicious civilian at the same convenience store Luisa came up missing from? You know, the one who shot at him?"

"We did follow up on that, Detective Rainwater. No such person driving the vehicle he described was ever located."

"Did you bother to stake out the store? I'm sure he told you about the discussion he had with an eyewitness who hung out there. The man claimed two men driving that vehicle frequented the store, often with unconscious women in the backseat. Then the guy ended up dead, thrown into a dumpster behind the establishment. I can't help but wonder what happened in that investigation."

"We're still working it."

"I bet you are."

Cole could see by the man's stiff posture and the resentment building in his eyes that this line of questioning was getting to him. His eyelids became mere slits, and Bancroft said, tightly, "What are you saying, detective?"

"I think the facts speak for themselves here, don't you? We have two men running around in an identified vehicle with passed-out women in the backseat; the brother of a missing girl who reported to your precinct that his sister called him from the same convenience store these men have frequented on several occasions and told you she informed him people were after her. Then there's an eyewitness who was privy to the suspicious behavior of these men, and that witness just so happened to end up in a dumpster behind the store, dead as a doornail. And now, my wife has been abducted by these men."

The storm clouds lifted from the sarge's eyes with a sigh and the lowering of his head. "Look, there's a lot of gang and drug activity in this area. It's something we've worked tirelessly to clean up. But it doesn't happen overnight. Because of that, we never would have suspected anything else was at play here. Don't tell me you, yourself, wouldn't have examined the facts where it concerned Ms. Florentino and came to the same conclusion I did."

Cole stared him down. "And now?"

"In light of what has happened to your wife, I think

you're right," Bancroft said. "We're dealing with something much different than I originally suspected."

"What we're dealing with is a sex trafficking ring. The evidence supports that theory. My question is, what are you going to do to bring my wife back to me unharmed?"

"Since you guys came into my office this morning, I've already sent my men out to do a little investigating. While they're working on that, we need to find out who this woman is who's passing herself off as Finch's wife. I'll need a description from you. I can have a sketch artist at my office by first light. Then, we start contacting CPS. We'll start with the branch office closest to the station. I'll also run a check on Julian Finch. If he's got anything in his background that can aid us in finding your wife, we'll find out about it. We're going to get Jenna back. I give my word."

Try as he may, Cole could not detect a single emotion in the man's face that wasn't genuine. Perhaps, he was overzealous in his prior suspicion the sarge may somehow be involved in this. Then again, it was too early to tell. He'd find out soon enough though.

Chapter Seven

It was the longest, most screwed up day of his life. It started with that Texas detective and his snooping wife, coming into the station and blabbing about some dead girl. Things went from bad to worse after that. Meredith and Julian couldn't pour piss out of a boot without directions on the heel. *They've royally fucked up everything this time.*

The man with the hook earring dangling from his left earlobe, sat in his driveway with his truck idling, every bit as ill-tempered as a rooster being chased out of the hen house. Now he'd have to babysit these incompetent assholes and make them do their jobs. How hard could it be to handle one woman who couldn't weigh more than a buck twenty dripping wet?

It wasn't like these idiots didn't handle more bitches than they could probably count. What was the issue with this one? If he had to go over there and hold their hands, heads were going to roll. He snatched his cell phone off the dash and scrolled through his contacts, looking for Simon's number.

It no sooner rang once than the imbecile answered. "What's up, Captain Hook?"

He hated that nickname as much as he despised the prick on the other end of the phone who gave it to him. If he'd never worn that damn earring, jerk face would have had to invent another name for him but he doubted the moron would have the intelligence to come up with anything creative.

"Where's the girl?"

"She's here at the red house."

"She talk yet?"

"We're working on it."

"Gawdammit, Simon. What the fuck have you been doing, playing rummy with the bitch? The clock is ticking, and that husband of hers is all over this like flies on stink."

"Word on the street is he's been talking to Luisa's brother. Any truth to that?"

"What's worse, he's put a bug in the sarge's ear. Bancroft had me scampering all over town today, running down leads to find out what happened to the bitch you shot. Speaking of which, if you'd have gotten the information we needed from her before you killed her, we wouldn't be going through any of this, now would we?"

"I told you, man. That was Leo's fault. The dumbass dropped the gun on the floorboard in the backseat. Luisa had it in her hands. She was about to shoot him. I had no choice but to bury a slug in her."

"Was he smoking that shit again?"

Simon snorted. "Leo's always smoking that shit. You know that."

"He's becoming a loose cannon to this operation because of his drug habit. If he can't leave the crack pipe alone, you're going to have to take him out."

"Okay, okay. I'll talk to him. If he doesn't take me seriously, I'll smoke his ass."

Captain Hook massaged his temples. Having to deal with these stooges was the icing on the cake.

"There's another problem," he admitted.

"What now?" Simon whined.

"We've confirmed Julian Finch is dead."

"Fuck! I knew when that bastard started running toward the boat and shooting at us, something must have happened to Julian. This Rainwater guy is gonna cause problems for us. I just know it."

"Let me deal with that. You handle getting the bitch to talk, you hear me?"

"She's not as easily persuaded as most of the girls who come through here. She's playing hardball because she knows we need something from her, and we won't harm her until we get it. Meredith is about at the end of her rope with her."

Annoyance wound its way around every one of Hook's nerve endings. The last thing he needed was some self-important woman giving them a run for their money. If these dopes didn't pull their heads out of their asses, and get control of the situation, they'd run out of time before they could find out the information they needed from the only person who could give it to them.

"Tell Meredith to find her weakness. Everyone has one. Find it, and she'll talk."

"Do I tell her what happened to Julian?"

"Not right now. I need her head in the game. If you tell her lover boy got creamed by this girl's husband, she might go off the deep end. There's no telling what she'll do to her. That's the last thing we need."

"Okay…but I don't know how much longer we can hold out. She's been calling his phone and she's getting antsy because he ain't answering."

"Just stick to the plan. Once we have what we

want, I don't care if Meredith ties a brick to the bitch's ankles and tosses her into the ocean for the sea creatures to nibble on. Get the job done. I'm not telling you again."

"You ain't my boss, Captain Hook. You don't get to talk to me like I'm your little bitch."

"If you don't take care of business, being someone's bitch will be the last of your worries."

"Yeah, yeah. I said I'd take care of it."

****

Meredith and the guy with the blond ponytail and the tatted neck whom Jenna assumed was Leo, sat at the table silently watching her eat.

A phone rang in the next room. The taller one, she now identified as Simon, answered it, then strolled through the kitchen and out the back door to talk to whoever called.

She did her best to ignore the vigilant stares, and bit into a wedge of cornbread. Although she didn't see much of the surroundings when Leo led her to the bathroom a few steps down the hall, allowed her a ten-minute shower, then practically dragged her to the other end of the house and planted her in a chair at the kitchen table, the back exit Simon stepped through to talk on the phone was all the discovery she needed. Now, if she was able to escape from the room they held her in, she wouldn't have to wander aimlessly through the house not knowing where an exit was. Mission accomplished on that front.

Meredith spoke first. "Now that we held up our end of the bargain, it's time for you to hold up yours. We know who the dead girl is who's been visiting with you, and we need you to get some information for us."

That so? "What do you plan to do with me once you get the information?"

Meredith's attention darted toward Leo who sat close enough to Jenna she could smell his rancid breath. The woman answered, "We'll let you go. It's as simple as that."

Sure, you will. "What guarantee have I got you'll stick to your word?"

Leo snorted as if he found the conversation amusing. Meredith said, "You'll just have to trust me."

"Because you've been so trustworthy up to this point." Did these idiots think she was born yesterday?

"You have no choice."

"I might not have a choice whether I live or die, but I damn sure have a choice what I am and am not willing to do for you."

Meredith appeared as if she wanted to tug out her hair. Jenna could tell she wasn't accustomed to dealing with someone who stood up to her. "I could make you miserable, you little twit."

"You already have."

Jenna was sure the woman was going to pick up her glass and throw it against the wall in a fit of rage. But Simon shuffled back through the door and motioned for the irate witch to join him. He pointed to the room beyond the kitchen.

She took the hint and rose from her seat. Simon left the room with Meredith sashaying not far behind.

Jenna glanced at Leo, and his attention drifted from her bare feet, all the way to her breasts. As hungry as she was, she lost her appetite. She clutched the material of the shirt covering her chest, tighter together. She didn't want to expose an inch of skin to this pig.

The disgusting animal aimed his stare at her face now. His eyes glazed over, and he ran his calloused hand up her arm, causing needle pricks of revulsion to twist in her gut. "You smell real nice," he drawled, closing in on her neck, and inhaling her scent as if breathing life into his rabid soul.

She squirmed and jerked in his grasp, but he clamped around her like a steel vice. "You ain't gettin' away from me, girl." He ran a wet tongue up her neck and whispered, "I'm gonna screw you better than your husband ever thought about doing."

Jenna swung the fork in her hand. It punctured his cheek, deep enough to hit bone.

He leapt out of his chair, let loose a tortured howl and danced in circles. Finally getting a tight grip on the utensil, he plucked it out and tossed it to the floor. The *ting* of the fork hitting the tile sounded more like an explosion. "You fuckin' bitch!"

He reared back his hand, and before Jenna could escape the oncoming assault, he nailed her square across the face. The blow knocked her backward. She and the chair hit the floor.

She scrambled to her feet, and the lunatic lunged at her. The shouting coming from the entrance of the kitchen stopped him in his tracks.

Simon advanced, towering over him, shaking with exasperation. "What the hell are you doing, you stupid motherfucker?"

"She stabbed me with that fork!" he wailed, pointing at the blood smeared utensil with bent tines lying on the ground.

Jenna could do nothing more than stand there trembling from head to toe. The spot where he slapped her was shrouded in a burning sensation. The ringing in her ears nearly cut off her hearing.

"Didn't I tell you to leave her alone?" Simon barked, shoving him back. "Why can't you just do what you're told?"

"She's just some stupid whore. Why're you taking up for her?"

"I told you to stay away from her. But you couldn't help yourself, could you? You don't know how close you are to being thrown out of this organization for good. You either straighten your ass up and get off the dope, or you're going to be done in more ways than you realize. This is the last warning you'll get from me."

The anger in Leo's eyes slowly evolved into apprehension. "What are you saying, Simon?"

"You got yourself one more chance. That's what I'm saying. Screw up again, and you'll never get another one. Got it?"

Leo rubbed the back of his neck, standing there under Simon's fiery gaze as if he was a child being admonished by a parent. His face glowed red with embarrassment. "Okay, okay. I won't touch her again."

Meredith entered the room and made a beeline for Jenna. She grabbed her by the arm, and jerked her across the floor, herding her down the hall and back toward the bedroom.

They approached the door. The woman twisted the doorknob, flung it open, and shoved her inside. Her heated stare slid over Jenna's entire body. "You are more trouble than you're worth." She snatched the roll of duct tape off the bedside table, tore off a long piece, and wound it around her ankles, doing the same with her wrists. "Here's the deal, Ms. High-and-Mighty.

You're going to find out from this little ghost of yours who else she told about us. We suspect she blabbed to more than her brother. So, you better tap into those psychic abilities of yours, however you do it, and summon that little bitch. If you don't have something for us by the time the sun comes up, we will make a phone call to our people in Texas and have them snatch Emily right out of her bed. That cute daughter of yours will make us a shitload of money."

Raw fear snaked through her like the lit fuse at the end of a stick of dynamite. "If you touch one hair on my daughter's head, I swear to God, I'll kill you."

"You don't strike me as a stupid person. You realize you're not getting out of here alive. The least you can do is save your daughter from a life of enslavement. Your choice."

Meredith left the room and locked the door. Jenna found it hard to breathe. She sat on the bed and tears spilled down her cheeks. Jesus, they were more than capable of making good on their promise. And she realized with every beat of her heart they'd do it. She couldn't, even for a second, imagine her daughter being forced to live a life of hell with these barbarians. If it was hers and Cole's life on the line, that was one thing, but her daughter? She was innocent in all of this. No matter the outcome, she could not let them take Emily. It was time to have a serious conversation with Luisa.

****

It was like a broken record. Disturbing theories about what these animals were putting his wife through spiraled through Cole's mind the entire night. He was living a waking nightmare with no relief in sight. And the pain in his stomach this morning, caused by the endless crying that racked his body throughout the night, was only a constant reminder this horror was as real as the rising sun. His heart ached for her in a way it hadn't for anything in his entire life and all he could do was hold out a desperate hope wherever she was, she never doubted he was coming to get her. *Just hold on, baby. I promise I'm going to bring you home safely, even if it kills me.*

He'd lay down his life if it meant saving hers, and the pressure to get her out of this situation as soon as humanly possible was a permanent knot tightening in his gut. God knows what kind of vile acts these criminals were committing against her. And the notion of her being at their mercy was intolerable. Every one of them would pay for taking her against her will. He just needed one solid lead to get the ball rolling in his quest to hunt them down.

He left the precinct after sitting with the sketch artist and stepped out into the early morning sunlight. The warmth of the day penetrated his skin as if nothing tragic in the world had taken place. How could the weather be this nice, and the activity of millions of people go on this monotonously when his world was in ruins, and his wife, trapped somewhere suffering God only knew how badly right now? But he couldn't rely on the Pensacola PD to do their job and find her while he locked himself away from the world and fell completely apart. So, he would fall apart while trying to find her.

Gathering what was necessary to press forward, he decided stopping by the convenience store where Diego's sister went missing from and chatting with the clerk would be a good place to start.

After taking the fifteen-minute drive across town, he wandered into the store. The person he planned to interrogate stood behind the cash register, attention honed-in on the cell phone in one chubby hand. "Excuse me," Cole said, sidling up to the counter.

The kid looked up; dull blue eyes behind lenses as thick as soda bottles were void of emotion. His countenance was the perfect picture of disinterest, as if being here was nothing more than another uneventful function he must perform in life, like slipping into his pants in the morning.

Cole flipped open his badge and held it up. "I'm Detective Rainwater. And I have some questions about an incident that took place here about a week ago."

"Sure," the young man said, his eyebrows lifting slightly.

Cole took the picture Diego had given him of Luisa out of his pocket and showed it to the cashier. "You seen this girl?"

He slipped off his glasses, leaned in and squinted at the picture. "Something happen to her?"

Ignoring the question, Cole said, "She was in here at night about a week ago. Were you working then?"

"She came in while I was here, all right. That girl was a train wreck."

"How so?"

He slid his glasses back up his freckled nose, and finally set his phone down. "I could tell she was on something. And I noticed the track marks on her arms. We get dopers in her sometimes, but this one took the cake. She came crashing through the door screaming they were going to find her."

"Who are they?"

The pudgy boy shook his head. "I have no idea. But about five minutes later two men came in here searching for her."

Cole braced his hands against the counter, preparing to fire off additional questions. "What do you remember about these men?"

"One was tall, could have been around six feet. He had dark hair, green eyes and wore a baseball cap. That was the one who said he was the girl's boyfriend. The other one was kind of short, brown eyes with a blond ponytail. The second guy was rough. He had a crater face and rotting teeth. I've seen both of them in here before. Sometimes separately, sometimes together. The girl was so out-of-it I told her to leave. She wouldn't listen. In fact, she refused to go until I agreed to let her use the phone. Of course, that was before those guys came in here searching for her."

Cole remembered Diego mentioning Luisa calling him from the store. That would account for the call she'd made.

"It was weird," the kid speculated. "The first call she made sounded like she was leaving a message for a business. I heard her say kids were being abducted from CPS and trafficked or something like that."

Cole's heart dropped to his feet. "Wait. She made two calls?" The mentioning of CPS instantly reminded him of Clara—or whatever her real name was—and what she'd stated she did for a living. Did Luisa know the woman worked for CPS? And even more disturbing, did she stumble across information that would implicate the woman acting as Finch's wife was smuggling children from Child Protective Services to turn them over to the traffickers she worked with?

"Like I said, she was out of it, paranoid as hell."

Irritation riffled through Cole. "She told you people were after her, and then two men show up to take her against her will, and you don't bother to pick up the phone and call the police?"

The guy appeared stunned. As if the possibility the girl may have been telling the truth never occurred to him. "But one of them was her boyfriend," he said in his defense.

"If one of them was her boyfriend, don't you think she would have gone willingly with them?"

He stared at Cole, speechless.

"Never mind." It was useless trying to get through to this guy. "What about the other call she made?" Though he'd guessed the answer, he needed to ask.

"To some guy she called Disantes."

"Diego?"

"That's it," he said, the first sign of life coming into his eyes. "Then this Diego guy showed up asking where she was."

Noticing the camera in the corner of the store, Cole pointed to it and asked, "Does that thing work?"

The kid nodded. "The police already took the recording for the night you're asking about."

This was getting more interesting by the second. "What department?"

"Dunno. A detective showed up here yesterday. He asked for the surveillance recording of the night that girl stopped in here. I gave it to him, and he left." The kid added, "The owner uses old school cameras in here. He hasn't upgraded since the 90s. It's analog surveillance. You know, VHS recordings."

The young man was right. That was about as old

123

school as it got for today's surveillance. He hadn't run across an outdated system like that in twenty years. But such a discovery wasn't surprising given the old-fashioned condition of the store. "And I assume you gave them the only tape you had?"

He shrugged, as if to say, "did you expect a place like this to keep multiple copies of each recording?"

"Did you hear the girl reference any names when she made the first call? Anyone who could possibly be involved?"

"Look, man, I was in and out of the back, taking care of inventory. I didn't hear the whole conversation."

"And she called on the land line, right?" Cole said, gesturing toward the old fashioned rotary phone hanging against the back wall near the checkout counter.

"Well, duh. I never let customers use my cell phone."

One thing was for sure, they needed to get a log of the outgoing calls from the store that night. Then they could identify the first number she dialed. "One more question. Tell me about the detective who came in here?"

Though the guy's furrowed brows told Cole he took the question as odd since Cole had presented himself as a detective, and should be privy to that information, he answered anyway. "Shoulder-length, wavy, brown hair. Dark eyes, maybe brown, maybe black. About your size."

The kid snapped his fingers. "Oh, yeah. He wears some kind of a hook earring."

An image of the detective sitting on the edge of his desk, acting suspiciously when he and Jenna stepped out of Bancroft's office sprang to his mind. Even from the distance of an entire room, the hint of gold in the guy's ear had been evident.

This was the same guy the kid just described.

Last night while talking to Bancroft, he recalled the sergeant telling him he'd sent a few of his men back out to reinvestigate the missing Luisa. Why didn't the sarge mention the confiscated video surveillance? Something like that would have been considered a major break in the case. It would have shown evidence of Luisa's abduction. And possibly the faces of the people who kidnapped her.

Were they purposely trying to hide information from him?

The bell above the glass doors leading into the store jungled, letting Cole know someone was entering the establishment. He swung his head toward the noise. A teenage girl and an older lady in a gray pantsuit strolled in. The younger one headed toward the beverage cooler in the back, while the other one wandered to the snack isle. "Hey, Mom, can I have an energy drink?" the teen asked over her shoulder.

"We talked about this, Daphne." her mother called.

Cole drew his attention back toward the clerk. "The next time someone comes into your store claiming someone is after them, you might want to pick up the phone and dial the police. That girl who was in here is dead. Just so you know."

The guy's mouth dropped open. Feeling a bit satisfied he'd made a point, Cole spun on his heel and stalked away.

He swung open the door of the rental car, digesting what he'd learned. So…Luisa had more information than he'd first realized. Perhaps, these animals didn't go after her simply because she'd escaped. Maybe they were trying to keep her from telling the wrong people what she knew—like a woman who worked for CPS was hip deep in missing girls. But who would she have called to relay that information?

The sooner he got back to the precinct, the quicker he'd find out.

****

Cole threw open the glass doors leading into the Pensacola PD, and marched straight to Bancroft's office. He didn't bother to knock, just charged in, temper pulsating like a jackhammer. He zeroed in on the sarge, who looked up from behind his desk. "When did you plan on telling me about the surveillance tape your men collected from the store where Luisa Florentino went missing?"

A blank expression stared back at him. "What in Sam's hell are you talking about?"

"One of your detectives took a surveillance tape from the convenience store where Ms. Florentino was abducted. Why didn't you tell me about this last night? Did you think I wouldn't find this out?"

The man abandoned his chair, anger chiseled into every crevice of his face. "Let's get one thing straight, Rainwater. Number one," he said, ticking off a digit on his right hand, "You don't work for me. Number two," he said, ticking off another digit, "Even if you did work for me, I'd never let you get involved in this case because you have close, emotional ties to the victim."

By the time he got to the third finger, he was incensed. "Number three, you don't charge into my office with a demanding attitude and start throwing accusations around."

Cole matched his fury. "These bastards have my wife. You're damn right I'm going to barge in here, and I'll keep barging in here and stay all over your ass and everyone else's in this place until you, or these clowns who work for you, find her. Do you catch my drift?"

"You wait one damn minute—"

"Oh, I've waited enough minutes. You're going to do your job. Or I'm going to rip one hell of a hole through this town doing it for you."

"What is your problem?"

"What was on the surveillance tape you neglected to tell me about?"

Bancroft looked like he'd been gut punched. "I don't know anything about any surveillance tape."

Cole hesitated for a minute. Was it possible Bancroft had no knowledge of the evidence his detective collected? There was only one reason he would have hidden that information from his supervisor. Because he was tied to the people who were responsible for committing the crime in the first place. "Why don't we call your detective in here right now, and get to the bottom of it?"

The sarge's attention darted away, as if he was working toward collecting his composure. "I can do that. Then we can discuss this calmly."

Calmly or forcefully didn't make a damn to Cole. One way or the other he'd get his answers.

Bancroft plucked the receiver from the phone on his desk and punched in a few digits on the dial pad. He cleared his throat and said, "I need you to get Benton in my office now."

After a few seconds, the man shifted the receiver in

his hand, appearing as if he wanted to jump through the line and throttle the person on the other end. "I don't give a shit what he's doing. Tell him he has five minutes to have his ass in my office or he'll be writing traffic tickets with Wesley for the next three months." He slammed the phone down and leveled his attention on Cole. "He's coming."

Cole nodded and said, "Did you get anywhere with CPS?"

"We've been in contact with two agencies within our vicinity. Unfortunately, there isn't anyone working at either office that matches the description you gave us. We have a few more places on our list, ones closer to Finch's home address. We don't know much about the woman he was passing off as his wife; I've got a few of my guys out knocking on doors to find out if anyone saw Julian with her, and if any of them happen to know anything about her."

It was a start, but Cole feared this investigation would not move quickly enough to save Jenna. Then there was the concern if some of Bancroft's men were involved in this, they'd sure as shit sabotage any leads that came in.

"We do know a little more about Finch," Bancroft offered, stepping around to the front of his desk, and leaning against it. "He was a Hurricane Katrina evacuee from the Lower Ninth Ward in New Orleans. He was involved in some petty crimes as a teenager and served twenty years in the state penitentiary for bank robbery when he was in his early twenties. Shortly after he was released, about the time Katrina hit, he resettled here in Perdido Key. He met a local man by the name of Jaxon Stoll, a Florida native, and a forty-two-year-old entrepreneur. From what I understand the two men became very close and went into business together fixing boats. A bad storm kicked up off the Gulf Coast one night five years ago. Stoll and Finch just happened to be out there in the crux of it in Saint Marie. One man made it back to shore. The other one didn't. Stoll's body was never recovered."

Cole remembered Julian mentioning his business partner dying, but he didn't say anything about the fact he was with him the night he perished. "Was the Saint Marie damaged in the storm?"

"That's the thing," Bancroft said, rubbing his chin, "Finch claimed the man was thrown off the boat and into the water by the high winds, but the vessel appeared untouched. There were other crafts caught up in the storm that night. All of them sustained damage, and a few even capsized. Not one of them made it out unscathed except the Saint Marie."

"So the vessel, and Finch, miraculously made it back to shore unharmed. And it just so happened that Stoll left the Saint Marie to Finch in his will. I smell a rat, Sargeant."

Bancroft stroked his chin with fat fingertips. "Perhaps, the case of Jaxon Stoll's death needs to be reopened."

"There's something else," Cole said. "I found out Luisa Florentino made two calls from the convenience store. On the first, she called someone and left a message, mentioning something about kids being abducted from CPS and trafficked. Both calls went out via the landline inside the convenience store. If we can get a log of the outgoing calls that night, we can find out who she called."

"You wanted to see me, Sarge?"

Spinning around, Cole noticed a wavy-haired detective stepping into Bancroft's office. Once his gaze settled on Cole, he stopped in his tracks and leaned against the doorframe with his arms crossed in front of him as if he was right at home, glaring at his adversary the way a wolf would stare down at a wayward mutt who stumbled into his den.

Not the least intimidated, Cole swaggered over and stood face to face with him. "Where's the video surveillance tape from the convenience store?"

The man blinked slowly, as if he was no more bothered by Cole's presence as he would have been by a pesky gnat flying around his head. He slid around him and approached Bancroft's desk. "You know, Sarge, some of the guys are talking. They can't figure out why you'd allow some detective from Texas to meddle in an active investigation on our turf."

Before Cole could open his mouth and fire off a single word, Bancroft said, "I'm wondering the same thing he is. Where's the tape, Benton?"

The guy took on a defensive stance, his hands settling around his hips. "What tape?"

"The one you collected from the convenience store clerk yesterday."

Benton chewed his lip. "There was nothing on it."

"What do you mean there was nothing on it?" Cole said, incredulously.

Benton turned, settling his gaze on Cole and frowned. "Just like I said, Sherlock, it's blank. There's nothing on it."

"Bullshit!" Cole said. "You erased the tape."

Benton threw up his hands, and faced the sergeant,

astonishment rolling off him in waves. "I don't have to take that shit, Sarge. For Christ's sake, he's accusing me of tampering with evidence."

"You're damn right I am." Anger flared unrestrained inside Cole like a lit torch. This asshole saw what was on that tape, then took measures to make sure no one else would.

Bancroft's expression froze like Mount Everest in the middle of winter. Cole could see he had no clue how to react.

Benton was on the move. His muscular frame advancing across the room until he stood so close to Cole, he could smell what the guy had for breakfast. "I don't know who the fuck you think you are, Texas boy, but you don't come in here and accuse me of shit."

The minute Benton's spittle landed on Cole's nose, it was his undoing, and he shoved the bastard hard enough to send him tumbling over the office chair behind him.

The detective scrambled to his feet, but Bancroft planted himself in between them, stiff-arming Benton to keep him in his place. "I think it's best you leave," Bancroft told Cole. "This has gone far enough."

Cole finally wiped the dirty cop's spittle from his face and headed for the door. He approached it, peered back, and said to the sergeant, "You need to ask yourself how the only surveillance tape that could identify the men we're after has come up blank. I'd wager it wasn't like that until your detective got his hands on it. That should tell you all you need to know."

By that time, Cole's pulse had returned to its normal rate and his breathing was finally under control—just the way he liked it before he started confronting a suspect. "I'd suggest you scrutinize the men who work for you because I'm not going to stop until I take down the ones responsible for my wife's kidnapping." Then he locked eyes with Benton and warned. "Give the goons you work for a message from me. Tell them I'm coming for them, and they had better hope and pray to God they haven't harmed my wife."

Chapter Eight

Benton checked every stall inside the precinct bathroom to make certain they were empty before locking the main door, then slipped his cellphone from his pocket. The adrenalin pumping through his system made it close to impossible to concentrate on the contact list. He scrolled down and when Simon's number came up, hit the call button.

The sluggish ring tone reminded him of a clock ticking in the background, winding down the seconds of his life as they spun out of control. He was smarter than this. Certainly smarter than that two-bit Texan who thought his shit didn't stink.

How in the hell did he learn so much so fast?

For years he'd worked this operation without a single glitch. Then out of left field comes this asshole barging into his territory threatening to throw a wrench into everything he'd worked so hard for. Something told him all along taking that bitch hostage wasn't a smart thing to do.

But what choice did they have? Through the woman's psychic abilities, they could get the information they desperately needed from Luisa. The young, untouched girls Meredith provided to the organization fetched top dollar. They would have never turned this kind of profit before. And he couldn't imagine all of that coming to an end because of the possibility some dead, ex-prostitute and drug addict ran her mouth to the wrong people. They needed to find out if Luisa had told anyone what she'd discovered before she escaped. And since she was deceased, the only way that would be possible was through the detective's wife who had a few screws loose.

"Hello," Simon said when he finally answered the phone.

Benton took a deep breath. "Tell me you got the information you needed out of that bitch."

"Meredith is due here any second. She's taking care of it."

"Where the fuck did she go? She's supposed to be laying low until we find out if she's been compromised."

"I'm not going to lie. Leo spilled the beans to her about Julian."

"Christ! When?

"Last night."

Anxiety seized Benton's gut in a vise. As if it was possible for his emotions to be driven any farther over the edge. "I can't believe you let her go like that. The sketch artist was here this morning. I'm doing my best to get the sarge to hold off on releasing the drawing of Meredith to the media. If anyone recognizes her, it's over for all of us. Bancroft has already called a few CPS offices in the area to see if anyone recognizes her as working there."

"Do they know her name?"

"Not yet. But it's only a matter of time."

"Listen, Meredith isn't from around here. Plus, the office she works for is so far away from Pensacola the only way they can find out which one it is, is if Luisa told someone."

"That may be so, but she's spent time here with Julian. Someone might recognize her."

"She's only come to Pensacola a handful of times. Julian has always gone to her neck of the woods. Besides, you know how paranoid she is about keeping a low profile. No one here will know who she is even if they see a drawing that resembles her."

Another knot seized his gut. "Well the sketch looks like her."

"It's a drawing for God's sake. How much of a resemblance could it have? And even if it is a close likeness, she's worked for that agency since she was eighteen. They treat her like family there. Who is going to turn her in based off a drawing that may have a few minor resemblances?"

Benton rested his palm against the counter, allowing the first wave of control to wash over him. Simon was right. It was only a drawing, taken from some goofball who worked a 7-11 for Christ's sweet sake. Meredith had a spotless reputation, and she was far enough away from Pensacola no one would put two and two together. She was so careful over the years she surely wouldn't have risked blowing her cover even when she found out Julian was dead.

Sure Meredith would be pissed as hell about losing Julian, but she understood business was business. Plus, she loved the money she made through the organization more than she loved Julian. She wouldn't do anything to hinder that.

As if in rhyme with Benton's train of thought, Simon said, "Meredith has got this under control. She threatened to kidnap Jenna's daughter last night. Told her she had until this morning to cough up the information we need."

Good. Meredith found the bitch's weakness. That should do the trick. "Listen, this Rainwater character is a persistent son-of-a-bitch. Until I can figure out how to deal with him, we need to move his wife to the cabin. No one will ever find her there."

"All right, as soon as Meredith gets back, we will make the arrangements. Just take it easy, man. As far as the agency knows, Meredith is on vacation this week. We'll get the information we need out of this psychic bitch no later than today, and then we'll know where to go from there. If worst comes to worst, and Luisa blabbed her mouth, and we know for sure Meredith's cover has been blown, we'll move the operation and make a few adjustments. The important thing is none of us will get caught."

"If her cover has been blown, we'll lose our supply of girls. Have you thought about that?"

"First thing's first, man. Let's figure out what damage may or may not have occurred."

"All right, fine. Today though, Simon. We don't have any more time to waste playing games with the bitch. Get her to talk and then wax her ass. Got it? I'll figure out how to handle her husband."

****

"I know what you want, *mujer blanca.* And I'm sorry. But I can't give you that information."

Jenna recognized Luisa's voice before she'd even spun around to stare at the girl she could sense was perched on the edge of the filthy mattress.

Jenna positioned herself to get a better view of the woman in the dim lighting of the room. She did everything she could to summon Luisa last night after Meredith threatened to kidnap Emily. But her reward was no response. Now she swallowed, attempting to wet her parched throat, but her voice came out a croak when she said, "Why didn't you show yourself to me last night? I know you heard me calling for you."

Luisa finally peered over at her, the woman's expression barely readable in the vague shadows cast from the nightlight. "You know why."

She certainly did. Luisa had information she realized these people wanted to save her daughter, but the dead girl was too caught up in revenge against the monsters that killed her to give a damn about the wellbeing of someone else. Her words yesterday haunted Jenna half the night. *I know what they want, and they can burn in hell before I'll ever give it to them.*

This dangerous game Luisa was playing by withholding that information was going to result in an innocent, eleven-year-old girl possibly being thrown into a life of living hell few could ever imagine. She'd be damned if she was going to stand back and let that happen.

"They are threatening to kidnap my daughter and force her into a life of sex trafficking. And you know they have every intention of doing just that. Yet, you have been avoiding me to keep from spilling the information you know they're after, even if it means saving a little girl, all because getting revenge for what they did to you is more important."

"Is that what you think this is about?" Luisa said.

The closer Jenna got, the clearer the wounded expression on the dead girl's face became. "I avoided coming back here last night because I didn't trust myself not to tell you what you wanted to hear. And once you gave that information to them, they would have killed you. You not knowing is the only thing keeping you alive."

"I'm already dead, Luisa. I've been dead from the moment they took me. I have no doubt about that now. But if giving them what they want can save my daughter—"

"It won't change anything," Luisa insisted. "Do you think these people have any honor? Do you think they care anything about keeping a promise to you? They are as sly as a coyote and will play on your weaknesses until they get what they want from you. And when they use you up and you have nothing left to give, they'll take you out like the trash. I've seen how they operate. I've watched them overdose girls on heroin when they no longer have any use for them."

Helplessness sank into Jenna's bones. She was right, and the knowledge of that stabbed into her heart. She lowered her head, and tears spilled from her eyes. She'd been so brave up until this point, determined to fight them, hopeful there was the tiniest chance she could win. But with Luisa's confession, all optimism flew out the window like a bird escaping through the iron bars of a prison window, leaving its owner to rot inside the walls of the dungeon.

"There's nothing I can do to keep them from taking my daughter, is there?"

That realization was the most disheartening consideration that ever occurred to her in all her life. Even when she'd been at her most despondent, lying in a pitch-black grave, knowing she was probably going to die, she still had the mindfulness to hold on to the fact

Cole and Emily would eventually be okay. But now with them vowing to hunt her husband down and kill him, and threatening to enslave her daughter, she didn't have any faith left to cling to. Once they murdered her with the knowledge her husband may be next, and her daughter would suffer the remainder of her short life, she wondered if that would be just the thing to keep her from moving on once they killed her. Would she be a spirit left aimlessly wandering the earth like Luisa?

"There's only one way you can save your daughter."

For the first time she noticed courage and hope reflecting in Luisa's eyes. "How?"

"By staying alive, getting out of this place, and helping the police put these animals behind bars. I give you my word, I will do everything I can to help make that possible. But if you just give up and don't fight for your life, your daughter, and thousands of young girls just like her will never be safe from these people again."

Jenna could not deny the logic in the dead girl's words. Jesus, she allowed these savages to twist reality, spin the truth into a clever illusion to suit their purpose. They used fear to plant the idea in her head the only way she could save Emily was to give them what they wanted and sacrifice her life in the process. But that was the opposite of what would ultimately keep her daughter safe. If she died at their hands, and Cole was eliminated as well, who would be there to keep Emily out of harm's way?

Swathed in a renewed sense of bravery and righteousness, Jenna resolved she must survive at all costs in order to take this sadistic ring down.

A shuffling noise outside in the hallway told her someone was approaching. A few seconds later, the click of the lock disengaging caught the breath in her chest. They were coming for her and would do everything in their power to wear her down, intimidate her with God knows how many dirty little tactics to get what they wanted from her and Luisa. She would have to be stronger than she'd ever been in her life to resist the threats they would place at her feet.

Meredith stepped through the door in an attractive, flowery summer dress, hair in a neat ponytail, silver earrings dangling from her ears, and smelling of fresh soap. She carried a tray over to the bedside table and set it down. Then, without a word, she marched over to the single window and threw open the drapes. Intense sunlight streamed through the window. Jenna winced and shrank away, giving her eyes time to adjust.

Footfalls echoed across the floor, telling her Meredith was advancing. She was finally able to open her eyes all the way, and the woman stood over her, staring down with an expressionless face. It was then she noticed the paleness of her skin, and the thin streaks of black mascara running beneath eyes that were pink and glossy. Was she crying?

Then the door creaked open again, and Leo stepped through the breach, slipped a pocketknife out of the pocket of his trousers, and before Jenna could react to the unexpected threat, grabbed her bound hands, and sliced through the masking tape, freeing them. He departed as swiftly as he arrived, locking the door behind him.

Meredith pointed toward the tray she'd carried into the room, and said, "There's toast and a cup of hot tea."

She cleared her throat and peered away. "It's a treat Leo put together for you."

Since when was Leo putting together treats for her? And what on God's green earth caused Meredith to come in here and serve it to her? This woman hated her guts. She was certain they were setting a trap for her. Nothing else made any sense.

"Well?" Meredith said, motioning toward the platter. "Aren't you hungry? Thirsty?"

"Not really."

Meredith let out an irritated sigh. "It's not poisoned if that's what you think." She stepped over and broke off a small corner of the bread and popped it into her mouth. "See?" she said, in between chewing.

Since they'd interrupted her dinner last night and left her to starve for the duration, the aroma of the toasted bread and freshly brewed tea was heavenly. Her stomach growled, and she couldn't resist grabbing a slice of bread and biting into it. She chewed slowly, glorying in the buttery flavor. Who knew a slice of toast could be this delicious? After taking a few more bites, she picked up the tea and sipped. She sat there, closing her eyes, enjoying the sensation of food and drink on her tongue.

She finished off the first piece and was working on the second slice. Meredith's voice intruded on her blissful state. "We heard you in here talking to Luisa and we know you asked her about the information we want."

Jenna stopped chewing and stared at the woman. "What, do you guys stand outside with your ear against the door?"

Meredith pointed toward the vent above her head.

And it hit Jenna all at once. They'd been listening in on her through a recording device they'd hidden in the ventilation. Her mind wound back to the discussion she'd just had with Luisa. Had she said anything incriminating?

"No more stalling. You're going to tell us what we want to know. And you're going to do that right now. Do you understand?" Meredith slipped her hand inside the pocket of her dress and snatched out a photo and tossed it in Jenna's lap. "Our guy in Texas took this photo yesterday. Emily seems to be enjoying time with her grandparents. It's up to you whether she continues to do so."

Oh my God.

It was like a gut punch from out of nowhere hitting her so hard it took her breath and left her struggling for a rational thought. Jenna stared at a picture of Emily nestled between her grandparents sitting on the front porch swing. She recognized the house as belonging to her parents, Amanda, and Robert Langley. The beaded hairclip she had bought her daughter for the wedding was fashioned in her hair, leaving no doubt this photograph was taken very recently. They'd gone to her parents' house and were stalking her daughter.

How had they known where to find her? Who would have given them that information? The people who ran this organization weren't stupid. She could attest to that. It probably wouldn't have taken much to have gathered that intel. Besides, she gave them a promising start when she stupidly told Meredith about Emily before she'd realized who the woman was. What would it matter though? If they planned to kidnap her all along, they would have figured out she had a daughter when she refused to do their bidding. And they would have used Emily against her as they were doing.

Luisa's earlier words echoed in her mind. *They threatened to kill my brother.* This was exactly what they did to weaken their subjects. Drag their loved ones into the middle of it and hold their wellbeing up as a negotiating tactic.

The small portion of food she'd just eaten soured her stomach. Desperation to do anything to save her daughter grew leaps and bounds. Then it hit her with the power of a wrecking ball. This was exactly why Luisa refused to give her the information she realized these people wanted. If she didn't know, she couldn't spill the beans in a moment of weakness and kill any chance she had to escape and turn them into the authorities. Luisa was familiar with their tactics, and she foresaw how they were going to play this.

You have to be strong, remember? Don't let them shake you.

Jenna swallowed hard, peering away, and taking a deep breath. "I'm going to need a little more time."

Before she knew it, the tea was slapped out of her hands, and the hot liquid burned her legs as the cup tumbled to the mattress. Meredith was on her like a junkyard dog, slamming her against the bed, hands wrapped around her throat, cutting off her circulation. Jenna fought for her life and tugged on the fleshy vice around her neck.

"I'm going to kill you, you worthless bitch! Just like your husband killed my Julian!"

Those words slammed into her, sending her mind reeling, and forcing her body into a state of paralysis.

143

But the pressure building around her throat forced her to snap out of it. With the fight in her returning, she managed to stretch out her arms as far as she could and thrust both thumbs into Meredith's eye sockets.

The woman finally released her, backing away with her hands to her face, howling in pain.

The door flew open, and Leo charged into the room. "What...what the hell is going on?"

Meredith backpedaled until she thudded against the wall. "I can't see!" she wailed. "That bitch tried to push my eyes to the back of my skull."

"Let me see," Leo said, approaching and slowly removing her hands from her face.

Jenna stared at the open door, then her attention swept over the two of them huddled in the corner. They were distracted, and if she was going to make her move, she'd have to be quick.

The first thing she'd have to do would be to rip the duct tape from around her ankles. Her trembling fingers gripped the end of the tape, and she worked quickly to unwind it. She was on her feet in a flash. Adrenaline propelled her down the hall, and her bare feet struck the linoleum like a stampede of wild horses.

Someone screamed, "Hey!"

She rounded the corner. The back door was in her sight. The second her hand fumbled with the lock she was thrown to the ground. Whoever tackled her wasn't letting up, and her struggles to free herself were reduced to the futile attempt of an animal trying to escape the steel teeth of a bear trap. She was weakened, defeated, and all she wanted to do was lay there and cry until she no longer existed. She was certain whatever they had in store for her now that she escaped the bedroom was going to be much worse than death.

Someone else entered the room, and she was lifted off the ground. "She isn't going to talk." She recognized Meredith's voice. "We should have already gotten rid of her and cut our losses. She's attacked both of us now."

"If it was up to me," Leo said, tossing her over his shoulder, "The little whore would be sinking to the bottom of the ocean right now."

He carried her out of the room and back down the hall. His footsteps jolted through her body. From her viewpoint, Meredith's shoes hobbled along behind him. The woman said, "It's time we have a serious talk with Simon. All she's doing is leading us on. She almost took out my eyes. I'm lucky I can still see."

Leo shouldered the door the rest of the way open, and the creaking sound sank into her bones like a death cry. Her body hit the mattress, and that familiar, foul odor crept up her nostrils. She couldn't be sure anymore what was worse, the dank smell of the tiny pine box Cole's brother had buried her in, or the rotten stench of this bed that was undoubtedly the final resting place of the many women they beat down and stripped of all human decency.

Out of the corner of her eye, she noticed Leo grab the duct tape from the nightstand. But Meredith stayed his hand. "I have a better idea. I think you should give that bitch what she has coming to her."

Jenna realized exactly what Meredith was referring to, and a gasp caught in her throat. *Oh God, please no.* The idea of that disgusting animal crawling all over her made her want to vomit. She honestly wasn't sure she could get through such a traumatizing experience.

Dead silence, then Leo said, "What do you mean?"

"C'mon. You know what I mean."

"But Simon said—"

"Simon's not here, now, is he? He left you in charge. I won't tell if you won't."

Leo didn't utter a word.

"Her fucking husband killed my Julian," Meredith said, her tone dark and volatile. "Make her pay for it, Leo. That's all I'm asking."

Jesus, this repulsive creature was going to rape her. Jenna sat up, thrusting her body against the headboard. "If you do this and Simon finds out about it, there's no telling what he'll do to you. You know that, right?"

Meredith slapped her across the face with such force, her head hit against the iron headboard. "Shut up! I've been patient with you, but that ended when I found out your husband buried a bullet in Julian's head. You're going to die a horrible death, just like you deserve, and your daughter will be my personal sex slave to do whatever I want with. But first, Leo is going to have his way with you." Then she faced him and said, "You've been licking your chops ever since we brought her here. You know you want to. So, go ahead. Screw the bitch until she drops dead for all I care."

****

"Hey, man, I don't think I've ever been more relieved to see you," Cole told Dylan Cruz.

The Ranger, sporting a pair of khaki shorts, light blue button up shirt, and dark shades stepped off the tarmac and headed his way. Cruz plucked the shades from his face and grinned his lopsided grin, approached Cole, dropped his travel bag, and gave him a man hug.

"Thanks for getting here so quick." The second his

buddy's arms gathered around him, it was Cole's undoing. He held on tightly, and the tears flowed as if a dam had burst. "This is so fucked up, man. One minute she was there with me, then she was gone."

He straightened up and backed away, swiping at his tears and attempting to get control of himself. "I'm running on fumes, bro. I haven't gotten much sleep, and I have no appetite, so eating is almost impossible. But I'm doing all I can to stay strong for Jenna."

Truth be told, his spirits lifted the second he saw Cruz's plane enter the runway. The man had been instrumental in finding Jenna after his brother kidnapped her, then buried her in a box. "I've got some updates since the last time we talked," he said, in an obvious attempt to move past his moment of weakness and get back to the business of finding Jenna. He eyed Cruz's duffle bag. "Is this all the luggage you brought?"

"I travel light, man. Always have." The guy stood there, his attention sliding up and down Cole. Then awareness reflected in his eyes, as if he could see inside his soul. "You could use a good meal and a shower." He spread out his hands as if to say, look in the mirror. "This whole 'I can take care of myself' thing is not helping Jenna one bit. You realize that, right?"

Cole shook his head. "Look I—"

"I know. I won't even pretend I can relate to the hell you must be going through. But there's one thing I'm certain of. We will get Jenna back. And we'll do it quickly. These animals are going to rue the day they took her. We are going to dismantle their enterprise and send everyone involved to prison. But if you don't keep up your strength and get your mind right, I'm afraid it's going to hinder us. You're a damn good detective and I need your brains in this investigation. So, let's go back to the resort, order a meal, and get you fed. I don't know about you, but I can't think on an empty stomach. Then, after you've taken a shower—so I don't have to deal with the stench rolling off you for the rest of this mission—we'll regroup and formulate a plan of action."

This was the Dylan Cruz he knew. Always ready with a plan of action and never one to mince words. Cole lifted one shoulder; after taking a long sniff, he retorted, "I don't stink."

They both headed toward the exit, Cruz leading the way. The man peered back at him and said, "That's the thing about stench. When you reek, you can't tell it. But everyone else can. Besides, how long has it been since you changed your clothes?"

He had him on that one. He was in the same garments he'd been in since Jenna went missing. Now that he stopped to think about it, he was feeling as grimy as he must have appeared.

"If you brushed your teeth, I'd consider that a bonus."

Cole lifted both hands to his mouth to blow in them and test how bad his breath was.

Cruz, not bothering to glance back again, said, "That shit never works. Trust me. Your breath stinks."

Once they rode the elevator down to the parking garage, and the doors slid open, Cruz asked where he parked. Cole snatched the key fob out of his pocket and clicked the button. A horn blared in the distance and headlights flashed. They headed in that direction.

After Cruz tossed his travel bag into the trunk, they both settled into their seats, and Cole fired up the engine. While driving back to the resort, he filled his buddy in on all that transpired in the investigation so far. "I have someone I want you to meet."

Cruz nodded, saying nothing, waiting for him to reveal who he was referring to.

"The guy I just told you about. Luisa's brother, Diego. I think he can be helpful."

Cruz slipped a pack of spearmint gum out of his shirt pocket, drew a stick out, unwrapped it and folded it into his mouth. "You mentioned he knows the area pretty well."

"He's lived here all his life, so yeah, he's a resourceful guy. He's been helpful to me, and I feel like he can continue to point us in the right direction."

"Why don't you give him a call and tell him to meet us at the resort?"

Cole couldn't describe the feeling of relief and comfort that washed over him now that Cruz was on the scene. He had been here alone, in unfamiliar territory, fighting to find his wife among people who could give a shit less if Jenna ever resurfaced again.

They were sworn police investigators for Christ's sake. Yet, they wouldn't know a clue if it stormed through the precinct and plopped in their lap like a dead cat. It especially peeved the hell out of him how Benton had conducted himself in Bancroft's office. That son-of-a-bitch was buried up to his slimy neck in this organization. It couldn't have been more obvious if the creep waltzed right up and admitted his involvement. But the sergeant couldn't see it. Or wouldn't see it. Then again, now that Bancroft knew his detective had gathered evidence behind his back, and said evidence just happened to be wiped clean, that might prompt the man to do a little investigating of his own.

At this point, now that the surveillance tape was taken off the table, their next best chance at gathering evidence would be getting their hands on the log of outgoing calls made from the convenience store to discover who else Luisa called that night. But since a subpoena or warrant would have to be issued to get the phone records, such a request could only be obtained through legal channels, which would undoubtedly involve the Pensacola PD. Even if the sarge agreed to pursue the telephone logs, it could take weeks to get them. They didn't have that kind of time.

"So, are you going to call this guy, or what?"

"I already did it on the way to pick you up."

Cole switched on his blinker, waited for traffic to clear, and swerved into the parking lot of the resort. He followed the valet parking signs around to the entrance of the establishment, and a tall, dark-haired man donning a familiar straw cowboy hat came into view.

Diego Florentino leaned against a cement column perched in front of the resort, working his jaw as if he was chewing something, probably gum. Recognition lit the cowboy's eyes, and he turned his head, spat out a wad, and strode in their direction.

"Is that your man?" Cruz asked.

They rolled up to the waiting valet attendant.

The young man swooped down and opened Cole's door; he handed the guy his keys. "That's him."

Cruz shuffled out of the car, and Diego got closer. Cole could tell something was on his mind. Luisa's brother opened his mouth, shut it, opened it again and said, "I've been thinking about the other call you said my sister made at the convenience store the night she was taken."

"Any idea who she called?" Cole asked.

He shook his head.

They strolled toward the resort entrance with Cruz bringing up the rear. Cole peered back at his buddy and said as a way of introduction, "Dylan, Diego." Then threw his attention on Luisa's brother and said, "Diego, Dylan."

Both men nodded at one another, and Cole continued his response to Florentino's statement. "The only way we can get our hands on the phone records from the store, is if the sarge, or someone in the department requests them. And even if they did, the phone company could take weeks to turn them over. As strong a lead as that may be, I don't think it will come in time to help us."

"But that's just the thing," Diego said, as all three men headed toward the bank of elevators. "My mother, rest her soul, had a good friend who worked for the local telephone company."

Cole stuck out a finger to hit the elevator call button. But his stance froze in midair at Diego's words. He peered back at the guy who stood alongside Cruz. "How do we know she works for the same telephone company the store uses?"

"We don't. But I'm betting if it's not the same one, she'd know someone working at the company that does. Ms. Estrella worked at more than one phone company back in the day. She knows a lot of people, *mi amigo*"

Cole hit the button. "Maybe we can cut out the middleman and get our hands on the logs a lot sooner," he speculated.

"You realize this is as illegal as hell," Cruz said.

"And how many times have you searched a

suspect's house without first obtaining a warrant when the opportunity presented itself?" Cole remarked, eyeing his buddy as if to say, *you damn well know the answer to that.* "Sometimes you have to pave your own way, or the job doesn't get done."

Cruz frowned. "Guess you got a point."

The elevator chimed, and the doors slid open. A young couple dressed for a day at the beach smiled from inside the bright interior of the cab. "Excuse us," the woman in the straw island hat said demurely, lowering her green eyes. She and her companion shuffled around them to exit the elevator. Cole nodded courteously and stepped out of their way.

Once they'd retreated, the trio entered the empty car. Cole hit the button for the floor he and Jenna's room was located on, and faced Diego, asking, "Have you called this friend yet?"

"I was waiting to talk to you."

"When we get to the suite, go ahead and give her a call. See if there's anything she can do for us."

"Sure thing."

The elevator doors slid open again, and they stepped out onto the third floor. There was a lot of traffic, vacationers trudging up and down the hallway, bellhops rolling luggage carts along as they led the way for new guests who were just checking in, and a few kids clutching beach bags jogging to catch up with their parents.

The sight of the children reminded him of Emily, and his mind reflected on the texts she'd sent him last night, worried about her mom when she'd not gotten a response from calling her. When he and Jenna left to attend the beach party two nights ago, they'd decided to leave Jenna's phone behind with her purse. There would have been little need for her to have lugged it around since Cole was with her and he'd had his phone handy in the event someone needed to contact them.

His wife's cell was still where she'd left it the night she went missing, buried in her handbag sitting on the nightstand on her side of the bed. The damn thing was a tormenting, constant reminder she wasn't there, along with her makeup bag and the small, diamond stud earrings lying on the bathroom counter she had removed before jumping into the shower and changing into the white sundress she'd chosen to wear to the beach party.

Every time his gaze brushed across something belonging to her, another chunk of his heart was torn out. He wondered how much more of this he could tolerate before he lost it and completely fell apart. All he wanted to do was close the world out, forget about all the responsibilities he had until Jenna was found. But he could not leave his daughter in limbo. And he damn sure could not have told her what happened to her mother. He refused to put that burden on her or anyone else who loved Jenna. He needed to concentrate on bringing her home before any of them realized she was missing. Emily would have fallen completely apart if he told her the truth.

So, he had lied answering his daughter's text last night, telling her they were fine. She asked if they could bring her back some souvenirs, and he promised he would. But the only souvenir he wanted was his wife back in his arms safe and sound. Without her, the world could have fallen into a fiery Armageddon, and he wouldn't have even noticed.

Cole slipped the keycard into the slot above the doorknob to their honeymoon suite and cringed. A hint of Jenna's perfume would still be lingering in the air just like it was last night, and again this morning, and he braced himself, realizing the intolerable stab of pain that was going to slice through him when it hit.

"Do you have room service in this place?" Cruz asked, shuffling in, and setting his duffle bag on the floor by the couch.

Cole pointed him toward the amenity's directory sitting on the glass coffee table, and his buddy hopped right on it, snatching it up, and leafing through it. Diego settled in on the loveseat opposite the Texas Ranger, and Cole took a deep breath, battling the demons that were the memories of his wife.

He headed toward the bathroom, saying over his shoulder, "I'm going to take a shower."

"All right, man," Cruz hollered out. "I'll order something for us to eat."

Cole did his best to draw his attention away from Jenna's belongings scattered throughout the bathroom. He honestly didn't know how much longer he could go on this way. There wasn't anywhere in this honeymoon suite she hadn't been, and no place she didn't touch. The memories burned into his mind like a permanent tattoo.

He snatched a towel out of the linen closet and undressed. But the moment he ambled toward the empty shower stall, he pictured her standing inside, just the way she was after returning from the day they had shared at the beach. She had that come and get me expression in her eyes. She had stared at him, water cascading over her face, and running down the length of her bronzed skin. He remembered the velvet of her skin under his roving hands as they roamed from her shoulders to her wrists, and then molded around her hips just before guiding her body against his and making love to her.

Waves of torment took over, and there was nothing in the world he could do to stop it. As he leaned against the glass encasement of the shower wall for support, his body gave in to the racking of tears again. "Oh, my God, Jenna," he wept. "I'm so sorry I let this happen to you, honey."

The second a thought of the bastards who took her entered his mind, he pulled himself upright, and his fists tightened into balls. He couldn't control the anger that ripped through him, and he punched the wall, shaking in rage. But as reasoning kicked in, his heartbeat slowed, and he closed his eyes, fighting to regain control of his emotions. He damn well knew losing his shit wasn't doing Jenna any good. Chastising himself to keep his cool had become a ritual every half hour. *Do what you have to do to find Jenna, pal.*

As he stepped into the shower, a stab of agony pierced him again. It was everything he could do to shove it aside and continue on. He twisted the knob and adjusted the temp of the water. It didn't matter if it wasn't warm enough. This was nothing more than a human necessity. It wasn't as if there was any chance he could enjoy it. The best thing he could do would be to get it over with. Without Jenna, nothing held meaning. He was going through the motions. And the sooner he could wash up, the quicker he could be back on the case, feeding his obsession to find her.

After finishing his shower, drying off, and

wrapping the towel around his waist, he stumbled into the huge, walk-in closet and rifled through garments until finding something decent to wear.

He slipped into the fresh clothes, grabbed a pair of sneakers, and carried them into the bathroom, setting them on a dressing stool. While brushing his teeth, his stomach growled again. And for the first time it dawned on him Cruz was right. If he didn't get a proper meal soon, his energy level would completely diminish, and it would undoubtedly affect his thought process. He needed to do everything he could to stay on task and focus, even if it meant allowing himself everyday necessities that were less than desirable at this point.

With his hands bracing the countertop, he leaned into the mirror and made a solemn vow to his reflection, "I will stay strong, and I will do whatever it takes to bring her home."

There would be no more teetering on the edge of falling apart, not another sliver of weakness attempting to convince him it was too late, and he'd never find her. She was still in the vicinity. He could feel her. It was high time to put all discouraging thoughts aside and hone in on who he truly was above all else. A damn good detective.

He stepped into the living room, and two starving men were leaning over their plates, practically inhaling fried chicken. His buddy peered over at him, licked his lips and said, "This is some badass grub."

Cole couldn't control the chuckle that escaped him. "As much as I just paid for that meal you're eating, it better be."

Cruz shrugged. "I'd offer to split the cost, but you can afford it."

Cole plopped down on the sofa across from Cruz and picked up a plate, filling it with two drumsticks, a heaping of coleslaw, and a dinner roll. The first bite was delicious whether he wanted to admit it or not. Around a mouthful of food, he asked Diego, "Did you make the call yet?"

The guy nodded, swallowed a lump of coleslaw, and said, "Estrella is checking into it for us. She'll call me back as soon as she knows something. I explained the situation and she understands the urgency. It's too bad we don't have that surveillance tape you mentioned."

"That's a dead lead. Nothing we can do about it," Cole told him. They would be wasting time chasing after evidence that was destroyed. What they needed was a fresh clue.

"So, it would be fair to surmise this detective Benton is definitely involved," Cruz put in.

Cole scooped up a forkful of coleslaw and slid it into his mouth. After swallowing he responded, "Without a doubt."

"And what was the sergeant's reaction when you accused this guy of tampering with evidence?" the Ranger asked before sinking his teeth into the dinner roll.

Cole frowned. "He was shocked and angry. But that didn't keep him from ordering me out of his office. It was hard to tell whether he believed me or not. To me, the fact Benton didn't bother to tell him he'd gathered that kind of evidence, or even mention the tape was blank is a sure sign he's hiding something."

"Right on," Cruz said, bobbing his head as if in deep consideration. "You and I know what it's like behind the scene of an investigation. Us detectives share information with each other. If a lead comes in, everyone assigned to the case knows about it from the top down. It's a joint effort. All the years I've participated in police investigations, I've never witnessed anyone on the team fail to mention a lead as promising as a surveillance tape. The sergeant in charge of the case would have been informed about the tape the minute it was taken into custody. There would likely have been more than one investigator viewing it. No one would have kept it to themselves unless they were hiding something."

"Exactly. I've been suspicious of this detective from the moment I laid eyes on him."

"What about the sergeant?" Diego said. "Do you think he's involved?"

"Try as I may," Cole answered, "I haven't been able to pinpoint any suspicious behavior from Bancroft that would lead me to believe he is a part of this."

"He's the one who gave you the recommendation for the captain and his phony wife who ended up kidnapping Jenna and nearly killing you," Diego provided. "And that was right after you and your wife showed up at the precinct telling him about a sighting she was having regarding my sister, who we can now say for certain was the victim of a sex trafficking ring."

Cruz stopped chewing and stared off into the distance as if he'd had an epiphany. "That's the connection," he finally said, slamming his fist down on the coffee table. The glass shook and everyone's plates rattled.

The crunch of the chicken Diego bit into became the only noise in the room.

"Sonofabitch," the Ranger said suddenly. "That's why they took Jenna."

"What are you talking about?" Cole asked.

"You told me Luisa was kidnapped by these people, right?"

Cole nodded, still not following.

"The day you and Jenna stopped in and informed Sergeant Bancroft your wife was seeing the ghost of Luisa, this dirty detective would have become aware of that fact."

"What's your point?" Diego added, sitting there appearing dumbfounded.

Cruz shook his head for emphasis, opening his arms to the obvious. "I worked a case back in my heyday. There was this rapist who walked into the establishment of a fortune teller and took the woman hostage. We all assumed he abducted her for the sole purpose of sexual assault. But when the guy let her go three days later, we discovered his motive had nothing to do with rape."

Out of the corner of his eye, Cole caught Diego setting the half-eaten drumstick back on his plate. His head spun around to glance at the guy, and he was as captivated by Cruz's story as a kid watching a Christmas special.

His buddy continued with his tale. "The suspect's father owned a ranch he turned over to his son before he died. The guy was old school. Never opened a banking account in his life. What he would do was bury money in glass jars all over the property. We're talking a spread of about fifty acres of land. That's why the rapist wanted the fortune teller. He was hoping she could tell him where the money was buried."

Right away Cole realized the point Cruz was making had been right there under his nose since his visit to the convenience store. He spoke even though the wheels in his brain were still catching traction. "Luisa made two phone calls that night. She'd left a message warning someone the organization was abducting young girls from CPS. That's what they wanted to know. Did she tell someone about that, and if so, who did she tell? That's precisely why they took my wife. She's the only one who has been in contact with Luisa.'

"And she is the only one who can give them that information," Diego finished for him, astonishment dripping from his face. "It makes perfect sense."

Cole wasn't sure how to feel about this latest discovery. It would certainly mean they didn't take Jenna with the intention of turning her into a sex slave, and they wouldn't harm her until they were able to bleed her for this information. He still had a chance to get to her before any permanent damage was done.

"As for the sergeant," Cruz said, "I have an idea how we can find out whether or not he's involved."

Chapter Nine

Buttons flew across the room, hitting the floor with a *ting*.

Jenna fought like an animal, landing a hard blow to the side of Leo's face. With a guttural moan, he gripped Jenna around the neck, applying such pressure, she feared she would faint.

"You won't get away with what you did to me last time. Do you hear me, you little whore!"

Realizing she was no match against this disgusting creature, Jenna ceased fighting. Staring into his soulless eyes, she was struck with the knowledge if she continued to resist, he would lose all control, and strangle the life out of her.

He leaned closer, and his fetid breath washed over her face. "That's more like it, girl." He ran a calloused palm that reeked of tobacco and onions down the front of her face before taking her chin between his fingers. "I haven't had a delicious bitch in a very long time."

As adrenalin pumped through her body, vomit threatened to rise in her throat. She swallowed it down, doing her best not to sink into sheer panic.

Don't lose control. You're going to survive this. Just close your eyes. It will all be over soon.

No matter how hard she tried, she couldn't block out the feel of his rough hands sliding across her stomach, then clamping around her breasts. His loud breathing was the only noise in the room. He slid his tongue up the side of her neck, over her cheek, toward her mouth. She locked her arms against his chest, fighting, thrusting with all her might to push him away.

From out of nowhere, the platter Meredith had left on the table flew up and smacked Leo in the face.

The pig leapt from the mattress with a shriek. "You!" he bellowed, pointing a trembling finger at her. "You did this."

Luisa appeared, stalking across the floor straight toward him. She looked ready to tear his face off. It dawned on Jenna that Luisa was behind the dish skyrocketing off the table and smacking Leo in the forehead. The ghost lunged at Leo, shoving him against the wall.

He instantly jerked forward, threw up both hands in a defensive posture, only to spin in aimless circles. "Who…who is in here?" he wailed. "Who did that?"

Luisa plucked a teacup off the floor. The unkempt man gaped in terror.

The crockery whizzed past Leo's head, crashed against the wall, and showered in pieces to the floor. Mouth quivering and eyes twitching wildly, his attention bounced around the room. "Is that you, Luisa?"

The room became eerily quiet; Leo backstepped, spun and pounded on the door like a crazed man. "Meredith! Get me the fuck out of here!"

Footfalls pounded down the hallway. Within seconds, the lock disengaged. Meredith swung open the door; the expression on her face was priceless. "What the hell is going on?" she asked, her attention skimming over the shattered teacup on the floor.

"That fuckin' dead bitch attacked me," Leo wailed.

"What? You're crazy."

Jenna watched as he shuffled around Meredith and stepped into the light of the hallway. Relief emanated from his body language now that he was out of the room. "Swear to God. That's what happened."

Meredith looked at Jenna. "What is he talking about?"

From the pit of her soul a smile blossomed. Although what Luisa did was totally unexpected, it had turned the tables on these monsters. "It seems like he saw a ghost. I'd believe him if I were you."

The irritation shrouding Meredith's face was a sight to behold. She kneeled to gather larger chunks of the china cup. "Go get a broom, you moron," she barked. "Jesus, Leo, you really need to get off the dope."

"I'm not high. I swear it."

She glared back at him. "I should have known better than to leave you unattended for more than a minute. You are nothing more than a total screw up, and I have no idea why anyone puts up with you."

He blew out a frustrated sigh and scampered down the hall.

"I don't know what happened here, but if you pull any more shit," Meredith warned Jenna, "I'll drag you to the bathroom, and chain you to the toilet. You can lay on the cold, hard floor in there and cry your little eyes out."

The warning went in one ear and out the other. Jenna was far too wrapped up in the picture of what just happened inside the cabin. If Luisa could move objects, it changed the dynamics of everything.

Leo approached the door, handed Meredith a broom and dustpan, careful not to step inside. The guy appeared skittish enough to pee his pants and burn a trail down the hallway if someone hollered *boo*.

Meredith snatched up Jenna's torn clothes. "Go find her something to wear, you imbecile. Then take her to the shower. We're leaving in less than thirty minutes."

Jenna felt her heart skip several beats.

Where were they taking her now?

****

Once he and Cruz swung into the parking lot of the Pensacola PD and found a place to park, Cole checked his watch. In approximately five minutes Diego should arrive. By then, the plan they'd hatched back at the resort would already be in motion.

"Now remember," Cruz said, pointing at the two-story building housing the PD. "We're here to get the information we need, not get involved in what's going on internally."

Cole nodded and climbed out of the rental car. His buddy was already out and standing beside the passenger door. "Once they see two of us, it'll sink in that trying to get to you again will pose a challenge. Eliminating you won't be so easy."

That was part of the plan. Psychological warfare.

Side by side, straight and tall, they strode down the precinct corridors. Stares followed them as they approached the door marked Sergeant. Cole raised a hand to knock.

Thirty seconds ticked by before the door swung open. Bancroft looked surprised to see someone standing at Cole's side. "You again. Haven't you done enough?"

Ignoring the sarcasm, Cole strolled into the office then stepped aside to leave room for Cruz to enter. As the two men settled in, Bancroft swung the door closed and wasted no time. "What do you want and who's this guy?"

"This is Dylan Cruz, a Texas Ranger, and a good friend of mine. I'm here to discuss getting a subpoena for the convenience store phone records. I mentioned it when I was here earlier." It wasn't as if he expected Bancroft to take the initiative to get that done, but he'd needed a ploy to kill time before Diego showed up, and operation *Pin the Tail on the Dirty Cop* could be deployed.

The sergeant shook his head, sighed, and wandered over to his desk. "Already done. The phone company is getting us the logs as we speak. Of course, you know how slow these things can be. It could take a few days or a few weeks before we receive anything."

After hitting one brick wall after another, Cole had given up any hope these jokers would do what the city paid them for. He couldn't control the skepticism that bubbled to the surface. "What about the sketch?"

"That'll hit the evening news. Anything else?"

Cole opened his mouth to fire off another question but shut it when Bancroft threw up a hand. "Before you ask, Benton has been relieved of his duties until I can get to the bottom of what happened with the surveillance tape. Does that satisfy you, Rainwater?"

Who put a busy bug up the sergeant's ass?

Cole was, until now, unfamiliar with this kind of productive behavior coming from the Pensacola PD. Obtaining phone records and publicizing the victim's sketch should have been priority from day one. At least Bancroft was finally taking this investigation seriously. "Has anyone found the video tape?"

The sergeant cut his gaze away, and the annoyance Cole was sure he caused, eased from his face. "I've got half the department searching for it. Benton claims he left it in the evidence room. But it's not there."

"What a surprise," Cole retorted.

Bancroft scowled. "Look, I realize this department isn't up to the lofty standards you think it ought to be, but we are doing the best we can with the information we have. I told you we'd do all we could to find your wife. And that's exactly what I'm doing. It isn't every day I have to put one of my best detectives on leave because I suspect him of tampering with evidence."

"So, you think he's somehow involved?" Cole asked, one eyebrow raised.

"No…yes. Christ! I don't know." The man ran his fingers through his hair. "I know something's up with him. He's been dropping little clues here and there."

"Like?" Cole encouraged.

Outside the door, loud voices drew closer. A crash sounded, then someone hollered, "If you don't get the hell out of here, we're going to throw your ass behind bars!"

"What the hell," Bancroft said, making a beeline for his door. He threw it open and stepped outside.

"Get your damn hands off me!" someone bellowed from inside the bullpen. "I demand to see the duty sergeant. Maybe he'll explain why you fools are doing nothing about my missing sister!"

"Aw, son-of-a-bitch!" Bancroft said. The expression on his face told Cole he was on his last nerve. "It's Diego Florentino. Let me deal with him. Make yourselves comfortable until I get back."

As the door shut and a large grin popped out on Cole's face, Cruz wasted no time. He hurried over to the sergeant's desk to shuffle through the drawers. As the noises outside the door intensified, Cole headed over to assist. He lifted papers and other items in search of Bancroft's cell phone. When the device was nowhere to be found, he cursed under his breath. Then his gaze swept across Bancroft's suit jacket draped over the back of his chair. He advanced quickly, digging his hands inside the pockets. When he tugged the phone from the right pocket, relief washed over him. Thank God. He hit the side button on the phone making the screen light up, hoping there wasn't a lock put in place to keep him from gaining access.

There wasn't, making this the second stroke of good luck he'd encountered so far. He immediately scrolled to the sergeant's most recent texts, looking for incriminating messages. He ran across a few from a contact saved as CB.

–When will you be home?–

–I'm on my way–

–Can you stop at the store and grab a loaf of bread?–

From the nature of the back-and-forth discussion, Cole assumed CB stood for Cheryl Bancroft, the sergeant's wife. More texts from a number with no saved contact.

–Your dry cleaning is ready for you to pick up–.

And a string of messages from *Little Cassie,* which upon closer inspection had to be his granddaughter. Nothing out of the ordinary. Nothing that would raise

Cole's suspicions.

Next, he scrolled through the most recent outgoing and incoming calls. Although he didn't recognize any of the numbers, he laid Bancroft's phone on the desk, and slid his cell from his pocket. He tapped on the camera icon and proceeded to scroll through the sergeant's calls while snapping pictures of them with his phone. He'd have time to sort through them later.

Meanwhile, Cruz was digging through a satchel on the floor by the leg of the desk. The Ranger glanced up and frowned, as if to say, "'I've got nothing, man." Neither did Cole. Perhaps Alan Bancroft was on the up and up after all.

"Let's get out of here," Cole said. He returned the sergeant's phone to the pocket of his suit jacket while Cruz stuffed documents back into the satchel.

Once they made their way out into the bullpen, the scene that awaited was amusing to say the least. Diego Florentino played the part of the disgruntled brother of a missing girl better than any Hollywood actor. The man was inconsolable, dead set on getting answers from a department that had done little to nothing to find his sister. Although this was part of the plan to distract Bancroft while Cole and Cruz snooped through his belongings, you could hardly tell it by the way Diego carried on.

The cowboy leaned over the receptions desk and jabbed a finger in the chest of one of the officers. "I'm tired of getting no answers. And I'm fed up with being told to go home while you incompetent assholes do nothing to find Luisa."

"Listen here, you prick." The officer behind the reception desk gave Diego a shove. "Lay a finger on me again and you'll find your ass thrown into that cell over there," he finished, stabbing a finger in the direction of the holding unit.

"All right, guys." Bancroft held out a hand in an obvious attempt to defuse the escalating situation. "Mr. Florentino, I can assure you this department is doing everything in its power to find out what happened to your sister."

"Then please," Diego said, throwing his arms wide, "explain to me what actions you've taken. Because from where I'm standing, I don't see anyone doing shit."

While Bancroft launched into an explanation of police procedures, and why it took time to get results, it became clear to Cole that now was a good time for him and Cruz to make their way toward the exit and slip out.

They stepped out into a parking lot baked by the afternoon sun. Intense heat rolled off the asphalt, distorting the view beyond the building. Cole snatched the sunglasses from the pocket of his shirt and slipped them on. From the corner of his eye he caught Cruz doing the same thing.

As they marched to the rental car, Cole used the fob to unlock the doors. Neither spoke until they shut themselves inside the cab. Then the Ranger broke the silence. "You're sure Diego is right about the time frame Bancroft's wife leaves the house for the homeless shelter?"

Cole nodded, starting the car, and sliding the seatbelt over his chest, locking it in place. "You heard him. He said Cheryl Bancroft has volunteered at the Saint Mark shelter for the last twelve years. She's there like clockwork every Monday and Thursday. She leaves her house at noon, and stays till three, which should give us plenty of time."

Cruz glanced at his watch. "Well, we'd better get a move on because it's twenty till. And we gotta catch her before she leaves the house."

"Roger that," Cole said, and shifted into drive, taking off across the parking lot.

On the way to the sergeant's house, he couldn't help thinking they might get caught red handed breaking into Bancroft's residence. If the sarge arrived home early, or his wife forgot something and doubled back to retrieve it and found them there, the jig would be up. They'd find themselves sitting in a jail cell with no way to rescue Jenna.

He had to admit, this was one of the most reckless and dangerous ideas he ever contemplated carrying out. It was sloppy and rushed. But he had to know for sure if Bancroft was involved in the kidnapping. So far what they'd found or lacked finding in the man's office didn't implicate him. But the sergeant couldn't be eliminated until they gathered enough proof to show he had nothing to do with this. Searching his home for clues was a good way to find that out. And unfortunately, time was not on their side. For better or worse, this was the only way to collect the intel they needed to scratch him off the list of suspects and move forward. Or discover his involvement and hatch a plan to bleed him for information on the whereabouts of Jenna.

Cruz's silence for the rest of the ride told Cole his buddy was just as concerned about all the things that could go wrong. From the first, Cole knew him to be a calculated thinker, always weighing his options, and carefully planning each move. They both realized this plan was rushed. And they were aware of what could happen when strategies were not thoroughly assessed. But the time for considering the consequences of a hasty approach had come and gone. The clock was ticking, and if they couldn't get to Jenna soon, there would be no getting to her at all.

As Cole veered off the street a few yards from the Bancroft residence, the crunch of the tires meeting the side of the road was a wakeup call to the idiocy they were about to pull. They shuffled out of the car, quietly shut the doors, and stared at each other over the hood. Cole wondered if the sight of Cruz standing there in his dark shades, with that stone expression on his face would be the last sight he'd remember seeing before they carted him off to jail for breaking and entering.

"Hey," Cruz said, snatching Cole out of his troubling thoughts. "We follow the plan. I sneak into the garage as she's backing out. Once I'm in the house, I'll unlock the back entrance and let you in. We're in and out, fifteen minutes tops."

Cole nodded, even though his better judgment didn't agree. "You ever done this before?"

Cruz frowned, slipping his sunglasses into his shirt pocket. "Which part? Sneaking into a garage before the door comes down and possibly crushes me, or breaking into a suspect's home without a warrant?"

"The sneaking into a garage part."

"Do I look like I have experience in dodging garage doors? It's never been a pastime of mine, and I haven't had the opportunity to rehearse before we decided to do this shit. But I've seen a few movies and I'm going on blind faith it can be done."

171

As good a response as any, Cole imagined. "Then let's do this."

Cruz marched around the car. "That's exactly what I'm talking about."

They inched toward Bancroft's house until they had a clear view of the closed garage. After slipping in the direction of a line of shrubs and crouching behind them, Cruz checked his watch one more time. He sighed and shook his head. "Dammit. It's five minutes past. I think we might have missed her."

The soft rumble of a motor ringing to life coming from inside the house alerted Cole that Bancroft's wife was starting her vehicle. He faced Cruz, whose stare reflected Cole's thoughts. *They were back in the game. Time to get into position.*

Cole remained behind the shrubs, and his buddy scurried across the lawn toward the house, taking up a position around the east wall, closest to the garage. He nodded at Cole, and then slunk back into the shadows.

An internal clock ticked off digits in Cole's mind while he waited for movement to start. Four ticks, five ticks, six ticks…nothing.

Then the buzz of a mechanism, followed by the clang of metal caught his attention. He instantly stepped back behind the shrubs, and after a moment, chanced a peek at the garage door. Through a breach in the small leaves, he caught a shrouded view of the metal door lifting, and the noise of a car door shutting. He closed his eyes for a moment, hidden well behind the bushes, and said a little prayer Cruz could get into the garage safely without being detected.

As a white suburban backed out of the driveway, he wondered where he could hide if Bancroft's wife happened to head in his direction.

He peered behind him; saw no other bushes or trees to serve as cover. It was an open landscape. In fact, if someone drove by right now, they'd surely see him crouched behind the shrubs. The only alternative would be to slip inside the bushes themselves. And by the appearance of the stiff, piney branches, it didn't seem possible.

Relief rolled off him in a gallon of sweat when the vehicle backed up and headed in the opposite direction. If their plan was successful, Cruz would already be hiding somewhere in the garage by now. The door was closed. Obviously, if his buddy was inside, Bancroft's wife didn't see him, or she wouldn't have continued out of the driveway. He realized one thing more than anything else though. He needed to get the hell out of this open space before somebody spotted him and called the police about the sighting of a suspicion person hanging around the neighborhood hiding behind bushes.

The second he saw the suburban rolling out of sight, he rounded the shrubs and made a beeline for the side of the house.

As the lock behind the wooden gate that led to the back of the residence disengaged, the quick pace of his heart slowed. Cruz peeked his head through the opening, motioning for Cole to hurry.

The Ranger's whistle indicated how close a call that was and swung the gate closed, securing the latch. He said, "Man, I accidently bumped into an oil can sitting on the floor of the garage. It clattered like hell, and I was sure she'd heard it."

Cole recalled hearing a clanging noise as the

suburban reversed out of the drive. But it was so slight he didn't take much notice of it. "I think when you tripped over the can, the garage door was closing, which is probably why she didn't hear it."

"Thank God. And it's a damn good thing she kept the garage door unlocked."

Cole assumed most people left that entrance unlocked, in the event a family member forgot their key and needed to get into the house when no one was home. It was common knowledge nearly all garage doors had an outside keypad with a code only close friends and relatives were privy to.

"Listen," Cruz said as he led the way across the manicured lawn, sidestepping the walking stones, "I spotted Bancroft's office near the front of the house. I'll head in there to search, and you check the master bedroom. Like I said, we don't have a lot of time."

They entered through the sliding glass doors Cruz, no doubt, unlocked from the inside. Cole's attention immediately zoned in on all four corners of the ceiling, as well as checking the walls for discoloration where a possible camera could be hidden. Because of the hurried plan of this break-in, he didn't stop to consider if the sergeant wired his house with surveillance equipment. If he did, they weren't in disguise and could be in some deep shit.

Damn, what an idiot. Why didn't I consider this before?

The reaction wasn't lost on Dylan, and he clapped Cole on the back. "I've scoped out the house. It's not wired.

"When did you have time to do that?"

"Before I came out to get you."

"And you call that a thorough search?"

"It's not like I had time to tear the place apart. But I'm confident there aren't any cameras."

"I'm glad you have more faith in a two-minute search than I do."

"And we just wasted one whole minute arguing about cameras that may or may not be in here."

"So, you admit there might be cameras."

"Are we on a mission to find Jenna? Fuck the talk about cameras, man. Let's get a move on."

That was that.

Cruz pointed him in the direction of the master suite, and they parted ways.

The master bedroom appeared every bit as drab as the rest of the areas he'd wandered through to get to this point. No pictures on the walls, not a single adornment, and sparse furniture; only what appeared to be a queen-sized bed, and a nightstand on one side with an ordinary lamp sitting on it. Guess the wife wasn't much for decorating. But the place was tidy. He'd give her that.

He headed straight for the nightstand and wrenched open the drawer. A few birthday cards lay in a neat stack. He quickly opened one up to discover it was from his granddaughter. *Happy birthday, Grandpa. All my love, Cassie.* Four or five business cards were scattered inside the drawer. An automotive shop, window tinting company, and a coupon for a free cake at the bakery. He snatched a small box out and opened the lid. Inside was a hollowed out, red-velvet mold in the shape of a pocketknife. Must have been a gift from his wife or granddaughter.

Dropping the box into the drawer and rummaging

through the rest of the items produced nothing incriminating. He shut the drawer and scanned the objects resting on top of the nightstand. A gold metal dish brimmed with pocket change, a few nuts and bolts, and some waded up gum wrappers. None of it was of any interest to him.

The dresser sitting in the center of the room opposite the bed appeared as ancient as one from the Wild West era. The mirror bolted on top was cloudy, and the wooden frame was as worn as old leather. He wasted no time opening one drawer after another and rifling through them. Nothing more than clothes and a wrinkled road map that had seen a few thousand miles.

He peered under the bed. Not so much as a dust bunny. He slid his arm under the mattress, hoping Bancroft hid a treasure there that would implicate the man. After lifting it halfway up, it became apparent, there was nothing here that would cast suspicion on the sarge.

Footfalls thumped down the hallway, and he stood up, glancing toward the door. His heart jumped into his throat. Jesus, did the sergeant come home?

"Hey, man," Cruz said, filling up the doorway.

Cole let out a sigh, allowing time for his heart to float back down to his chest. "Shit. You scared the crap out of me. I thought you were Bancroft."

"I didn't notice it before, but are you always this paranoid?"

"What we're doing could land us in jail, bro. Then who's going to save Jenna?"

His buddy frowned and leaned against the doorframe as if to say he had a point. "I really didn't think of it that way."

"Welcome to reality. I'm glad you could join me."

"I found something. "Cruz handed him a scrap of paper.

On closer inspection Cole realized he was staring at a list of satellite offices for Child Protective Services. Handwritten notes appeared beside each inscription. *Emailed sketch of suspect. No one recognizes her. Talked to Abigayle Wright yesterday. She emailed a copy of the sketch to all caseworkers in the area and will let me know if any of them know the woman in the sketch. Check back with her tomorrow.*

Cruz said, "Seems like Bancroft is on the up and up. This is proof he's investigating the case and trying to identify the caseworker responsible for kidnapping Jenna. I searched through everything in his office and couldn't find anything that would raise my suspicions."

"Neither could I."

Although Cole wasn't sure what he would find when they stumbled into Bancroft's home, he had to admit he was relieved to learn the sergeant wasn't part of this, and the guy was genuinely trying to solve this case.

Maybe.

Chapter Ten

To her count, Jenna pounded on the door for the hundredth time. "Hey, assholes, I told you I need to use the bathroom!"

"Shut up!" Meredith's voice floated down the hallway just the way it had done for the last thirty minutes. "Piss in your pants for all I care."

Despite that the side of her hand was bruised and aching, Jenna continued to pummel her fist against the door. "I'm not going to stop!"

For the first time since she'd been abducted, she realized she'd gained the upper hand on these creeps because of what Luisa did to Leo. They were afraid of her, terrified of what the ghost of a girl they trafficked and murdered would do if they pushed the boundaries with their captive. Because of that, Jenna had a new and powerful weapon she planned to use against them. My, how the tides had turned compliments of a shattered teacup and a flying food tray.

"I swear, if you don't let me out to use the bathroom, I'm going to sic my dead friend on the both of you! Do you hear me out there?" She followed up her threat with more pounding on the door for good measure.

Footfalls hammered down the hall, then the creaking of a door opened in the distance. "Leo!"

It was obvious Meredith swung open one of the

bedroom doors and was beckoning for him to come out of hiding. "Get your ass out of bed and let that bitch out to use the bathroom."

A few minutes of silence followed, then some rustling, and then, "You're crazy as a loon if you think I'm going anywhere near that ghost summoning psycho!"

"Listen, buddy. You're getting paid to do this job. If you don't get out here and take care of this, I'm going straight to Simon and telling him you're too afraid of a ghost to take care of business. You're already on his shit list and you know it."

Jenna pressed her ear tighter against the door. Thumping sounds told her Leo was off the bed and storming out into the hallway. "I don't care what you do. You weren't in the room when that shit went down. You don't know what that dead bitch did to me."

"I'll tell Simon I caught you in there trying to rape her. He told you what would happen if you pulled that shit again."

"You dirty, lowdown snake! You're the one who put me up to it."

"Who's he going to believe?" Meredith taunted. "You or me?"

A wide grin lifted Jenna's cheeks. She'd managed to cause distrust and animosity among them on a level that didn't exist before. As long as they were on edge and at odds with one another, she had a much better chance of escaping right under their noses if need be.

"I can't go back in that room," Leo whined. "Luisa's gonna kill me. I just know it."

"How's a ghost going to kill you, dumbass?"

"The same way she threw that fuckin' cup at my

head!"

"You're crazy."

"I'm telling you, she's out for revenge. We're all responsible for her death. After she finishes with me, who do you think she'll come after? Ever stop to think of that, Meredith?"

The ensuing silence lasted long enough for Jenna to wonder if the two went separate ways. Then, "Yeah, that's what I thought," Leo's gruff voice said. "If you think I'm so full of shit, why don't you go in there and get her yourself?"

"That's it. I'm calling Simon right now."

More silence, then steps down the hallway.

"You bitch!" Leo roared.

"Just let her out of the room," Meredith ordered. "If she tries to pull any shit, I'll be right out here."

"That's real comforting."

"What's it going to be? I call Simon, or you let her out of the room?"

"Fine, gawdammit. I'll do it. But if I holler for you, you better come running, you hear?"

The lock clicked in the door, and it swung open as wide as a barn. Jenna leaped back to keep from falling out into the hallway.

Looking white as a ghost, Leo stood in the light. Beads of sweat dotted his forehead like a case of measles. She had the feeling if she'd made a noise, he would've vaulted back hard enough to slam against the wall and crack his skull.

He didn't say a word, only slipped out his pocketknife with a hand that trembled so badly she feared he might cut her as he sliced the binding. Somehow, he managed without drawing blood, then tugged on her arm to drag her out of the room.

"Wait a minute," she said, pulling back. "I'm starving. And I need a shower."

"What?" Leo stared at her, that same deer in the headlight's expression chiseled into his face.

Did she rock his world, or what?

"A meal, then a shower," she repeated. "Please."

His gaze darted in all directions as if he was looking for someone—or something. "I uh…It's uh…"

"Not going to happen, princess," Meredith said, slithering into the hall like a serpent and looking quite pleased to be the bearer of bad news.

We'll see about that. "You animals have fed me one piece of toast and one bite of cornbread since you dragged me into this Godforsaken hellhole. After lying on a filthy mattress that smells like rotting corpses and piss, I need to bathe." Jenna gestured toward the open doorway. "I'd like to do that now."

"Look at you, all demanding and full of yourself. You make peasant girls like me seem like trivial pissants the way you throw your weight around." Meredith circled her as if admiring her wits, stopped, and swiveled on her heel. "I think you've forgotten where the fuck you are, and who has complete control here."

Anger coiled around Jenna's gut. She wanted nothing more than to snatch the witch into the air with one fist, then mop the floor with her.

Then a much better idea occurred.

"You're right," she said, feigning defeat. "I am a prisoner here, and I'm at your mercy. But I have a little ghost of a friend who must be floating around here somewhere, and I'm willing to bet if I called on her, she'd help me out in a pinch. What do you think?"

Witnessing that condescending glower melt from Meredith's face was the icing on the cake. The woman fought to regain a frosty stare, but her eyes twitched, giving away the fear lying just beneath the surface.

"Would leftover pork and beans be okay?" Leo wanted to know.

"With a slice of bread if you have it," Jenna answered, then spun and sashayed to the bathroom all on her own.

****

Cole was standing inside the honeymoon suite and peered out the window, surveilling the parking lot. When a knock on the door interrupted him, he lowered the binoculars and approached the door.

From the other side of the door, Diego grinned and held up a bag. "I got everything you asked for."

Cole rummaged through the bag while strolling back to the window and found a blond-streaked wig, paste-on mustache, and two pairs of glasses. One pair had a thin, metal rim, the other was framed in thick, brown plastic. He peered back at Diego. "Man, where'd you find this stuff so fast?"

"When you told me you guys were being tailed, I remembered I'd inherited a bunch of stage props from my mom after she passed away. She was a theatre director, and always had these kinds of things lying around for the performers. I figured it would be perfect for what you guys needed."

You saved our asses, bro," Cole told him. "I really appreciate it."

"The car still there?" Diego Florentino asked, pointing at the window.

Cole nodded. "We noticed it sitting on the side of the road about a mile from the resort on our way back from Bancroft's house. When I drove by, the driver pulled out behind me. I went past the resort and veered into a gas station, and sure enough, the car followed. Once I got out of the store and rolled back onto the highway, the son-of-a-bitch was behind me again. Now he's sitting in the parking lot and hasn't moved since."

Diego took the bag and dropped it onto a nearby table. "Any idea who it is?"

Though Cole couldn't be positive, he had a good idea the guy following them was connected with Detective Benton, whom he suspected had tampered with the "lost" videotape. "It's got to be Benton or one of his henchmen."

"Do you mind?" Diego motioned toward the binoculars resting on the windowsill.

Cole handed them over. "Knock yourself out."

For a good two minutes Diego stared out the window, not saying a word, then out of the blue said, "Holy cow. Are you talking about the red hatchback with the banged-up tailgate?"

Cole took the binoculars and stared out the window. They were talking about the same vehicle. He rambled off the license plate, then handed the surveillance apparatus to Diego to confirm.

After a moment, Florentino said, "That's the one."

"Why do I have the feeling you know who drives that hatchback?"

"Because I do." Diego handed the binoculars back to Cole. "His name is Ron Lewis, and he's an officer at the Pensacola PD. You know, the fat bastard who always sits behind the front desk. The one who was giving me such a hard time earlier today. We got into a heated argument, and he shoved me, remember?"

The moment an image of the chubby man's face formed in Cole's mind, he wondered how many more dirty cops were involved in this mess. Of course, Benton put his fellow officer up to following him and Cruz since he couldn't do it himself.

"Did you call your buddy like you said you would?"

"Of course, man." Diego stared at him. "I told him my car won't start and asked him if he would drive me and a pal to the nearest car rental."

Cole pointed to the bag of disguises. "What's he going to say when you hop into his car wearing that?"

"Listen, I've known this guy since grade school. He just got out of the pen. He's always up to his ears in some shady shit. He's not going to ask too many questions. Don't worry."

After the seat-of-your-pants B and E he and Cruz recently executed, Cole didn't want to risk having their plan blow up in their faces because of some overlooked technicality. "Let's go over the plan again just to be safe."

Looking as though he considered it unnecessary but was willing to go along solely to appease his more nervous partner in crime, Diego sighed. "Me and Cruz slip out, wearing disguises. He rents a car under his name. Once we have a set of wheels, we're all set to tail Benton, and scope out where he goes. With any luck, it'll lead us to the location where they're hiding Jenna."

"And?"

Florentino rolled his eyes. "If we identify the location, we're to call you for backup before making any moves."

A toilet flushed and both men stared in the direction of the bathroom. Cruz waltzed into the room. "Having a party without me?"

"And here are the favors," Cole replied, stepping over to the table and emptying the contents of the bag Diego carried into the suite. "What would you like to be today, a blond or a brunet?"

"I'm feeling kind of sexy, gentlemen. I'll take the blond wig."

****

"I hope everything was to your liking, Miss Priss," Meredith said as she herded Jenna down the hallway, stopping long enough to open the bathroom door before giving her a brutal shove inside.

The impact sent her flying forward. She had to grab the front of the porcelain sink to keep from slamming into it. Although shock and anger hit her system like a rock, she managed to straighten up, and paste on a satisfied grin, just to spite the goddess Meredith. "Perhaps, you can fetch me some bath salts."

Meredith's eyes narrowed and her hands balled into fists—until the blood drained from her face. Perhaps a ghost with an axe to grind was enough to keep her captor's anger under control. "I'm giving you five minutes to take a shower. Simon is on his way here right now. And he's bringing backup. When he gets here, we're taking a little trip. All I can say is you better be prepared to tell him what he wants to know or find yourself sinking to the bottom of the ocean. Then your daughter will take your place." The look on Meredith's face spoke volumes. "I'll be right outside this door, so don't try anything stupid."

The door slammed, and Jenna's heart lurched. *Emily. Did they kidnap her? What if they had her in their clutches right now?*

"They don't have your daughter."

Jenna jerked in the direction of the voice. There, perched on the edge of the tub sat Luisa, elbows propped on her legs, chin resting on her fists. "I heard Meredith talking on the phone earlier. Not sure who she was talking to, but they were discussing whether to abduct Emily. With all the unexpected crap that's happened so far, they're afraid kidnapping another victim right now will bring too much heat. They're using an empty threat to scare you into telling them what they want to know."

Jenna blew out a sigh of relief, then jabbed a thumb in the direction of the closed door, whispering, "She's out in the hall."

"I know."

"I've gotta' get out of here," she said, keeping her voice to a minimum. "Simon and some others are coming. I think they're going to take me out to the ocean and throw me in."

Luisa frowned, shaking her head. "They're taking you to the cabin. Another conversation I overheard."

"A cabin where?"

"It's not in Florida," Luisa said. "I'm not exactly sure where it is, but I've heard them mention the cabin before. It's where they take girls before they ship them out of the state."

Just great. If they took her that far away, Cole would have zero chance of finding her.

"We have to do something," she told the dead girl, panic rising in her voice.

Luisa put a finger to her lips to signal for silence. "Don't worry. We'll think of a way out of this."

"Wait. We now know you can move objects, right? Why not unlock the door and let me out?"

"Meredith is standing right outside, remember? Besides, since I moved those things in the bedroom, I've tried to do it again, but haven't been able to."

"What do you mean you haven't been able to? You already did. I saw it."

"I know. But I can't do it anymore. I don't know why, but nothing I do to make it happen is working."

A pretend buzzer sounded in Jenna's mind, like the kind on a gameshow when a contestant gave an incorrect response. *Wrong answer. Try again.* She desperately needed Luisa to tap into whatever superpower she'd wielded against Leo when he attempted to rape her. It was her only hope to escape this place.

She took a few steps over to the sink and gestured toward the faucet. "Turn on the water."

The dead girl's initial response was to shake her head, her mannerisms speaking volumes. Then, she lowered her head with a deep sigh, rose from her position, and stepped over to the sink. If nothing more—Jenna imagined—than to prove she couldn't do it. Luisa's hand wrapped around the knob; she twisted, but nothing happened. She stared at Jenna with sorrowful eyes. "See. I told you. I can't do it anymore."

Jenna wasn't giving up. There must be something she could do. She needed to reflect on the time when Luisa sustained the ability to attack Leo. An idea occurred to her. She once watched a movie where a ghost, when becoming highly emotional, was able to achieve enough mind control to move objects. The name of the movie didn't matter. The only thing of importance was what the spirit was able to accomplish.

"What were you thinking when you swung the tray at Leo and threw the cup at his head?"

Luisa paused for a moment. "I…it reminded me of when he raped me. In that same room. I felt such rage thinking about what he'd done and how helpless I was, all of a sudden, I picked up the tray and it lifted off the table. Then I swung it at his head."

And it hit him smack in the forehead.

"It was anger that came over you, Luisa," Jenna said, throwing out her arms in an *ah ha* moment. "The energy of the fury you felt must have given you the ability to lift a physical object and swing it at him. Now, I want you to imagine what he did and focus your energy on turning the knob."

In Luisa's eyes was profound realization. She bowed her head, and Jenna imagined she was conjuring emotions from deep inside. The color of her face transformed into an angry shade of red; she began to shake with rage. This time when she twisted the knob, it turned. And water poured out of the faucet.

Oh my God, it worked.

While Jenna turned off the water, Luisa stepped away from the sink. Her expression reflected disbelief and laughter bubbled out of her. "I can't believe it. It was anger. That's what I was missing the whole time."

Before Jenna could respond, the doorknob clicked. She ran to the toilet and flushed it just as the door swung open.

Meredith stepped into the room, her roving stare examining every square inch of the tiny room. "Did I hear voices in here?"

Jenna made no comment but continued with the business of turning on the shower and unbuttoning her shirt. "I didn't hear the shower running," Meredith said, "but I know heard you talking to someone."

"That's because I was using the toilet and humming to myself. You've kept me locked in that room so long it seems like singing is the only way to keep my sanity."

The doubtful expression hugging the witch's face told Jenna she didn't quite believe her, but she couldn't disprove her either. "Well, hurry up, your majesty. We don't have all day. Got it?"

She was right about one thing, they didn't have all day. It was time to shower up, get back to her room, and formulate a plan of escape now that Luisa was back in action.

****

Cole's departure from the resort was delayed by an unexpected call of nature. Cruz and Diego were long gone by the time he walked out the front door toward the parking lot. A sound alerted him. He looked up and saw Officer Ron Lewis, in the red hatchback, booking out of the parking lot like the very devil was on his ass.

As he headed to his ride, Cruz called. They had a hit on Benton's car. Cole was still reeling with a mixture of elation and anxiety after his buddy informed him the dirty detective led them straight to the Pier 21 Marina. There, Benton piled out of his car, headed down the boat ramp, and climbed into a small cabin cruiser matching the description of the one Cole had taken shots at the night Jenna disappeared.

His hands shook so bad it became a challenge to

simply turn over the ignition then shift into Reverse. *Get it together, dude.*

It was the moment of truth, what he'd been waiting for since this nightmare began. The sense in his gut told him he was on the cusp of finding Jenna. If they needed information from her—like Cruz suspected—there was a good chance she'd still be alive.

As the image of the resort faded in the rearview mirror, Cole wondered if the perpetrators were still holding Jenna on the boat. Although his first instinct told him they'd taken her to a remote place, he now reconsidered that scenario. Perhaps keeping her on the movable vessel enabled them to shuffle her quickly from place to place. If there was one thing he understood about traffickers, holding captives in one area too long only increased the chances someone would notice suspicious activity and call the authorities. Moving these girls on a constant basis is what made it possible for them to continue to fly under the radar.

Adding to that, Jenna's abduction was different than the others. They didn't take her to traffic; they took her to bleed her for information. Therefore, it made sense they may not have taken her to one of their stash houses. He could only hope and pray she stayed strong and refused to give them the information they wanted.

Her silence was the only thing keeping her alive.

****

Heart pounding like a jackhammer, Cole pushed the car twenty miles over the speed limit, weaving around vehicles, narrowly avoiding fender benders a couple of times. Although he realized going this fast risked a traffic stop, he'd have to deal with that if it happened. Right now, Jenna was out there, and she needed him.

Up ahead, a red hatchback switched lanes, swerving in front of him then braking at a four-way stop. Since he saw no damage to the tailgate, it couldn't be Lewis. At the same time, it took Cole back to the same question: What happened to their tail and why did he take off just as Cole came out of the resort? What was important enough to cause him to abandon his post?

For the moment, Cole didn't have to deal with that. The thought of Benton being in control of whether Jenna lived or died sent his fists into spasms. He reflected on the outburst they had at the precinct when Cole shoved him hard enough to send him tumbling over the chair in Bancroft's office. Although he had a hunch at the time the piece of shit was involved, he couldn't prove it—then.

Now that it was confirmed, the things Cole would do to that son-of-a-bitch would leave him either dead or unrecognizable. The only thing that would stop him from finding his wife was a bullet to the head.

As the marina came into view, he swerved into the parking lot, scouting out the different vehicles for the one Cruz rented. He found the white SUV sitting near the front of the parking lot. He rolled past it and parked in a spot a few spaces down. The last time Cruz was on the phone with him, he'd assured Cole that Diego would stay behind as lookout while the Ranger checked things out.

As Cole climbed out of the rental, his sixth sense told him something was very wrong. The driver's side door was slightly ajar; Diego's cell phone lay on the ground cracked. He hastened his steps, picked up the cellular device, and wrenched open the door. Diego was nowhere to be found. But his hat lay on the floorboard, and the review mirror was positioned in such a way to indicate a struggle. The keys still hung from the ignition.

Without a doubt someone forcefully removed Diego from the blazer. But where was Cruz? Nothing appeared disturbed on the passenger side. His buddy must have vacated the automobile before the kidnapping took place—just like he'd told Cole he was going to do.

Unable to deny the truth, Cole headed down the boat ramp in a steady jog. If the traffickers got Diego, they also had Dylan Cruz. His hope of finding Jenna diminished by the second.

He approached the slip number that Cruz told him housed the cabin cruiser and was surprised to find the boat still there. Secured by ropes to several posts, the craft rocked gently with the waves.

He immediately released the Glock from his waistband and stepped onto the rear of the cruiser. He waded through a rat's nest of discarded ropes on the floor, stepped around plastic storage boxes, and wandered past the cracked, leather seats. Straight ahead was a set of Plexiglas folding doors which served as the barrier between the upper deck and the interior of the cabin. There existed only one way to find out what was below: open the door and check it out. Anyone could be down there. Cruz and Diego might be tied up; Benton might be waiting, holding a gun on the door.

It had to be a trap.

And maybe he was overthinking it.

It didn't matter. The decision to enter the cabin was made before he'd wrapped his hand around his gun and yanked it free. He certainly didn't plan to walk away and leave it a mystery.

He stepped down into the cabin, and the boat swayed with his advancement. There was a small fridge off to his right, a few shelves, a mini stove to the left, and the view of horseshoe seating toward the back of the vessel with a table in the center. The wall to the right told him there was more to this space than what met the eye. Knowing someone could be holed up behind the structure, he proceeded with caution.

He rounded the corner quickly, his gun trained in front of him. An open door shifted with the rocking of the boat, the hinges squeaking as it tottered back and forth. From the appearance of the small toilet, he realized he'd found the bathroom.

He wandered back to the upper deck to see if there were any clues out there. It wasn't until he peered over the side of the vessel, his gaze brushed across another cell phone lying on the wooden walkway separating the slip from the next one. He climbed off the boat to investigate, and picked up the phone, realizing instantly it belonged to Dylan Cruz. But even more disturbing was the splatter of fresh blood dripping down the side of the vessel, not a foot away.

Cole's breath caught in his chest. Jesus, what could have gone so wrong from the time he'd gotten his friend's call, to the ten minutes it took for him to drive out here?

Shit! Dylan was always so careful. He was skilled at performing surveillance without being spotted. How the hell did this happen?

Based on his inspection, there wasn't a single shell casing at the scene. And with the attention a gunshot would have caused, it was common sense the perps wouldn't have risked that out here in the open. Even though there weren't a lot of people around, the marina was still open, and there was a store and a restaurant within a one-minute walking distance from where he stood on the dock.

He doubted they'd have confronted Cruz. They would have snuck up behind him. Which meant they were aware he was there. At what point did they become privy to that information?

With scenarios swirling around Cole's brain, he ambled back down into the lower cabin, hoping he'd find clues he'd missed on first inspection.

On the second scrutiny, he noticed how filthy and battered the small space was. The air was stale, and a pungent order came from the oval booth style seating arrangement. He rambled around until he found another light switch and flipped it on.

A naked bulb cast unforgiving light across the place. Roaches scattered from plates holding uneaten food. A cold shiver ran down his spine when distant recall brought up pictures of crime scenes involving trafficking victims. The filth and depravity the women and children had been subjected to turned his stomach—and he was a seasoned officer.

The people who committed these crimes were the worst of humankind. They were the evilest among us. They had no conscience, and he imagined there was a special place in hell just for them. The urgency to get Jenna out of wherever they were keeping her burned in his gut like gasoline.

But now he was without the aid of the only people who could've helped him locate her. Damn if it didn't feel like the end of the road. He lowered his head and fought tears of hopelessness. He wanted to shrink down on the dirty floor, hold his head in his hands and cease to exist. If he closed his eyes and opened them again, maybe it would have all been a dream and he would discover he was back at the resort, his beautiful wife lying in his arms.

He needed to straighten up, battle this overwhelming fear, latch on to the first shred of courage he could muster, and get on with the task of finding her. She needed him, damnit. He was her only hope and there was no way in hell he would let her down.

The recollection of the way she had gazed up at him that dreadful day he hauled her out of the coffin his brother put her in and resuscitated her back to life, came over him like an angel giving him hope in his darkest hour. When her eyes had sprung open, and she recognized his face, she was so grateful and relieved. He imagined he'd never again witness anything as profound as that in all his life.

He realized what he had to do. Turn to the only person left who could help him find Jenna.

Cole plucked out his phone and searched for Bancroft's number. He placed the device against his ear, and the ringing pulsated straight through him.

The second the man answered, Cole blurted, "I need your help."

****

Bancroft's sigh came over the line loud and clear. "What's going on, Mr. Rainwater?"

"Listen, Dylan and Diego tracked Benton down to the Pier 21 Marina. He was here on the same boat that took my wife that night. I know he's involved with her disappearance."

Another sigh sounded. "I have the same suspicion. Ever since you accused him of tampering with evidence, he's been acting squirrelly. That was the reason I suspended him. Not only that, but I think another officer may be involved as well."

Like the chubby bastard who was tailing them at the resort. Cole decided to keep that under wraps until he determined what information Bancroft had. "What makes you think that?"

"I really can't say until I know for sure. But trust me, I have my reasons."

This would have to be another discussion for a different time. Right now, Cole needed to get to the reason for the call. "I'm in a bit of a pickle," he admitted. "I'm on the boat right now. Luisa's brother and my buddy Cruz who arrived before me are missing. The vehicle they drove here is out in the parking lot; I can tell a scuffle took place inside it. Additionally, there's evidence of foul play near the boat. No one is here but me."

"I take it you haven't spotted Benton or anyone else out there?"

"There's no one here and I haven't seen anyone. Can you meet me out here?"

The man didn't respond, and Cole picked up the noises of traffic and the rush of wind through an open car window. "I didn't want to say anything because I didn't want to get your hopes up," the sarge said, "but we got a lead on the whereabouts of the CPS case worker we've been searching for, and—"

"What the hell are you saying, Bancroft? You *know* where my wife might be, and you didn't tell me?"

"That's not what I said. Someone called the station and reported seeing a lady who resembles the one in the sketch. I'm headed out to the general area of the sighting now, but being an investigator, you know how these things typically go. It's probably nothing, which is why I didn't want to alert you until I had a chance to check it out."

"That's bullshit. If you got a lead on the possible whereabouts of my wife, I have every right to know."

"We don't even know if the suspect is anywhere near your wife even if it turns out to be the caseworker. I'm the one who took the call, and to be honest, from the sound of it, I'm doubtful it's going to pan out."

"Tell me the location." Cole spun on his heel and took the first step out of the cabin. The hammer of a gun clicked, and he stared up at a man standing over him, a weapon trained on him.

The phone slipped from his hand.

Chapter Eleven

"I unlocked the back door," Luisa told Jenna, leaning over to peel the duct tape from her wrists.

Jenna busied herself with removing the tape from her ankles. "You're getting really good at moving things."

"It's getting easier. I keep the anger right here." Luisa placed one hand against her chest. "For what that animal did to me, and the others."

Jenna stopped her activities to stare into the ghostly eyes. "I promise you when I escape, they're all going to pay for what they've done. Every one of them."

The spirit searched Jenna's face for a moment, then nodded and stepped toward the door. "I'm going to check on Meredith and Leo, see where they are. If they haven't gone into the kitchen, I'll come back here and unlock the door." She pointed toward the bedroom exit. "Once you're out of the room, I'll go ahead of you to make sure the kitchen is still clear before you make your escape."

As Luisa floated through the wall, Jenna was overcome with emotion. She was on the verge of breaking free. The dead girl had already made the trek through the woods once. She'd be able to guide Jenna as far as the road. Then it would be up to her to flag down a ride and get to safety.

Of course, the first call she made would be to her

husband. The thought of seeing Cole's face again made her want to break down in tears. She was so thankful for Luisa. Without her, Jenna would never have survived this ordeal.

The lock disengaged and the door creaked open. Luisa strolled back inside, all business. "Let's go. We have to hurry. They're in the living room."

That was all the encouragement Jenna needed. She rose from the bed and quietly followed the dead girl down the hallway. The moment they approached the end of the hall, a floorboard creaked under Jenna's foot. She halted, fearful her captors heard the noise. Peering back at her, Luisa put a finger to her lips, then marched ahead to scope out the situation. She reentered the hall and swiped out her hand, gesturing all was well. It was time to continue.

When the back door came into view, Jenna approached, heart fluttering and adrenaline pumping like fire through her veins. Blessed freedom was through that door. All she had to do was open it and slip out. Her hand wrapped around the knob. For a moment she froze, thinking this was too easy.

"What are you doing?" Luisa hissed. "Open the door. Hurry."

Putting her fears aside, she swung open the door and stepped out.

Straight ahead, four figures approached the house from the back yard. They were close enough to identify.

The shady detective Cole had complained about was positioned in front. The other three were directly behind him. A chubby uniformed officer she'd spotted behind the front desk at the precinct, the Spanish cowboy who'd given her the creeps, and Simon.

The men advanced. The overweight cop and Simon had their hands clasped around the cowboy's arms.

She froze.

One of the men caught sight of her and signaled the others to stop.

The Spanish cowboy's scream sliced through the night. "Run, Jenna, run!"

Her body reacted to the demand, even though her brain was caught up in a fog. She practically flew over the two steps and scurried across the patio, sharp rocks cutting into her bare feet. She didn't care. She hit the lawn, forcing her legs to sprint so quickly her muscles burned.

Shouting fanned out among the group of men, and one voice overshadowed the others, "Get her, you idiot!"

The grunts of exertion were so close the sounds prickled the hairs on the nape of her neck. Whoever was back there was gaining speed. She drove her muscles to the brink, but she somehow sensed it wouldn't be enough.

She was snatched in mid-air and thrown to the ground. The feel of the earth against her cheek was a cold reminder these bastards weren't ever letting her go. The recollection of Luisa's words the day they'd taken her here hit her like a freight train. *These guys are very good at what they do. No one will ever catch them.*

It was true. She did everything she could to escape. But in the end, she was still their captive. Meredith was right. The traffickers owned her.

She was plucked from the grass by the hair of her head. "You're not going anywhere you little bitch."

Although she couldn't twist her neck far enough

back to see the face of the person herding her toward the back door, she managed to direct her attention downward recognizing the color of his shoes and the bottom of his pants legs. It was the detective her husband believed had acted suspicious. Jesus, it was impossible to stop these animals when the police were so deeply imbedded in it.

She was prodded through the doorway and shuffled into the living room.

Meredith gaped when the dirty detective shoved Jenna into an old, ragged lounge chair. "You asshats should have been watching her closer," the detective said. "I caught her in the backyard trying to escape."

"That's not possible," Meredith spat.

"Well, here she is, isn't she?"

"Where's the dead girl's brother? You said you caught him."

Jenna was dumbfounded. *Luisa's brother? Who was she talking about?*

Before the detective could answer, footsteps approached the living room. The other three men piled into the room. The pudgy cop forced the Spanish cowboy into a chair opposite Jenna, and stepped behind him, placing a knife at his neck. "Try anything stupid, motherfucker, and I'll slit your throat."

It dawned on Jenna there was more going on here than she realized. The Spanish cowboy was Diego, Luisa's brother. He wasn't a suspicious character as she originally guessed. But what was he doing at the police station that day?

Simon stepped to the corner of the room where he rested his back against the wall. "If it wasn't for me spotting that guy," he said, pointing at Diego, "and the other guy rolling into the parking lot of the marina, we never would have known they'd been tailing Benton."

Jenna's ears were on fire. So, the name of the detective was Benton, and Luisa's brother had been following him. But who was the *other* one Simon mentioned? Christ, was it Cole? And if it was, what on earth did they do with him?

"Who was the other guy?" Meredith asked.

"I saw him at the precinct with her husband," the detective sneered, giving Jenna's hair a hard tug. "Some guy he knows from Texas, name of Dylan Cruz, a Texas Ranger. Evidently, Rainwater called for backup, and this Cruz guy caught a flight out here."

"You're sure he's dead?" Obviously with all that happened, Witch Meredith couldn't be sure of anything anymore.

This time it was Simon who spoke. "I knocked him out and threw him over the bridge and into the ocean myself."

Before that horrifying news could sink in, the chubby cop restraining Diego said, "Are we going to get on with this shitshow or what?" He repositioned the knife against Diego's neck. "I'm ready to cut this bastard's head off if that dead sister of his doesn't respond to our demands." His mouth lifted into an evil grin. "Hey, Luisa. Where are you! As you can see, we have your brother. I'm gonna slice his fuckin throat if you don't tell that bitch you've been talking to who all you called the day you escaped. We're pretty sure you called more than just your brother from the store you ran into."

The psycho whipped his attention from one end of the room to the other. Jenna figured he was searching for a sign. "You hear me, bitch? I'm not fucking around."

From out of nowhere, a loud crash ricocheted throughout the room. Benton loosened his hold on Jenna enough to allow her to move her head to one side. She stared at the glass table in the corner now shattered into a thousand pieces.

Luisa stood over the broken item. The dead girl bent and wrapped her hand around the lamp that had fallen to the floor. In one smooth motion, she lifted it, then whizzed it straight at the chubby cop's head.

The impact was so hard the guy flew backwards, dropping the knife and colliding into the corner of the room. Diego was out of the chair in a flash, but he didn't get far before Simon and Meredith tackled him and dragged him back over to the chair and forced him into it.

With all the action, it dawned on Jenna she could make a run for it. She jerked forward but Benton clamped both hands on her shoulders. "Don't even think about it," he warned, pinning her to the seat.

While Simon held Diego down, Meredith bound his hands and feet with duct tape. Loud moaning came from the corner. The cop who'd held Luisa's brother at knifepoint struggled to his feet. He stepped toward the weapon lying on the ground.

But it was too late. Luisa plucked the knife from the floor and poised it above her head. The guy's eyes became as large as saucers as she plunged it into his chest. Screaming in agony, he stumbled back and hit the wall. He slid down the wall, landed on the floor, legs spread and unmoving.

"Oh my God!" Meredith came to her feet, mouth

open and gaping like a fish.

"I'm afraid God's not going to help you now," Jenna said.

Luisa crossed the floor in front of Jenna and marched into the kitchen. A drawer opened and slammed.

A deafening silence fell over the room while five—now four—felons stood around like lambs being led to the slaughter. Luisa was going to pick them off one by one. It was time for them to pay the piper.

The spirit returned, with two kitchen knives in one hand, a pocketknife fully extended in the other. Luisa faced the detective holding Jenna hostage and raised the pocketknife like she intended to throw it at a dartboard.

And let it fly.

It hit dead center of his forehead. Jenna jumped out of the way before his weight took her with him to the floor.

"Go!" Luisa said. "Get out of here now. I'll meet up with you as soon as I can."

Jenna sprinted into the kitchen and out the back door, wary of Leo since she didn't see him among the crowd in the living room. With the coast clear, she took off across the lawn.

With her heart beating a mile a minute, she jogged to the front of the residence. Beyond the driveway and parked cars, there was nothing but dense woods. The cars didn't just appear out of nowhere and certainly hadn't been flown in by aircraft which meant they'd been driven here.

In the darkness any path wasn't easy to spot, but the farther she wandered toward the rear of the automobiles, and a few feet beyond the enclosed clearing, she noticed two wide impressions running about six feet apart from one another in a straight line. The grass in the middle of the ruts was flattened out, as if, over time, the bottom of a vehicle wore it down.

She winced with every stomp of her feet against the dead grass and compacted earth. She knew by the stinging pain in her soles, she'd sustained deep cuts from the jagged rocks she ran across earlier. Now, the slightest bit of pressure sent pinpricks of agony up her legs. But she couldn't think about that; she had to make her way through the woods as quickly as possible.

After maybe fifteen minutes, she needed to stop and rest. Placing her palm against a large tree trunk, she sucked air into her lungs so rapidly it burned. Past the point of exhaustion, her body sagged. Her heart hammered so hard, she feared it might leap from her chest.

She half sat half fell against the hard ground. Her hands worked their way down her calf, massaging the muscles that cramped so severely she wanted to cry out.

No one would hear her if she did. It was so dark out here, it was getting nearly impossible to tell if she was still following the vehicle tracks. Every patch of ground and tree appeared the same as all the others. There were no landmarks, no breadcrumbs left behind—like in the fairy tales—to ensure she wasn't running in circles.

It was no use. She didn't have a clue where the hell she was and wouldn't know the way out if the answer flew through the darkness at the speed of light and smacked her in the face.

Am I going to die out here?

Tears racked her body, and she lowered her head,

shaking it. She was foolish enough to believe she was free when she ran out of that hell house and put a distance between her and the people in it. But she wasn't free at all, only locked in a different kind of prison. And the enormous forest swallowing her up wasn't going to come to her aid.

"What are you doing?"

She looked up and stared straight into Luisa's eyes. A sound tumbled out of her mouth but Jenna couldn't be sure if it was a laugh or a whimper. "Oh my God, you came for me."

The dead girl frowned. "I told you I would."

"I got lost. And I was so tired." Jenna shook her head to clear her mind. "The truth is, I was overcome with fear I would die out here. I was alone and I panicked."

"You were never alone, Jenna. I have been with you the whole time. I promised you I would do everything I could to get you out of there. I don't turn my back on people I care about."

Tears streamed down Jenna's face, and she couldn't have been more grateful Luisa had found her in the chapel the day of her wedding, even though at the time she didn't understand what a true blessing the girl would turn out to be. "I can't tell you how fortunate I am you came into my life. Thank you for never leaving me when I needed you most."

The expression in the spirit's eyes told Jenna she was proud to have meant so much to someone. "I've grown kind of fond of you, too. And I'm going to miss you when this is all over."

Those words hit Jenna like a ton of bricks. Would this all be over? Could she find her way out of this forest and back into the loving arms of her husband?

"Let's get you up and out of here. I know the way to the main road. It's not much further."

Jenna struggled to her feet and grimaced in pain. "My feet," she said, "They're in pretty bad shape. I don't know how much farther I can go."

Although she could see sympathy hidden in Luisa's eyes, the girl put on a stern front. "Listen, I'm a ghost, I can't pick you up and carry you out of here. You're going to have to walk on your own. Do you hear me? You've come too far to give up now."

Luisa was right. But she honest to God didn't know how much harder she could drive her body before she collapsed. "All right. I'm going to try."

"Trying is for amateurs. You've told me about how you survived being stalked by a serial killer once, and how you lived through being buried alive. I thought you were a pro at this kind of thing. Was I wrong?"

It was at that moment Cole's words struck a chord deep within her. *Bravery is the actions you take when you find yourself in those predicaments.*

He had told her that, and she attempted to convince him she wasn't courageous at all, she was simply doing what she had to do to survive. And he assured her what she did in those situations *was* the definition of bravery. Now, it was time to shove the pain and doubt aside, stand up on her feet, and stumble her ass out of this jungle.

"I have to know one thing," she said, and took her first few steps to test her injuries and analyze how well they would hold up under the punishment she was about to put them through. "Do I have to worry about the ones back at the house hunting me down out here?"

"Simon and Meredith are tied up. Thanks to my brother. I had the knife in my hand, and I almost killed them. But I decided they deserved a life in prison for what they did to us and all those other girls. Besides, the feds are going to need their testimony to get all the ones involved. We can't trust the local police now that we know they're in on this."

"So, your brother is okay?"

"He was about to call the FBI before I left to go find you."

An idea occurred to Jenna. "Why don't we go back to the house then? If there's a phone, I can call my husband."

"The house is at least twenty minutes from here on foot. We're much closer to the road. And I'm afraid in your condition you'll never make it back there."

"What if it's like it was when you escaped, and no vehicles come to my rescue?"

"Jenna, we're still closer to that convenience store than you are to the house. You ran farther than I thought. This is the only way."

Now that she realized she was heading in the right direction the whole time, and wasn't far from the road, what Luisa said made the most sense. If a car could not be flagged down, she'd make it to the store and finally call Cole. It would all work out. Everything would be okay. She'd gotten past the most difficult part...escaping from captivity.

She nodded, and continued on, this time slowing down a bit, and being a little more careful where she stepped. Jenna was able to use the trees for support. More minutes ticked by, and thankfully, as they wandered a few more yards through the thick forest, there was a break in the trees up ahead, and the road below came into view.

She crawled as far as she could down the embankment and rolled the rest of the way. Her tortured feet were nearly to their breaking point. She managed to scramble to an upright position and stumbled to the bottom of the hill. The road was silent. The only noise within earshot was the serenading of crickets and other night creatures. Her heart sank. After all this, she was going to have to somehow stumble to the store.

"It's okay," Luisa told her, "I'm here with you and we're going to get through this. Let's just keep moving. You'll be there before you know it."

Jenna scrambled to the center of the road and crumpled to the asphalt. "I can't." She lay on the cold blacktop, not caring if a vehicle did show up and run her over.

"Get up."

Her eyes fluttered shut, and the dead girl's words faded into the distance. "Just give me a minute. I need to rest."

"Open your eyes right now, Jenna. Don't do this. Please. You're almost there."

"Leave me alone."

Something nudged her, and her eyes opened to mere slits. Another shove, harder than the first. Luisa was crouched down, her face only inches away from hers. "Get up!"

The shouting jarred her from the slumberous state she was succumbing to. Her mind teetered on the edge of giving up or gathering the will to keep moving.

"All you have to do is sit up. Brace your hands against the pavement and haul yourself up. Your daughter and your husband are counting on you to make it through this."

Emily. Oh my God. My daughter will never understand if I don't come home because I refused to do everything I could to make it back to her.

When she was lying in that grave Cole's bother put her in, she didn't have a choice whether she lived or died. She had been trapped and forced to rely on outside forces to rescue her. But now...she was essentially in control of getting off the ground, or choosing to lie here, eventually expiring, and becoming a meal for the buzzards.

It took herculean effort to thrust herself upward. But she managed, and sat on the road, taking deep breaths, and mentally building her strength.

"You all right?"

"I'm minced meat, but I have to keep moving."

"That's the spirit."

She grunted in exertion to stand all the way up. "Let's go," she rasped, slowly putting one foot in front of the other.

The rumble of an approaching vehicle caught her attention. She peered behind her, and the glow of headlights ascended the hill. Oh, thank God. Help was coming.

The closer the automobile got, the better Jenna could make out the outline. The jeep rolled up beside her and came to a stop. She was surprised at who was sitting behind the wheel.

"Oh my God," Sergeant Bancroft said, a stunned expression washing over his face. "Where the hell did you come from? We have been looking everywhere."

Jenna opened her mouth and then shut it, a tidal

wave of fear rushing over her. Was the man also involved in the trafficking ring? She'd seen both a uniformed officer and a plain-clothes detective at the house who worked for him.

She turned to run, but the car door opened, and the scrambling of feet told her he was quickly approaching. He grabbed her from behind. "Hey, it's okay, Mrs. Rainwater. I'm here to help you. Why were you running?"

She discovered she didn't have much of a fight left. "Because you're probably involved with the people who took me, just like that detective and the big cop who mans the front desk at the precinct. They work for you, don't they?"

He released her and stepped back. "Jesus Christ, I knew it."

She stood there and the man paced back and forth. The mannerisms of his gate told her he was agitated. "Rotten bastards," he cursed. "Your husband was right about Benton all along. I had a feeling about Ron Lewis, too. Hell, he follows Benton around like a lost puppy. That's what raised my suspicions about Lewis to begin with. It appears those two weren't on the job as much as they let on to be. When I checked into it, I discovered they'd go missing half the day."

Her heart slowed its pace. Judging by his outraged reaction when she mentioned the names of those involved, he was probably not a part of this. But a nagging suspicion danced around the recesses of her mind. She couldn't control the undertones of accusation in her question. "What are you doing out this far?"

"We got a call from a concerned citizen in town. Said they saw a lady resembling the CPS caseworker in the sketch that was broadcast on the news, and they witnessed her leaving the store up the street" he said, pointing in that direction. "That's where I was headed when I saw you."

"You mean Meredith—I don't know her last name," Jenna said, just as it was sinking in her husband must have told him about the couple they were hanging out with on the beach when she came up kidnapped.

Of course, he would have shared that information with the police. That was probably before he found out some of the authorities were involved. And the sketch Sergeant Bancroft mentioned wouldn't have been possible without Cole's description of Meredith. Her loving husband was doing all he could to find her. She never doubted him.

"Where is my husband?"

"Last I talked to him he was at the marina. Diego and Cruz, who were evidently tailing Benton, tipped him off the detective was there. So, he drove over to the marina. But when he arrived, he said his buddies were missing, and it looked like foul play was involved."

That matched with the little bit of information she was able to gather at the house when Simon, Meredith, and Benton were discussing what happened to Cruz.

"You mentioned the name Meredith," Bancroft pressed. "Is that the name of the caseworker?"

"She and another guy named Simon are tied up at the house."

"Tied up?" He stared at her as if to ask, how the hell did that happen?

"It's a long story," she said, in lieu of *my dead friend flew into a rage, stabbed Lewis and Benton, then freed her brother so he could tie them up.* "I was able to

212

escape, and I've been running through the woods ever since."

The burst of energy she gained when Luisa encouraged her to get up was draining fast. She staggered over to the jeep and slumped against it.

"You seem like you're in bad shape, Mrs. Rainwater. Let me help you into the passenger's seat."

"It's my feet. They're cut up pretty bad. And I'm just so tired."

He managed to get the door open, and Jenna practically fell into the seat.

Before she realized it, he was propping her up and strapping her into the seatbelt. "It's all right. I'm going to get you to the hospital."

"You need to call my husband," Jenna insisted.

"I will. Don't worry. But the first thing we need to do is get you some medical attention. I'm afraid you're going to collapse."

Chapter Twelve

The tall guy in a blue windbreaker flashed his badge. "Special Agent Marshal Young, FBI. Who the fuck are you?"

What was the FBI doing here?

Since the man didn't look like he was about to lower his weapon, Cole figured the smart thing to do was drop to his knees and lace his fingers behind his head. "Detective Cole Rainwater, Farmersville PD, in Texas. My creds are in my back pocket."

The agent stepped into the cabin, warning him not to flinch a muscle, and dug into Cole's pocket for the badge. After verifying Cole was who he said he was, the man tossed his creds on the floor, slipped his gun into his holster, and helped him stand. "Texas, huh? What are you doing in sunny Florida?"

"My wife thought it would be a great idea to come to Florida for our honeymoon." he said, leaning over to collect his badge from the floor. "Since we've been here, she ended up getting kidnapped by sex traffickers. I've been searching for her ever since."

Agent Young took a step back and surveyed the surroundings. "Wait a minute. You say traffickers took your wife?"

"After conducting an investigation, me and two buddies discovered a Detective Benton of the Pensacola PD is involved in my wife's disappearance. We tracked him down to the marina."

"His name is Benton Reyes," Young clarified. "Thirty-seven years old, worked for the PPD for the last seven years. He lives with his girlfriend and a golden retriever named Ralph in a one-thousand square foot, brick home on the east side of town. He's got a degree in accounting but couldn't cut the mustard and lost his license within one year of opening a firm. So, he became a cop."

Impressed, Cole nodded. "You've done your homework. It seems you know this guy."

"He's been on our radar since we started this investigation. There's word on the street he's been involved in some illegal drug activity. And his name has come up in certain circles connecting him to the prostitution of young women."

Since the agent mentioned *investigation,* Cole could easily guess what prompted this probe. "Did you receive a call from a woman named Luisa Florentino that tipped you off to what's been going on?"

The agent appeared a little surprised Cole would know that. "She called our field office. Said she suspected a CPS caseworker by the name of Meredith, who in fact worked for this sex trafficking operation, was kidnapping teenage women from the custody of Child Protective Services and turning them over to these goons."

"Meredith, huh?" So that was the woman's name.

"Meredith Foster. We've been searching for her for a week. She's been on vacation from work. Nobody's seen her."

"She's been passing herself off as Clara Finch, wife of Captain Julian Finch. Me and my wife booked a cruise with them. Then they invited us to attend an intimate beach party, and that's when she kidnapped my wife. I haven't seen either of them since."

"We've been searching for the young woman who placed the call that initiated this investigation. But we've had no luck finding her. It seems she's—"

"Dead."

"Missing," Young corrected.

Cole shook his head. "Nope. She's dead. My wife is a psychic, Agent Young. Six months ago, she died, and I resuscitated her. Since that happened, she's been able to communicate with those who have passed on."

He stopped there in order to gauge the guy's response. In his experience, most people assumed that kind of talk was out there. Way. Out. There.

But Young didn't flinch, didn't blink. He simply said, "My aunt on my mother's side was psychic. I was close to her growing up. And I've seen enough to believe such things exist."

Good. Now that he got that out of the way, Cole went on. "My wife, Jenna, got a visit from the spirit of Ms. Florentino. This led us to Pensacola PD to find out if they'd launched a missing person's report on this girl, and to dig up more information about her. While we were there at the station house, I think Benton overheard our conversation. He would have known my wife was psychic, and that she'd been getting *visitations* from Ms. Florentino. What you said about receiving a phone call from Luisa? The info I've uncovered so far leads me to suspect Benton was aware she'd called someone the night she escaped, but they couldn't be sure who she called. And they had no chance of finding out that information because Luisa was—"

"Dead, but your wife has been in communication with her," the agent finished for him, an expression of *ah ha* written all over his face. "So, they took your wife."

"Wait. Does the Pensacola PD know anything about your investigation?" Cole asked. If they did, he was being led around by a chain this entire time.

Agent Young shook his head. "We couldn't be sure of their involvement if any. I've been working human trafficking cases for a while now. Unfortunately, we've discovered the local police are tangled up in it more often than most people know. It's an opportunity to make a lot of money they can't seem to resist. Plus, the traffickers often times need assistance from local law enforcement to keep the operation running smoothly and eliminate any chance of getting caught."

Of course, they did. Cole already realized as much. But there was something he was curious about. "What brought you here to the marina?"

The agent leaned against the open cabin door, peered at the heavens, and shoved his hand into his pocket. Then he returned his attention to Cole. "We've been tracking Benton, but we lost him." He blew out his breath. "Being that we intercepted the police scanner, we heard the call come in about a disturbance at the Pier 21 Marina. Apparently, the guy that owns the store here heard a scuffle and some loud shouting on the dock. He witnessed what he thought were two guys dragging something heavy across the deck. We assumed it was connected because when our guy lost sight of Benton he was headed in this direction. I came to check it out."

"That had to have been my buddy, Dylan Cruz, they attacked. I found his cell phone and blood splatter on the side of the boat out there," Cole pointed toward the opening beyond where the agent stood. "The other guy who was helping us had parked in the lot up there. They grabbed him as well."

"Who's the other guy?"

"His name is Diego Florentino, the dead girl's brother. I met him the night they kidnapped my wife. We were both searching for her."

"Who's this Dylan Cruz?" Young asked.

"A buddy of mine from Texas. He's a Texas Ranger and has aided me in cases there. He flew to Florida to help me find Jenna when she went missing. I wasn't getting a lot of cooperation from the Pensacola force." As he finished the last sentence, something struck him as odd. He cocked his head at the agent. "Have you seen the police out here?"

The guy stared at him a moment, appearing confused, then said, "What do you mean?"

"If a call came into dispatch about a disturbance, wouldn't the cops have arrived on the scene?"

He could see the wheels churning in the agent's mind by the solemn expression on his face. "I arrived here about ten minutes ago. I didn't see them, did you?"

Cole frowned and shook his head.

The agent said, "Then we have to ask ourselves why they didn't show up?"

"You said you heard the call. Who was dispatched to come out?"

The guy scratched his chin. "Some sergeant agreed to take the call since he was already out this way."

"A Sergeant Bancroft by any chance?"

218

Young snapped his fingers. "That's the one."

It had bugged Cole from the start that Bancroft mentioned nothing about receiving a call to come out to the marina when Cole spoke with him earlier. All he'd said was he'd gotten a lead for a possible sighting of the CPS worker and was headed out to check on it. Perhaps Bancroft planned on going to the marina after he investigated the lead. Wouldn't it have made more sense to send someone else to the marina while the sergeant investigated the sighting? It wasn't standard protocol to ignore an assault call. Why would Bancroft agree to take the call when he was already on another call?

Young's cell phone jangled, ripping Cole away from his thoughts.

Agent Young answered his cell, stood up straight, eyeballed Cole, then wandered out onto the rear of the boat, shutting the door behind him.

Cole fought the urge to follow the guy to the upper deck and listen in on his conversation, but he'd been an investigator long enough to know how it was when you got a call in the field. Stepping away from others to get a little privacy was customary. All detectives did it.

He didn't have to wait long before the door slid open, and the agent poked his head inside. "You'll be happy to know your buddy Cruz is alive. He's at the county hospital."

"Do you know what happened to him?" he said, coming out of the cabin while the agent stepped aside.

"He was thrown into the ocean. Luckily there was a fisherman with his boat parked under the bridge when he was tossed. The man saw it happen and jumped right in after your friend, saving his life."

"Jesus, is he okay?"

"He's asking to talk to you. I'll take you to him if you want."

"How about I follow you."

****

The agent led Cole into the hallway of the hospital toward the nurse's desk where two other FBI agents stood dressed in similar blue windbreakers. They leaned against the snack machine chatting. The male sipped from a Styrofoam cup, and the female with the dark hair and ponytail smacked gum appearing as amused as a motorcycle enthusiast in a tricycle race.

"Andy and Christina, this is Detective Rainwater," Young said, introducing them. "The guy I told you about on the phone."

Christina offered a uh-huh as a greeting, and Andy merely blinked, with a half nod.

"Which room is Ranger Cruz in?" Young asked.

They pointed down the hall, and then continued with their conversation as if no one had interrupted them.

What a warm welcome that was, Cole thought as he and Young strolled down the corridor. Guess the FBI sports a different culture than Texas law enforcement, although Young was cordial enough.

"Ouch, Doc, be careful. This shit is killing me." Cruz's voice floated down the hall, marking the room where they took him.

Cole stepped through the doorway, and his buddy locked eyes with him, his head slightly bowed due to the procedure being performed on him. The doctor threaded another stitch along the top of his noggin. "This hurts like hell."

"I offered to give you another shot of lidocaine, but you refused." The doctor looked to be at the end of his rope when it came to dealing with this impossible patient. "So, here we are, Mr. Cruz, doing this the hard way."

"I told you, doc. That stuff doesn't work on me." He eyeballed the agent at Cole's side. "I guess you've been introduced to the FBI. They seem to be crawling all over this place. Are the local police not doing a good enough job? I'd give them a one star rating myself, but that's me."

Cole wouldn't have given them that much. "I hear you went for a swim."

"The ocean isn't as nice as everyone says. Of course, when you're going into it unconscious, it's a little hard to enjoy."

"They say the fishing around here is out of sight though."

Cruz chuckled. "I'm living proof they're pulling some big ones out of the ocean."

The doctor sighed with annoyance. "Mr. Cruz, you need to stay still. I can't work with you moving around like this."

"Ouch. Can you hurry, doc?"

"Believe me, I'm trying."

"So, what happened?" Cole demanded. "I saw blood on the side of the boat, where I found your phone."

"After I'd climbed out of the cabin cruiser, they snuck up behind me and hit me over the head."

It happened just as Cole thought it did. "I imagine you didn't see what they did to Diego."

"They do something to him, too?"

221

"There was a scuffle at the Blazer. He's missing."

"Oh shit," Cruz said, pursing his lips.

The doctor blew out a huge sigh, dropped what was left of the suture equipment onto a metal tray, and stepped away from his patient. "You're all fixed up. Keep the area clean and come back in two weeks to have the stitches removed."

"I won't be here in two weeks," Cruz said. He sat up with a grunt.

The man appeared relieved at that news, gathered his chart, and made a beeline for the exit. "Then, may I suggest you check in with your primary care provider when you return home."

"Listen, Cole," Cruz said, and slid off the exam table. "You know how we concluded that Bancroft wasn't involved?"

Cole nodded, but in the back of his mind a small seed of doubt was already flourishing given what he'd learned from Young about the disturbance call at the marina, and how Bancroft ignored it, let alone didn't mention it on the phone even after Cole told him he was there.

"The sarge is a smoker," Cruz said.

"I know."

A memory surfaced in Cole's head. He and Jenna had just arrived at the Pensacola PD and as they strolled up the walkway, they found Bancroft smoking in front of the building. Cole had recalled the sergeant explaining how he didn't care for filtered cigarettes but hated the flavor of the tobacco from the unfiltered ones. So he'd formed the habit of tearing off the butts.

"I found a pack of cigarettes in the sergeant's briefcase while we were combing through his office earlier today," Cruz said. "The weird thing about them was, the pack was already open, and all the filters were missing. The first time we arrived at the precinct, I noticed a bunch of torn off butts in the ashtray outside, along with stubbed out cigarettes with no filters."

"What's the point here, Cruz?" Cole asked. "Tell me there's more to this story."

"I had an opportunity to search the boat before those bastards knocked me over the head. In the bathroom, I ran across a small trash can. Inside I saw what appeared to be a dumped-out ashtray. It was a bunch of cigarettes with no filters and torn off butts."

Bancroft's tendency to tear cigarettes apart was an oddball habit that set him apart from other smokers. Therefore, the existence of those smokes in the boat meant Bancroft had been there recently. And if he spent time on that craft, he was well aware of the goings on and who all was involved in the criminal activities. He recalled spotting an empty ashtray next to the stove when he searched the cabin. There was no telling how many times Alan Bancroft was on the vessel taking care of business. He could have even been there the night Jenna was taken for Christ sakes.

Son of a bitch. Was there anybody in that police station who wasn't wrapped up in this?

****

The crackling of a radio—or something like a radio—woke Jenna from a sound sleep. She stared out the windshield, scarcely remembering what had happened.

Then the flashback of escaping into the woods and making it to the road with Luisa's help came to her. Sergeant Bancroft happened along and was taking her to the hospital for treatment. How long had she been asleep? She must have zonked out shortly after he helped her into the jeep. She couldn't remember ever being so drained in all her life.

But the more she considered how much time might have passed since she first climbed into the car, the more she was puzzled by the scenery whizzing past. Tall weeds and limbs smacked against the body of the automobile. It resembled the very forest she escaped from. Was the way to the hospital through the woods? If it wasn't, then where were they headed?

Before she had time to raise concerns, a voice from the radio clipped to the review mirror, boomed from the speaker. "Hey, Sarge, come in. It's Mayor Romero. Do you read?"

Bancroft snatched the radio and pressed the button. "I can hear you, Mayor, loud and clear."

Jenna caught the slightest shift of the sergeant's attention rotating in her direction, and the awful awareness building in her gut intensified. Something told her to shut her eyes before he glanced at her. For a reason she couldn't identify, she sensed the importance of acting as if she was still asleep.

After a moment of silence—probably long enough to ensure she was not awake—he continued the conversation. "When was the last time you heard from anyone at the red house?"

"Well, as you know we had some major problems out there. But Leo has assured me everything is back in order. Thank God he was hiding in the back bedroom and was able to sneak up on Mr. Florentino before he had a chance to call anyone."

"I assume Meredith and Simon have their shit

together?" Bancroft asked this Mayor person. "You realize they nearly blew it this time."

"Noted. They will be dealt with. You can bank on it. As of now, we are back on track though. If you have the detective's wife, we can pick up where we left off. Ms. Florentino's brother is safely tied up. We will be ready for the dead bitch this time when she tries to pull her shit."

Bancroft said, "I have the Rainwater woman. She's sleeping right beside me. That run through the woods knocked it out of her. She's so exhausted I can guarantee she won't be a problem."

"How long before you reach the red house?"

"Just a few more minutes."

"Good. Good. Call me when everything's done. And Alan, I'm sorry you had to be brought into this. I know we were hoping to keep your identity a secret."

"It would have been best if Benton and the rest of them had been kept in the dark about my involvement. Less concern any of them could have pointed a finger at me in the event they'd been taken into custody. But I guess desperate times call for desperate measures. Not much we can do about that now."

"It's unfortunate. But I suppose you're right. They've blundered this so badly someone with authority had to step in and take control before everything went off the rails."

"Roger that, Mayor. I'll be in touch."

A paralyzing fear swept over Jenna. He was taking her back into the clutches of those monsters. *Why didn't you heed your initial instincts when they told you to run?* Trusting any of the police was foolish. Yet she allowed Bancroft to deceive her. Freedom was so close she could almost taste it. And now it might as well be on another continent.

She sat, still slumped in the passenger's seat, too afraid to open her eyes and alert him to her conscious state. Her mind frantically worked through a plan of escape. She could unsnap the seatbelt, swing the door open and jump from the jeep. But the impact would surely kill or seriously injure her more than was already the case. Fighting him would be useless. Although the little bit of rest she'd gotten helped replenish some of her strength, it wouldn't be enough to allow her to put up much of a battle.

From out of nowhere the jeep braked so hard, her head slammed against the windshield. Her eyes snapped open to hear Bancroft cussing and see Luisa holding her foot to the pedal while yanking on the emergency brake. The dead girl opened her mouth to scream, but Jenna was out of the vehicle before the word *run!* could be issued.

There was no intended direction, only a desperate need to clear a path as fast as her tortured feet would take her.

Bancroft's voice echoed through the forest. "Where are you going, Jenna? You'll get lost out there. Your feet are in no condition to get you very far. If you come back, you have my word I won't kill you. We just want to know who Luisa called. That's all."

She knew who all of them were now. She'd seen them and could identify them by face if not by name— real or assumed. They'd have no choice but to get rid of her.

She sprinted forward until the sound of Bancroft's screaming faded. Now that the hollering ceased to exist, she assumed she'd put enough space between them that a quick rest could be safely taken.

She shrank down next to a tree. It was worse though, with her feet now in unbearable pain. Maybe she'd stay right here and fade away. It was better than dying at the hands of those animals. Tears racked her body, and she did her best to stifle the crying noise. It was hopeless. Rescue really wasn't coming this time. She'd overheard what Bancroft said to…the mayor. They were only a few minutes away from the house. It would be easier to cross the Rio Grande than it would to run through the forest again.

The fucking mayor for God's sake.

"Jenna." Luisa stood over her. "We need to go now. The sergeant ran off into the woods to search for you. He left the keys in the jeep."

"God, I'm so glad to see you," Jenna said, and gingerly got to her aching feet.

"For some reason you keep doubting I'll come back for you, *Chica.* I told you, I don't leave the people I care about stranded."

"If I could hug you, I would."

"How about we get your ass to the jeep before that old *bastarda* finds you."

Jenna took her first step, although she realized hiking to the vehicle was going to be hell in her condition, at least she had the most wonderful person to help her along the way. She'd get through this. Hope was back, and it was time to fight for her life again.

"Lead the way. I'm right behind you."

By the time they made it to Bancroft's vehicle, Jenna was completely spent. She hobbled to the driver's side door, used the window frame for support to swing herself around, and struggled into the seat. Luisa was right. The keys were hanging there. She could picture laughing in Bancroft's face as her hand curled around the ignition.

But no sooner had she twisted the key than the sergeant bounded through the forest up ahead. He tore down the path directly in the glow of headlights, at full speed, straight for her.

"Go to hell, you son-of-a-bitch!" She released the emergency brake, threw the gearshift into Drive, and floored it.

Jenna braked hard and rolled the window down. Bancroft's moans carried on the night air. She adjusted the rearview mirror to better see the ground behind her. He was crawling on his belly in an effort to get away. *Oh no you don't.*

She put the transmission into Reverse, grabbed the back of the seat, and peered through the rear window, driving until she felt the huge bump under the tires. Then she put the jeep in drive and ran over him one more time for good measure.

No more sounds or movement came from Alan Bancroft. After tonight, there wouldn't be another young woman forced into slavery, be sold for sex for his profit, and eventually die at the hands of that man.

In the dead silence that followed, Luisa said, "*Santa mierda.*"

Jenna flexed the wrists that had been locked onto the steering wheel and peered over at her new friend. "You'll have to translate. Spanish wasn't one of my electives."

"I said holy shit."

That about summed it up.

Chapter Thirteen

The number that popped up on his phone was familiar, though he couldn't quite put a name to it. "Rainwater," he said, after placing the device against his ear.

"Oh, my God. Cole?"

He felt his heart stop, then kick in with an abnormal beat. "Jenna?"

"It's me." Her tone broke on a whimper. "I thought I'd never hear your voice again."

"Honey, where are you? Are you safe?

"A convenience store called Henry's Quick Stop. Hold on, let me ask the clerk for the address. I don't even know—"

"It's okay, sweetheart. I know where it is."

Now he understood why the number seemed so familiar. It was the same place where Benton's crew had grabbed Luisa. The number was the same one they were attempting to get the logs from. The same place where Cole had stopped and questioned a chubby kid behind the cash register.

Though he didn't yet know how she got there, he remembered all too well what happened to Luisa the night she arrived at that place. He wasn't about to take the chance those savages would run her down like they did the dead girl. "Listen, Jenna. I want you to go into the bathroom and lock the door. Don't open it for anyone but me. I'm leaving now."

Her voice broke. "Please hurry, Cole."

"Don't worry, I'll be there."

He stared straight at Cruz, hardly believing what just happened. "Jenna's at Henry's Quick Stop. We need to go now."

As he and Cruz trudged out into the hallway, Young called out. "Can you wait? I need a moment to gather my staff. These people are dangerous and it's not safe to go without us."

"I don't care what you do," Cole said over his shoulder. "I'm going to get my wife, and screw everything else."

****

By the clock on the wall, ten minutes ticked by at an agonizingly slow pace while Jenna walked the floor inside the small, filthy bathroom. She'd killed Sergeant Bancroft before he was able to get back to the stash house; his partners would be expecting him. When too much time expired and he didn't show, they'd go searching for him.

They would discover his body, and know she'd gotten away. That's when the search for her would ensue. The first place they would come would be this convenience store. It was the nearest public place to the house. It was the location Luisa fled to the night she escaped.

The tense situation was getting to the dead girl, too. Anxiety pinched the corners of Luisa's face. The woman realized what these people were capable of as much as Jenna did. Neither one of them could count this ordeal over until she was safely in Cole's arms.

"He's coming," Luisa said. "Your husband. He'll

be here."

Although the encouragement spilled out of her mouth, Jenna sensed the unspoken words behind it. *If he makes it before they do.*

She couldn't help but wonder what it must have been like for Luisa that night. Waiting on pins and needles for Diego to arrive and save her, all the while knowing those pigs were coming. Actually, Jenna could relate, at least a little. She was overcome with the same fear, she imagined, the dead girl went through at that time.

She kept eyeing the door, waiting for the crash against it that would warn her the goons were out there trying to get in. The dreadful idea no sooner left her head, than someone pounded against the door. She let out a startled gasp and backed away.

"Jenna, honey, are you in there? Open the door, baby."

Indescribable relief flooded over her. She couldn't turn the lock quick enough.

She swung open the door, and he was standing there, the expression on his face as his gaze took her in was one of warmth and raw emotion. Not a word was spoken between them as she fell into his arms.

He held her so tight she could hardly breathe, and the extraordinary heat of his body penetrated deep into her soul. God, how she longed for his touch, the opportunity to once again gaze upon that wonderful, handsome face. He was magically here with her right now. He came to her rescue yet again.

"Oh my God, Jenna." He set her away long enough to look into her face. Tears filled his eyes; she felt him shaking like a leaf in a storm. "I didn't know what they were doing to you. I was sick with worry."

"I'm all right." She lost the battle to keep the tears from spilling to the surface. Her chin quivered, and she wept, leaning against him for support. "I knew you were coming for me. That's the only thing that kept me going."

"Oh, honey." His trembling lips kissed her cheek, and her forehead. Then he rested his chin on the top of her head as he held her. "I would have gone to the ends of the earth to bring you back to me. I can't live without you." He rocked her in his arms, and she clung to him.

After a while, he let her go long enough to brush back her hair. His long fingers worked her face from side to side, examining her skin for what she imagined were abrasions, cuts, and any other injuries. Then his attention slid down the rest of her, ending at her feet.

Her stare drifted in the direction of his. And for the first time she got a good glimpse at what was the mess of her toes. They were purplish and bloodied with deep lacerations. She couldn't even imagine the pathetic condition of the soles.

"What happened?" he asked, easing back a few steps to position her on the toilet.

She sat on the lid, and he knelt, lifting her leg to inspect the wounds. He continued his observation, and his face transformed into a shade of white, then an angry red. It was clear he wanted to rip someone's head off.

"It's okay, Cole," she said in an effort to quiet the rage growing in his eyes. "I did it to myself when I ran away.

As if the weak explanation was going to calm him. He must realize as well as she did if the traffickers hadn't captured her, there would have been no need to run away and sustain these kinds of injuries.

But he didn't go completely mad and tear the bathroom apart like she feared he was about to when the dark clouds floated over him. He kept it together like a pro, and she was thankful for that. She needed his head in the game if they were going to bring these criminals to justice. There was still work to do. These animals were not behind bars yet, and she'd promised Luisa. The clock was ticking.

"We need to go. I can lead you back to the house where they've been keeping me. They're still there, Cole. And we can get them if we hurry."

"Whoa, just hold on a minute now." He lowered his head, she imagined, to gather his wits. "Your feet are in bad shape, Jenna. You can't go anywhere like this. I'm going to have Cruz take you to the hospital while me and the FBI go to the stash house. Just draw me a map of the location and I'll get these bastards."

FBI agents?

What was he talking about? The last time the feds were mentioned was when Luisa informed her Diego would be calling them. But she later discovered through that radio chat between Bancroft and the mayor that Leo got to Luisa's brother before he made that call. She'd also heard Simon describe how he'd thrown Dylan off a bridge into the ocean. Did she imagine that whole discussion?

"Cruz is okay?" she asked, shocked. "But Simon said he tossed him into the ocean."

"Simon, huh?" Anger tugged at his face again. "Who is Simon?"

"One of the guys who was holding me hostage.

There was also a guy named Leo, and of course, Meredith. Her real name isn't Clara Finch, by the way."

"I know. I've been told. It's Meredith Foster. And she's been abducting children from CPS and turning them over to the traffickers for Christ knows how long."

"How do you know this?"

"The FBI told me. The night Luisa Florentino escaped she called them from this store and warned them about what Meredith was doing. They've been investigating this case without the knowledge of the Pensacola PD."

So, that was the information Luisa wouldn't tell her for fear it would end up getting Jenna killed. The dead girl knew the atrocities Meredith was committing against children in foster care. She'd reported it to the FBI the night she escaped.

Cole marched to the door, spoke with someone outside the room, and then returned, kneeling beside her again.

"Who's out there?" she asked.

"Cruz and a team of feds. I asked Dylan if he could get me some sterile water and bandages for your feet. We need to doctor you up or those cuts are going to get infected."

Well, I guess he's not going to force me to go to the hospital right now.

Good, because the only place she planned to go was back to that hell house to take those assholes out. With her husband in tow.

"How did you get here, Jenna?"

The question took her back to what she'd done to Bancroft. She had never taken anyone's life before. But she understood the way it was with these savages. Either you take them out or they'll come back to get you. She learned that lesson the hard way when she escaped the first time, and they caught her, and dragged her back into the house. That was exactly where Bancroft planned to take her. She had no choice but to stop him permanently.

She could not live in regret over what she did to survive. It was either him or her. "I drove Bancroft's jeep after I killed him. I had already escaped, and he found me on the road. Even though I'd seen that suspicious detective, Benton, at the house, and the chubby cop who sat behind the front desk the last time I was in the police department, I let the sergeant fool me into thinking he wasn't involved." She shook her head in disgust at herself.

Just then, Cruz waltzed in with some gauze wrap, medical tape, and a bottle of sterile fluid. He stood there staring at Jenna, and the slightest hint of a grin broke out on his face. "We have been looking all over for you."

She had heard that line before from him the day Cole heaved her out of the ground and resuscitated her back to life. She had opened her eyes, and he stood over her, making that same remark. She grinned a little and said, "How is it that you guys keep losing me?"

He shrugged. "I'm beginning to think you get bored and decide it's time to seek out another crime. Maybe you should work for the police department so we can retire." He set the items on the floor next to Cole. "I was able to drum up these supplies from the first aid kit in the back."

Her husband opened the bottle of fluid, lifted her

foot, and got to work cleaning the wounds.

She winced in pain but held her foot in place like a trouper. The sooner he got this over with, the quicker they could be rounding up some wicked and corrupt people who deserved to spend the rest of their lives behind bars.

"So, what happened when he ran into you on the road?" Cole asked, taking her back to the discussion they were having before Cruz entered the room.

She still couldn't believe she'd killed someone, even if he was going to take her to her death. *You didn't have to run him over as many times as you did. He was far too injured to have been a threat to you the first time you ran him down. All you had to do was drive off.*

It was as if Cole could see into her soul. He stretched out his hand, touched her cheek, and slid his fingers down her face. In his eyes was an understanding that shot straight to her heart. If anyone knew who she truly was and was familiar with all the ghosts that haunted her, this man was.

"Jenna, whatever happened out there wasn't your fault," he told her. "You need to believe me when I say that. These people took you against your will. And they forced you to make decisions no one should have to make. They're the bad guys, not you, honey. You have a beautiful heart, and I love you so much for it."

He always reached her in a way no other person could. Tears streamed down her face again, and she sobbed against his shoulder the second he gathered her in his arms. "I ran him over three times, Cole. Once would have been enough. It was overkill. If I'm honest with myself, I know I did it because of the anger in my heart. I hated them so much for what they'd done to those other girls...what they'd done to me, and what they did to Luisa."

"I would have done a lot worse. You couldn't have run him over enough times to make up for all the innocent lives he was responsible for taking."

Cole broke the embrace and said, "Can you tell me what happened?"

She nodded, and he tore open the gauze, continuing to bandage her foot. "Bancroft talked me into the vehicle. Said he was going to take me to the hospital. I was so exhausted I fell asleep. The next thing I knew, I heard him talking on the radio to Mayor Romero. It became clear they were in on this together. The sergeant was to take me back to the house, but before he could, Luisa slammed on the brakes so I could escape. She found me a little while later in the woods and told me Bancroft left the keys in the jeep. That's when we went back, and I started up the vehicle. Bancroft ran out of the forest straight at me. So, I floored it."

"Wait. Luisa slammed on the brakes?" In his eyes was an expression that, even though he accepted she'd had visits from a dead girl, the fact she was slamming on brakes was going a bit far.

She wasn't about to launch into that drawn-out explanation. Jenna eyed the dead girl who currently lounged against the sink. "Luisa, why don't you say hello."

The girl winked at her, spun around, and twisted the faucet knob. Water poured out and Cruz, who was standing beside the sink nearly shit his pants.

Cole stopped what he was doing long enough to shake his head, and then threw his attention back into doctoring her other foot.

Jenna said, "You might need to know she killed Benton and the chubby cop."

"How in the hell did she do that?" her husband wanted to know, putting the finishing touches on her bandages by tearing off a strip of medical tape with his teeth and applying it to her foot.

"She got a hold of some knives. Benton wouldn't let me go, and the other cop was holding a knife to Diego's throat."

"Diego?" he and Cruz said in unison.

Before Jenna could utter a word, Dylan rushed toward her. "Are you saying Luisa's brother was at the house?"

She nodded. "I figured you guys were working with him to find me. They planned to use him as bait to get to Luisa, so she'd tell me who she'd called the day she escaped. And then they were going to force that information out of me."

"You and the FBI need to head over there now," Cruz said.

Cole stood. "Honey, I'm going to grab some paper and a pen from the clerk. I need you to draw me that map. Cruz will stay with you," he said and headed out the door.

"Wait!" Jenna got to her feet, flinching in pain and limping toward Cole as fast as she could. "I told you, I'm going with you."

"Jenna, that's crazy. You can't even walk."

"All I need is a pair of shoes, and I can manage."

"I am not dragging you over to that house. Let me and the FBI deal with this. You stay here with Cruz where I know you'll be safe." An expression of *that's final* was chiseled into every crevice of his face.

"Cole Rainwater, you are not leaving me here. I've been through hell, and I want to see their faces when they're hauled out of that house in handcuffs. Besides, I'm going to need Luisa in order to get back to the house, since I can't remember the way there. And I'm the only one who can communicate with her." *How do you like those apples?*

Cole peered toward the heavens and blew out a sigh. "Where do you suppose we can get you a pair of shoes out here in bumfuck?"

"What size does the clerk wear?"

"Are you kidding me?"

She stood unmoved while Cole adopted an *I can't believe what I'm about to do* expression.

She hobbled out of the bathroom door behind him and limped to the front of the store.

"Hey, man," Cole said, approaching the kid behind the counter. "What size shoes do you wear?"

The chubby cashier glared at him and said, "Excuse me?"

"Your shoes. What size are they?"

The guy tugged his glasses down his freckled nose. "Who wants to know?"

"Listen, kid," Cole said, flashing his badge. "I don't have time for this. I'm going to need your shoes."

He appeared as if he was going to throw his head back and laugh at any moment. "What is this, like one of those movies where the cops demand someone's car, only with shoes instead?"

By the expression on Cole's face, it was clear he wanted to throttle the kid. Instead, he shoved his hand into his back pocket and produced his billfold. He counted out five twenties and slammed them on the counter. "Will this cover the shoes?"

"Is this a joke?"

Cole simply grabbed for the money in a show of taking back the offer.

"Now, wait a minute. If you want the shoes that badly, they're yours." The clerk swiped the bills off the counter before Cole could change his mind.

Jenna spoke up. "Good. Take them off and hurry please."

****

They piled into an unmarked van and made their way to the site, guided by Luisa, where she'd left Bancroft. Once there, she defined the outline of Bancroft's lifeless body through the beam of headlights. The man's crumpled form and the tire marks surrounding him told a clear story of what happened.

A hand squeezed her knee. She was surprised to peer over and find Luisa staring at her. "It's okay, *Chica*. You did what you had to do."

Jenna nodded. "I know." It was high time to put any guilt she had to rest concerning the man's demise. None of these people deserved an ounce of sympathy.

"What?" Cole asked.

She shook her head. "Sorry, Luisa was talking."

"Where do we go from here?" the agent driving the van asked.

Luisa spoke up. "Tell them to keep following the path. When they come to a clearing, they'll find the house."

"Keep on the pathway," Jenna said. "The house is after the clearing."

Although it was a tight squeeze, the driver

managed to veer around the dead body.

They continued until Jenna could clearly identify the clearing at the edge of the thick forest. And she recalled from memory, the house was just past the parked vehicles directly ahead.

"If you go much further," she told the driver, "they may be able to spot you."

After exiting the van, Jenna stared on as several FBI agents gathered their gear, slid magazines into their weapons, and met at the front of the vehicle, discussing the point of entry.

An arm slid around her waist. She set her sights on the movement, and her husband was beside her, drawing her close. "Did I tell you how much I like your new shoes?"

She peered down at the dirty, oversized sneakers and let out a snort. "Good God, if Cecilia could see me now."

Cole leaned over to place a warm kiss on her forehead. After he cleared his throat and ducked his head, she knew his demeanor changed to serious. "God, Jenna. Every day that passed and I couldn't find you was like pure hell. Even now that you're with me, I'm almost too afraid to ask what they might have done to you. I think I probably wouldn't be able to stop from killing them."

She reached up to clutch the sides of his face. "I understand. Luisa stopped—she kept me safe. After they saw her physical powers, they were too afraid to do much of anything except cower."

He munched on his lip for a moment, then said, "Leo's in there, right?" He pointed straight ahead.

She took hold of his arm, worried he would storm

in there, take the bastard out, and possibly land in a boatload of trouble. She gestured to the crew of federal agents who now were getting into position to approach the house. "Why don't we wait out here together, and let the FBI deal with them?"

"I'm not leaving your side, sweetheart."

Even as the words left his mouth, she saw storm clouds brewing in his eyes. His jaw was taut, his shoulders tense, legs braced. She wanted her own revenge against them. A lengthy jail sentence wasn't enough.

They stood side by side in the silence of the night. "The number of local government officials involved in this mess is endless," she said. "It goes all the way to the mayor, for God's sake. There's no telling how many above him are entangled in this too. How could people who served the community commit such an unforgiveable depravity?"

"As awful as it is to say, the trafficking of human beings is more lucrative than the trafficking of drugs," Cole murmured. "With narcotics, the more you sell, the more it becomes necessary to replenish your product. But when you're dealing with the sale of people, the same person has the potential to turn a profit many times."

"There must be so many more organizations just like this one out there."

Cole nodded. "Until our government takes more aggressive steps to crack down on sex traffickers, it's a crime that will continue to grow by leaps and bounds." This time when he spoke, he stared dead into her eyes. "It's the bigger guys...the politicians, world leaders, and top government officials who drive the bus for sex trafficking to exist. People like Meredith and Simon are only there to fulfill the demand for services. The demand wouldn't be there if it weren't for those with deep pockets willing to finance it."

It was a sickening scenario, and something Jenna wouldn't have ever considered if it hadn't been for her present situation. At least her kidnapping wouldn't have been all for nothing. This ring was going to be disbanded. And the perpetrators from the bottom up would be exposed for who they were.

The van door slid open, and Cruz poked his head out. "They just radioed. They have the criminals in custody, and they're ready for us to bring the van around. Y'all hop in." He then stumbled toward the driver's seat.

Dylan carefully maneuvered through the tall weeds and shrubbery until the van's headlights illuminated a clear path to the front of the house. FBI agents filed out of the front door of the residence, and in the bright light of the high beams, Meredith, Simon, and Leo were in cuffs, trudging along as the feds escorted them to the vehicle. Jenna threw open the van door and jumped out with her husband following close behind.

With the door of the house still ajar, Jenna witnessed, through the light spilling out from the doorway, two more silhouettes making their way out onto the front lawn. Since she'd already identified the ones presently hiking toward the van, she imagined the two lagging behind must be Luisa's brother, and another agent.

The agent leading the pack called out to them. "Hey, is that one Diego Florentino?" He pointed in the direction of the house.

Jenna cupped her hand to carry the sound of her voice, confirming the federal agent's assumption. The agent who had Diego by the arm released him.

"Meredith!" Jenna said, when the witch was close enough. Though there were a thousand things she'd love to say to the bitch, when she got within arm's length, she changed her mind, deciding actions spoke louder than words. She balled up her fist and let the woman have it.

Meredith's head snapped back from the impact, and when she straightened up, Jenna took immense pleasure in the blood dripping from what appeared to be a broken nose. She grinned at her handwork, spun on her sore heel, and moseyed up to Leo.

Cole must have been fast on his feet the way he grabbed her arm and held her back. She wrestled to break free, but the expression on his face gave her pause, and she stopped resisting.

He ambled over to Leo and swung a mighty punch to his gut. While the guy balled over in agony and screamed obscenities Cole said, "That's what you get for putting your hands on my wife."

After her husband finished, Jenna strolled over and spat in Leo's face. "Luisa asked me to give you a message. She's going to become your cellmate in prison."

The scumbag bucked and kicked as agents hauled him into the back of the van along with Meredith and Simon. "No. Not that…please, I can't handle that."

As Diego sauntered over, Cruz said, "Man, we are tickled pink to see you're okay."

The cowboy rolled his eyes. "Those people are loco, let me tell you."

When he focused his attention on Jenna, he said, "So, you can talk to my sister, huh? Is she okay? I mean, I know she's dead, but is she—"

"She's an amazing soul," Jenna told him, overcome with a torrent of warmth. "If it weren't for your sister, I never would have made it out of there alive. She stayed with me, encouraged me, and gave me hope when I didn't have an ounce to spare. It was her who made it possible for me to escape. I can see why you love her so much."

The sight of this big guy breaking down touched Jenna deeply. "It was just me and her growing up. We did everything together, but when Mom and Dad passed away, she got lost somehow, and I just never could get her back again." His big hand swiped his eyes.

"Tell him not to blame himself," Luisa said, standing next to Jenna and staring lovingly at her brother. "Tell him it was because of his love for me I found the strength to get clean before Simon kidnapped me. He doesn't realize I overcame my addiction. I was going to wait a few more weeks before I told him, until I could be sure I was strong enough to withstand the temptation of going back to that life, but I was taken before I had the chance to let him know. No one else believed in me like he did. It was my own stupidity that put me in the position of doing the wrong things and being around the wrong people. If anything, Diego did his best to try and dissuade me."

Jenna repeated the message, and her brother lowered his head. "God, I didn't know she got clean. I wish she would have told me. But I'm so glad she did, even if I didn't get to see her after she worked so hard to battle her demons. I'm so proud of her."

"Oh, Diego, my kind-hearted, little brother." Luisa sighed, the tone of her voice weakening, and catching on a sob. She straightened up, appearing as if an amusing recollection struck her. "He should be jealous because I'm going to see Gus again."

Not sure what she meant by that, Jenna asked Diego, "Who's Gus?"

Her brother's attention locked on an object in the distance, as if pondering that question. "Huh," he finally said, awareness lighting his eyes. "We had a pug named Gus. He was an ugly little thing, but he had the biggest personality of any dog we knew. He ran out of the house one day and got hit by a car. Me and Luisa were devastated. That little dog was really something to us. I don't think either one of us ever got over losing him."

"Well, your sister thinks you ought to be jealous because she says she's going to get to see him again."

A light-hearted grin crossed his face. "She would say something like that."

"It's time for me to go, Jenna."

When Jenna peered at Luisa, she could see a bright glow encompassing her. Although she realized her friend's work was done and God was ready to take her home, her heart beat in double time. The woman became such a close companion, and she would give anything to be able to keep her. But Luisa Florentino was nobody's property.

"Thank you," Jenna uttered, a tear sliding down her cheek. "I will never forget you. And I will hold you in my heart always."

"I love you…" The voice floated in the air, and the soul of Luisa lifted into the sky, disappearing.

"Oh my God," Diego said, staring into the sky with amazement. "I heard her say 'I love you.' "

****

Jenna sat at the kitchen table, sipping her coffee, and Cole tossed the morning paper in front of her. He kissed the top of her head, stepped around behind her, and wrapped her in his arms, giving her a bear hug. "How's the omelet?"

"I'm glad I married a man who knows how to cook."

"Well, don't get used to it," he said, stepping away. "We'll be heading home today, and the chefs at the Blazing Saddle Ranch will be having none of it."

"Ugh. Don't remind me."

"I'm going to pack, honey. I suggest you finish your coffee and do the same. We have a plane to catch at eleven. Emily will be waiting for us at the airport."

Butterflies danced in her stomach at the idea of seeing their daughter after all the hell they'd been through over the last week. Truth be told, even though the staff at the ranch drove her to madness, she would be glad to touch down in Texas and be home at last.

When she glanced at the newspaper, the headline jumped out at her. *Politicians, Local Authorities Involved in Human Trafficking.*

According to the article, the mayor as well as a handful of senators in several contiguous states were arrested for their part in trafficking minor girls. Seven officers from the Pensacola PD were presently sitting in jail awaiting a preliminary hearing. Other locals were also involved, including a caseworker for Child Protective Services.

Mugshots of Meredith, Simon, and Leo sat side by

side staring up at her. The feds raided a cabin nestled in the hills of Arkansas, rescuing over twenty teenage girls who were previously in foster care. The raid in Arkansas led to the discovery of another five stash houses, where an additional seventy-five women and underage girls were released from captivity. Due to a confession from one of the locals working for the traffickers by the name of Leo Ward, the remains of Luisa Florentino, a young woman who died at their hands, were uncovered two days after his arrest was made. Her friends and loved ones will be laying her to rest on Saturday.

A phone rang. Jenna's attention was drawn to the device sitting across the table from her. It jangled again, and she got up, stepping over to it. She recognized the phone as belonging to Cole. The name Diego popped up. She peered around for her husband, but he was nowhere to be found, and she remembered him telling her he was going to pack.

She slid her finger across the screen and answered the call. "How are you holding up?"

"Is that you, Jenna?"

"I'm sorry, Cole's in the room packing."

"No, it's all right. I was just calling to say thank you. I didn't have your number, so I called your husband. There were so many questions I had concerning my sister and what happened to her before her death. You made it possible for me to communicate with her and say goodbye. I'm finally able to put those terrible thoughts behind me, knowing Luisa is okay. And it's all thanks to you."

"You have nothing to thank me for. If it wasn't for your help, Cole would never have gotten as close to finding me as he did. I should be thanking you."

"Hogwash. Your husband is a smart man. He would have found his way without me. In fact, he told me if I came to Texas and graduated the police academy, that I had a job in his department waiting for me."

"From what Cole tells me, you'd be really good at crime investigation."

"I'm seriously considering it."

"I think you should."

"Well, I have to go. I'm at the funeral home and we're making arrangements for my sister's memorial. I'm sorry you guys can't make it."

"I would like nothing more. But I've been away from my daughter too long. And after my ordeal…"

"I understand completely. Hold her close for as long as you can. You two have a good flight. And tell that husband of yours, I'll be calling him."

"I will. Take care, Diego."

Cole appeared behind her. "Who was that?"

"Diego." She set the phone down. "He called to thank me, and said you offered him a position in your department."

"I think he'd make a fine investigator."

"I agree."

Her husband glanced at his watch, and then examined her with one raised eyebrow.

"What is it?" she asked.

"It's nine thirty. We have an hour and a half to kill before we have to catch the flight."

She recognized that mischievous grin. "Oh, no. I still have to pack and get ready."

"I'll help…"

"I'll never have time for a shower."

He slid his gaze up and down her body. The softness in his dark eyes as he stared into hers was a dead giveaway for the intimacy he sought—and was much more than sexual gratification. When he held out a hand, she slipped hers into it, allowing him to lead her into the bedroom.

As they stood at the foot of the bed, he brushed the back of his hand against her cheek, then cupped her face, drawing her to him. When he took her lips with his, the kiss was different from what she was accustomed to. This was slow, meaningful. When he slid his mouth to her ear, the heat of his breath penetrated her skin like the glorious heat of a summer sun. "Oh, God, Jenna. I was so afraid I'd lose you forever."

He planted a trail of feathery kisses down the base of her neck while his hands glided up her arms and he gently drew the spaghetti straps of her sundress over her shoulders. The moistness of his mouth brushed against the spot where the thin material once lay. "My heart is beating so hard. Feel."

With that, he slipped his shirt off and placed her palm against his chest. As his heart hammered beneath her fingertips, he murmured, "This is what you do to me, my love. When you went missing, there was such an aching right here, I couldn't bear it. And it wasn't just the fear and the worry that something unthinkable would happen to you and I'd never see you again. It was that it felt like half of me had been ripped away and was dying." His expression became even more somber. "Keeping you safe was my responsibility. I failed you and can never forgive myself for that."

The tears sliding down his sculpted cheeks shot a hole straight through her heart. She dropped tender kisses on the glistening streaks. "What happened was not your fault, Cole. I should have listened when you warned me that you had a bad feeling. You were right and I was a fool. You did everything a good husband should have done to keep me safe. I made that very difficult for you. You should know as frightened as I was, I never doubted you'd search for me for as long as it took."

"I would never have stopped until I found you." He brushed a stray wisp of hair off her face, then ran his long fingers down her cheeks, across the flesh of her neck and around the curve of her shoulders, as if drawing a tantalizing map of her body. "Let me assure you, Mrs. Rainwater, by the time I'm through with you, you'll know the lengths I would have gone to get you back. You're mine, and no one takes you away from me ever."

He snatched her up and laid her across the bed, his heated gaze never straying from hers. She couldn't take her eyes off him as he unzipped his pants, then stripped down naked. He was a beautiful sight standing there, hard and lean. A hot flash of desire swept through her, threatening to turn her to ash. It only intensified when he advanced toward her, drew her panties down, and let them drop to the floor.

Her breath caught in her throat as his piercing stare burned a trail aross every inch of her body. When he slowly climbed on top of her, kissing her from her ankles to other things, she knew she was as good as beathen…again.

A word about the author...

Although not a native Texan, Donnette Smith has spent more than half her life living in the Lone Star State. She is an entrepreneur and former business owner of Tailor Maid Services LLC. After spending a few years working as a journalist for the Blue Ridge Tribune, she realized her love for writing romantic detective novels. Her stories cover a wide range of genres, from horror, time travel, mystery, fantasy, paranormal, and thriller. But one theme stays the same, there is always a detective solving a crime, and a gorgeous victim he would lay down his life to protect.

Donnette's biggest fascination is with forensic science and crime scene investigations. Her novels include, *Cunja*, a horror/mystery/suspense that debuted in 2012. Book 1 of The Spirit Walker Series, *Killing Dreams*, a fantasy/romance story with a paranormal element became available in September of 2021. Book 2 of The Spirit Walker Series, *Buried Alive*, was published on March 14, 2022. Her latest, Book 3 of The Spirit Walkers Series, *The Taken*.

Thank you for purchasing
this publication of The Wild Rose Press, Inc.

For questions or more information
contact us at
info@thewildrosepress.com.

The Wild Rose Press, Inc.
www.thewildrosepress.com

www.ingramcontent.com/pod-product-compliance
Lightning Source LLC
Chambersburg PA
CBHW05163026066
47170CB00004B/1114